COME TOMORROW

CASTAWAY CHRISTMAS SERIES, BOOK ONE

TESS THOMPSON

COME TOMORROW

For Violet Estrin.
My best friend and Christmas decorating queen. May we have many
more holiday celebrations together.

A NOTE TO READERS

Dear Readers,

I'm so excited you found my holiday historical romance. I hope you enjoy Wesley and Luci's story as much as I loved writing it. This is the first of the Castaway Christmas books. If all goes well, I'll have another one for you next December.

One note, I used a little creative liberty by including snow globes, which may not be totally historically accurate. They weren't mass produced as they are today. However, I wanted to use the imagery of the snow globe and what it represents to Wesley. Forgive me my creative license.

Thank you for choosing my book when there are so many out there. I appreciate it more than you can know. I'm truly living my dream because of readers like you.

I love to hear from you, so don't hesitate to reach out via email at tess@tthompsonwrites.com.

Much love to you and yours,
Tess

PART I

DECEMBER 1904

1

esley

I WAS FOURTEEN THE FIRST TIME I CAME UPON LUCI QUICK ON A stark late-December afternoon that smelled of woodsmoke and pine needles. Atlas, my dog, was also fourteen. However, in the unfairness of things, he was already an old man.

Our warm breath made clouds as we ran across a thin carpet of frozen leaves. The light was lonely this time of year, dull and gray, full of shadows. Icy snow fell from a low sky. White frost covered leaves and grass. Only last week, the sky had been blue and the last leaves of autumn had clung to the branches as one would an old friend about to depart for a long trip. Overnight, a cold front had arrived, freezing everything. But isn't that the way of the world? In an instant, everything changes.

We'd come farther into the woods than usual. Atlas led the way, as if he had a reason for taking us off our typical path.

3

Who was I to disagree? Atlas asked for nothing. Never complained. He loved me unconditionally. All my life, it had been me and him. Wesley and Atlas. Boy and his dog. Whatever path he chose, I would follow.

Lately, he'd slowed, his once youthful yellow Labrador body now stiff. He could still jump onto my bed, but it pained him, so I lifted him instead. Atlas wasn't one to complain. Still, despite all that, when he entered the outdoors, he came back to life, seeming to forget his arthritis and creaky bones. He was as game as ever for our roamings through the wood. Our escape from my family's estate where we could breathe.

If rage and secrets had a smell, it would be my parents' home. That morning, a crash had woken me in the early dawn, followed by the raised voices of my parents. I'd pulled the covers over my head and scrunched my eyes closed, willing it to stop. Atlas had whined and pressed his bulky warmth against my legs. We couldn't make out the words, only waves of anger. Even so, this felt different. Usually, they didn't argue out loud. No, their disdain was the quiet kind, like the frozen dirt under these leaves. After breakfast, Atlas and I made a run for it. We knew danger. Could smell it. *Stay away,* the instinct whispered. Whatever had angered them would be taken out on me one way or another. Father's strap across my back. Or Mother's cold banishment to my room. She was like the frozen ground, unmoving, impenetrable. Father was more like the unexpected cold front. A violent temper that came from nowhere and without warning.

We came out of a thicket of trees into a clearing. Nestled between firs, pines, and maples stood a shack. Atlas went perfectly still, then sat back on his haunches. A girl held a crying baby close to her chest as she paced over the frozen dirt. In truth, she was more waif than a girl, as thin as the winter light. She wore a tattered coat the same gray as the boards of the sad dwelling. As motionless as a deer, I watched her. Beside me, Atlas did the same.

I took in the shack. The roof sagged. One dirty window had a crack in the shape of a claw. A thin trail of smoke drifted weakly out of a tin stovepipe. In contrast, as if to make up for the sag of the roof, the girl's back was straight as a board. Pink cheeks glowed from the cold. Snow settled on top of her head and shoulders.

The baby continued to cry—not loudly, more like a kitten's mew. She couldn't have been more than a few days old, as she was no bigger than a loaf of bread. I didn't think the girl old enough to be the baby's mother. She seemed about the same size as my sister, Lillian. I guessed her to be about twelve. The time between a girl and a woman.

A mound of freshly turned soil caught my eye. A crude cross made of tree limbs marked it as a grave. Someone had been recently buried. The mother of this girl and the baby?

She moved the baby into a different position, cradling her in her arms instead of against her shoulder. The mewing creature seemed to like this better and stopped howling. A muscle in Atlas's backside twitched. He inched forward little by little as if a rope tugged him to the girl. The small movement rustled the leaves underfoot, exposing us. Her head jerked up, toward the noise. We locked eyes. Hers were green and shaped like almonds. Her small pink mouth formed a circle before she stepped backward.

I put up my hand in a gesture of friendship and attempted a smile. "Hello there."

She bobbed her head in greeting. Even under the dull sky, her hair was the color of wheat in the fall.

I put up a hand in deference, hoping to reassure her. "Don't be scared. I mean no harm."

The muscles of her face relaxed. She drew closer. "What do you want?" Her voice sounded raspy, as if she was tired and thirsty. With only a few feet between us, I could fully appreciate the beauty of her oval face and high cheekbones.

"Nothing. I was here walking with my dog. We didn't know anyone lived back here. I didn't mean to disturb you. Or the baby."

The sharpness in her eyes softened as she turned her gaze toward Atlas. "What's his name?"

"Atlas. What's yours?"

"I'm Luci Quick."

Atlas sat back on his haunches and held up his paw. A trick I'd taught him after many days of tutelage.

"Sorry, boy. I can't shake with you right now with this baby between us." She smiled for the first time. My knees weakened at the sight. An angel right here in the middle of the forest. Had she been here all along and I never knew?

She returned her gaze to me. Neither of us spoke, but we didn't look away. Seconds ticked along. Or was it years? Who knew? I was lost in her, swept into the tide pool of her green eyes. "Where have you been?" I asked finally.

Another smile lit up her face. "Have you been looking for me?"

"Not until I found you." The clouds seemed to open suddenly, changing the snowfall from icy shards to flat flakes.

Her thin brows drew together. "Can you search for someone you don't yet know?"

"Yes, I think so." I touched my jacket where it buttoned over my heart. "In here. There's an empty space that some-one's supposed to fill, but you don't know who they are or where they are, maybe looking for you too." How could I explain? All my questions were answered by this encounter. I now knew my purpose. And that purpose was bigger than just myself. These two were meant for me to find. Meant for me to care for.

A fine layer of snow already covered the ground like a lacy

handkerchief. The afternoon had grown so quiet I imagined I could hear the flakes landing on the dirt.

We both jumped when a crash from inside disrupted the quiet. "You should go. Pa's mean when he wakes up after the bottle. He won't like it if you're here."

Those words pierced through my chest. *Pa's mean.* Her mother was dead. She had this baby to take care of all by herself. How would they survive the winter?

"Will you be all right?" I asked, unable to think of anything else to say. A crushing instinct took hold. My hands twitched at my sides. I would take them away from here. Someplace where they would be safe and warm. But where? My home was also fraught with turmoil. Mother wouldn't take kindly to a stray cat, let alone a girl and a baby. When I'd brought home a baby bird last summer, I'd been punished. Who knew what had happened to the bird?

"I have to be." She spoke no louder than a whisper, yet in that simple sentence the grit of thousands of women before her shouted in solidarity. "There's no one for Sadie but me."

"I'll bring you food. If you want?"

A wariness like a startled animal came to her eyes. "Why?"

"Because . . . because I want to." What else could I say? *Because you're my purpose.*

"I'm ashamed." Her eyes grew glassy with unshed tears. "But I'll say yes."

"Don't be. Sometimes things are bad for no good reason."

"Mama kept us from starvation. Now, I don't know what will happen." What had her work been? Probably a domestic like the ladies who worked for Mother. We had more staff than we did family members.

"I'll come back tomorrow. Mollie will have the cook put together scraps . . . whatever we don't eat." I flushed, imagining how that must sound and how she would probably hate me for it. No one likes to feel indebted to another.

7

A shout from inside the house caused the girl to once again jump. "That's Pa. You have to go."

"I'll put the basket right here by the tree. Empty it and I'll pick it up later. We'll do it that way, all right?"

"Step behind the tree," she said. "He's coming out."

I did as she asked, peeking from behind the tree as a man stumbled out to the porch. He wore faded red long underwear. It was baggy around his hips, with holes in the knees. Greasy hair stuck up on one side of his head. A full beard covered most of his face, but his small, hard eyes were starkly evident. "Luci, get in here and make me something to eat."

"Please go. I don't want him to see you." The fear in her eyes chilled me. Every good instinct I had told me to haul her and the baby out of there. But again, where would I take them? Where were a lone girl and a baby safe in this world?

"I'll come tomorrow, Luci." I turned away, and despite my urge to stay and fight, I darted back into the forest.

I needn't have worried about getting lost. Atlas knew the way home. We gathered speed as we wove in and out of the trees. By the time we were back to the edge of my family's property, I was out of breath.

I opened the back gate to our estate. We ran past the empty vegetable boxes and dormant flowers to a bench near the rose garden.

"Whoa, now, Atlas," I said as I plopped onto the bench. "Let's catch our breath before we go inside." I lifted him up to sit next to me. He sat upright like a person. I put my arm around him. "I don't want to go in there."

Atlas sighed in sympathy.

My back still stung from the strap my father had used on me the night before. I'd been punished for leaving a book open in the library. Father took the care of his books very seriously. I'd spotted a bird while exploring, and I'd been looking up the type of bird in the big book of fowl. He had gray feathers and a white throat and a face with black stripes around his eyes. After some searching, I discovered he was a red-breasted nuthatch. I'd been so excited I'd run out to see if I could spot him again and left the book on the table. For my carelessness, I'd received two lashings from the strap Father had hung on the back of the door for just such occasions.

Snow fell in earnest now. At least an inch covered the lawn. It was nearing dark, and the lights of our brick mansion shone brightly through the windows. From this vantage point, I could see the silhouette of my mother in the window of her upstairs bedroom. A shadow moved behind the curtain in my father's study.

Atlas shifted to put his head in my lap. I petted him as gently as I could. He let out another sigh, this one shaky, as if he couldn't quite catch his breath. "I know, boy. You're tired. We went too far today." I tucked my chin, trying not to cry. The truth had crept into my chest of late. Atlas had lived a long life. I knew he would leave me soon, but I sensed he was worried to leave me alone. "When it's your time to go, don't worry about me. I don't want you staying here just for me." Tears leaked from the corners of my eyes. I lifted my face to the sky and closed my eyes. Snowflakes cooled my warm cheeks and wet eyes. I looked back at him. He'd closed his eyes. The fur around his eyes had turned white. "Don't be gone for long, though. Come back to me, all right? Come back in a puppy's body, and we'll take up where we left off."

Atlas lifted his face and rose up to give me a lick on my hand.

I smiled down at him. "All right, then. I'm glad you agree. But for now, let's go inside. Mollie will have a good dinner waiting for both of us."

2

L uci

AFTER THE BOY DISAPPEARED THROUGH THE THICKET OF TREES, I remembered I hadn't asked his name. How was it possible to feel as if you knew a person without even knowing what they were called? With Sadie cradled in my arms, I went inside to answer Pa's bellowing. He'd awakened from his drunken sleep mean and hungry.

"Girl, where's supper?" His hair stuck up on one side. He hadn't shaved in weeks, and his beard had grown in patchy and uneven. I could smell his unwashed body from several feet away.

"I don't know." My words came out as wooden and numb as I felt. "We don't have anything to fix."

"Tomorrow's Christmas Eve. Are we supposed to go to bed hungry?"

Christmas? I'd completely forgotten. I rubbed my tired eyes. They felt as if I'd been in a sandstorm.

How had Mama kept us from starvation? I'd not thought about it much when she was alive. I'd lived in the shadows to avoid my father's fists. But now it was up to me to keep us all alive.

Pa grabbed his jacket from the hanger by the door. "I'm going into town."

"Pa, what about Sadie? She needs milk."

He whipped back around to look at me, his eyes alight with anger. "That baby's got nothing to do with me. Ain't even mine."

I stared at him. Was it true? He hadn't been here when she was born. Was that why? The reality of what this meant chilled me to the bone. I was truly on my own.

He turned and walked out the door, his boots heavy on the rickety porch.

Ain't even mine. Who was the father, then? Mama had had secrets. And she'd gone to the grave with them.

Reeling from this latest truth, I drew in a deep breath to steady my nerves. If I was going to take care of Sadie, I had to be strong and smart.

I walked to the window to watch him lope across the yard toward the path we took to the dirt road that led to town. Once I was sure he was gone, I lifted the loose floorboard where Mama had hidden money. There were two nickels. Enough for the next few days. I'd go to town and buy flour and milk.

I returned to the window, afraid he might have turned back for some reason. No sign of him. My gaze fell upon the old chicken coop. When Mama had started laboring, she'd told me she would have the baby outside in the empty chicken coop. "It'll get real messy."

I'd had no idea exactly how messy.

I shuddered as an image of all the blood came to me. After Sadie had come out, Mama had grown so pale I could see the veins through her skin. I'd held on to her as the life drained from her. The utter stillness of her body had been the opposite of the wriggling baby in my arms.

By the time Pa had come home from the bar, Mama's body was already cold. I'd tried to clean her up, but there was too much blood. I'd wrapped her in the bloody quilt and prayed that Pa would come and at least help me get her into the ground. I closed my eyes, remembering the last words she'd ever said to me. "Please, Luci, take care of the baby. I'm begging you."

"Yes, Mama. I'll never let anything happen to her."

I blinked away the memories and warmed the last of the milk for the baby. Our only hand feeder was still in the pot on the stove. When she'd been carrying Sadie, Mama had told me how important boiling water was to kill bacteria and germs. Sadie was only a few days old, but I'd already come up with systems. Feed, sterilize, sleep, and repeat.

I fed her in Mama's old rocking chair. She'd brought it to the marriage, she'd once told me. The only thing she had of her own mother.

"We have to survive," I said to Sadie as she squeezed her hand around my thumb. I thought about the boy and his promise. Who was he, and where had he come from? I'd never seen him in town or during the time I'd attended school. At least I didn't think so. Unfortunately, because of his cap and scarf, most of his face had been covered. It was only his dark-blue eyes that I saw clearly. Those eyes were seared into my memory. They were familiar, too, as if I'd known him my whole life.

Then again, maybe I'd made him up. Had I been delirious with exhaustion and hunger and invented him?

Not that it mattered. Even if he managed to make good on his promise, I had to come up with a plan. I was on my own.

To keep us alive, I needed to make more money. How did a girl with no skills do such a thing?

First things first. I would walk into town before it got dark and get supplies. If Pa came home, I'd have something to feed him. Carrying Sadie all the way into town and back would be hard, especially if I had flour and milk in my arms.

Suddenly, I had an idea. I'd make a sling for her that would keep her close and safe but free up my arms. Working quickly, I cut up Mama's old nightgown. The middle section was big enough for Sadie, and the sides narrowed into ties.

I laid her on top of the newly cut pouch, then scooped my hands under the fabric to lift her into my arms. Sitting with her on my lap in the rocking chair, I tied the ends around my neck. I was pleased with myself, and my spirits lifted.

The walk to town was a good three miles, so I had to go now or it would be dark by the time I started back home. With the nickels held tight in my hand, we set out.

THE TOWN OF DEVON HAD A POPULATION OF A FEW THOUSAND. Brick storefronts lined each side of a main street. I kept my head down, avoiding eye contact with anyone who passed by going the other direction. As we approached the dry goods store, I clutched my nickels tighter and quickened my pace. Seconds later, we reached the front door. I tugged open the door and slipped inside the warm room. Sadie had fallen asleep during our brisk, cold walk. Although the ties around my neck seemed to be holding fast, I kept one arm under her.

I hadn't come to town often in the last few years. Since Mama had taken me out of school, I'd had rare occasion to make the trip. In fact, Mama had discouraged me from doing so. She'd said town was no place for a little girl. I wished she'd remembered that before up and dying on me.

The store smelled of sawdust and brown sugar. Barrels with everything a person could want were lined up in rows with aisles between them. I passed by sugar, brown sugar, pecans, oats, and finally found the flour. A woman behind the counter watched me suspiciously, as if I might steal something. I wanted to run out of there and never look back, but I couldn't. I had to be brave. Trembling, I dragged myself up to the counter.

"Can I help you?" The shopkeeper was a stout woman with gray hair and small gray eyes. Her cheeks were round, like white pincushions. An apron covered most of her drab brown dress.

"I . . . I . . . need some flour, please."

"What you got there? A baby? At your age?" Her small eyes bored through me.

"No, ma'am. This is my sister. My mama died. My name's Luci Quick, and I'm trying to figure out how to take care of Sadie, and I don't know much of anything about babies or making bread." All this tumbled from my mouth, as if this woman cared.

Her jaw muscles twitched as she looked at me even harder. "You're Connie Quick's daughter?"

"Yes, ma'am."

"I hadn't heard she was dead. Childbirth, I suppose?"

"That's right." I swallowed past the painful lump in my throat. "She never even held Sadie here. Now it's up to me."

"How old are you?"

"Twelve."

"What a shame she left you alone with an infant. That's what happens when you live the kind of life she did."

I wasn't sure what she meant. Was being poor shameful and punishable? "I have these." I put the nickels on the counter. "I don't know what it'll get me."

She shook her head, as if trying to make sense of what I was saying to her, then spoke in a tone that was flat and mean. "Where'd you get those? Are you already in the family business?"

Was she talking about Pa and his drinking? She must be. Maybe she thought I was asking to buy drink. "I wouldn't use it to buy whiskey like Pa. Not ever."

She folded her arms over her chest. "We don't want your kind in our town."

My stomach churned with nerves. "Excuse me, ma'am?" If only Pa would stay home and drink instead of coming into town to go to the saloon and gamble away all the money Mama had managed to make.

"Your mama wasn't welcome in my store. I don't take money earned from whoring around."

I flinched as if she'd smacked me. *Whoring around?* I only had a vague notion of what that was, but I felt almost certain it was when a woman lay down with men who weren't her husband. Why would she say that about Mama? "I don't understand what you're saying." I sounded like an idiot. Dull and stupid.

"Everyone knows what she did. For as long as I can remember, she's been the town whore. How do you think she kept your pa in his whiskey? Have you ever seen him work? Did you ever wonder where she went at night?"

My legs weakened. I grabbed the edge of the counter to keep from falling. "He says poker is his work." I said this under my breath, as shame flooded through me, made me hot and sweaty despite how cold I'd been only minutes before. Tears blurred my vision. Mama took money for lying with men? Everyone knew? "I was asleep at night." Sadie. *She ain't mine.* He'd known of her work and hadn't cared? "How many men?" I had to know the truth now.

"More than the wives of this community think. My own husband, may he rot in hell, used to be one of her regulars."

"I didn't know," I whispered, more to Sadie than to the angry shopkeeper. *Keep your wits about you*, I told myself. I swiped away my tears and straightened my spine. Survival was all that mattered. I had to get this woman to sell me flour. Even if it took groveling, I had to leave with a sack of flour or we weren't going to make it until next week. After wiping my tears with the sleeve of my coat, I looked up at her. "I'm sorry for what my mama did, but she's left me with this baby, and I'm all she's got. I can assure you I didn't get that money from offering up my body to a man." I didn't even have breasts yet. What man would even want a girl? "Please, can you sell me some supplies?"

Her small eyes softened slightly. She placed her hands flat against the counter and sighed. "I don't suppose it's your fault. It wasn't mine either, you know."

I didn't entirely understand, so I stayed quiet.

"I'll give you five pounds of flour and a pound of kidney beans for one of your nickels."

"Thank you, ma'am." My stomach growled at the thought of warm beans.

"I'll throw some lard in too. Fried-up pieces of bread will stick to your bones. Also, biscuits made with lard are quick and easy. Be sure to soak those beans overnight, or they'll give you a stomachache. Once the baby's big enough, you can soak pieces of bread in milk and let her suck on them."

"Do you know where I could get milk?" I asked.

"Moore Brothers dairy delivers to folks who don't have a cow."

More money.

"Stop over there on your way home. Mrs. Moore sells it a penny a quart. Tell her Mrs. Adams sent you."

"Thank you. I will. You know of any work around town?" I asked.

"Not for a girl with a baby."

"Thank you, Mrs. Adams. I should go now."

"Take care of yourself, girl. We're in for a long winter."

I needed a miracle. That's all there was to it.

3

Wesley

WITH ATLAS AT MY HEELS, I TOOK THE OUTSIDE STAIRS DOWN TO the kitchen entrance. A blast of warm air hit my face as I entered, as did the aroma of garlic and roast beef. I tore my newsboy cap from my head and stuck it on the rack near the door. Mrs. Walker, our cook, and June, one of the new maids, were busy preparing treats for tomorrow's Christmas Eve supper. Mother liked to have a variety of pies and cakes.

The kitchen had two cookstoves, which were both lit up tonight to cook the pies and a few loaves of sourdough bread, plus a chocolate cake. Gingerbread cookies were piled high on a plate on the buffet in the corner. We would eat well tonight. I thought again of Luci's wan face. Surely I could take some of our leftovers out to her?

"Good evening, Mrs. Walker. June."

June nodded, then looked away, shy. She wasn't much older

than me, but as the oldest of seven children she had to go to work as soon as she was able.

Mrs. Walker, stout and white haired, wiped her hands on the front of her apron. Her full cheeks were rosy from cooking over a hot stove, but that didn't diminish her smile. "Young Wesley. Are you ready for Santa?" She tugged at her cap, which made it slightly lopsided over one ear. My presence was expected in the kitchen at least twice a day, where Mrs. Walker and I fed Atlas his breakfast and dinner. Both Lillian and I adored the staff, and they didn't seem to mind that we obviously came down for refuge from the upstairs.

I grinned. "I know there's no Santa, Mrs. Walker. I'm practically grown."

"You're breaking my heart."

"I have to grow up. Otherwise, how will I ever get out of here?"

She tutted but didn't comment. There were things no one could speak of in this house. The treatment of young Wesley was one of them. Everyone knew what went on in Father's study. If they were to say anything at all, they would surely be dismissed immediately. Thus, we all pretended the strap didn't happen. I liked it that way. To see pity in their eyes would have been as bad as the punishment itself.

"I've been wondering where you got yourself off to. Your sister's been looking for you."

Alarm bells chimed in my head. "Was she all right?"

"Yes, I believe so." A flicker of concern showed in her eyes, but again, she didn't comment further. "She's like a lost puppy without her brother, that's all."

Mrs. Walker walked into the pantry and came out with some kibble for Atlas. He wagged his tail, but it lacked enthusiasm. His appetite had diminished lately. Just a year ago he would have rushed over to Mrs. Walker and waited, watching her every move as she set his bowl on the floor.

She set it down near his water bowl. "Come on, boy, time for your dinner," I said.

Atlas, more to please me than anything, ambled over to his dish and began to eat.

"He didn't eat much this morning," Mrs. Walker said. "But he's hungry tonight. Maybe traipsing all over the forest was good for him."

My own stomach grumbled, reminding me of my purpose. "Mrs. Walker, do we have a lot of food left over after our meals?"

"Sometimes, yes. Why?"

"No reason, really. Curious, that's all." I couldn't get Mrs. Walker involved until I had permission from our head housekeeper, Mollie. Getting our sweet cook in trouble was not on my list of Christmas wishes.

"Curiosity killed the cat." Mrs. Walker returned to the stove. "Mollie said for you to stop by her office before you head up to change for dinner."

"Thanks, Mrs. Walker. I'll go now." I wondered why Mollie wanted to see me. Not that it mattered. I needed to see her too.

With Atlas trotting obediently behind me, we headed down the narrow hallway to Mollie's office. She was always there this time of day, doing whatever needed doing.

Mollie kept everything running like clockwork. She managed the inside staff with a firm but fair hand. Dax, her husband, was our head groundskeeper. They shared a small cottage not far from the main house.

I knocked on the door, and she called for me to come in. Dax was there too, having a glass of beer. They had the same routine every day. After he'd cleaned up from his outside duties, he had a beer while Mollie finished up for the day. The office was small, with dark walls and no windows. She kept her broad desk tidy, and the room smelled of the dried lavender Mollie kept in a vase.

"Hello there, lad." Dax had been in America since he was a young man, but his Irish brogue remained strong. To look at his slim frame, one wouldn't guess his physical strength and endurance. He worked ten-to-twelve-hour days in the summer, ensuring the grounds and gardens were tidy and watered. A mere look in a plant's direction and it grew as if under a spell. "Have you been out and about?"

"Yes, I've come from the woods," I said, slightly breathless from nerves. If I couldn't get Mollie to agree to my plan, I didn't know what I would do. Atlas flopped on the braided rug near Dax's chair.

"And I have to ask you something," I said to Mollie.

She lifted her gaze from a notebook where she'd been making a list of some kind. Her dark-blue eyes flitted from my head to my toes. "Your coat looks damp. Where's your hat and scarf? You'll catch your death." With her fair skin and pink cheeks, she reminded me of a ripe peach. My favorite fruit, just as she was among my favorite people. Her black-and-white curls were pulled back into a bun at her neck, but a few had escaped, framing her heart-shaped face.

"You'll be getting the floors wet with your boots," Mollie said.

I looked down at my feet. They appeared dry to me.

"And that dog smells to high heaven."

I couldn't smell Atlas at all. "Sorry, Mollie."

"I don't like your running around like a wild animal in the woods. Who knows what kind of trouble a boy your age could get into? There are people in this town who mean you harm. Not to mention the animals." Her Irish lilt often made a statement sound like a question.

"Staying in here all day . . . I just can't . . . " I trailed off, unsure how to explain that the woods were the place I was free.

"I don't want any reason for your dad to do what he did last night," Mollie said in a softer tone. "We worry about you."

I hung my head, shocked that she'd spoken of it aloud. "I know, but I'm all right."

"How's your back?" Mollie asked. "Do you need me to put the salve on again?"

I'd been sent to my room after my punishment. Mollie, somehow, had known that I needed her, even though she should have already been retired to her cottage for the evening. I'd heard the floorboards creaking in the hallway and had known it was her. Because it was too painful to lie on my back, I'd been facedown on the bed when she came through the door with her medical kit in her hand. I knew it hurt her and Dax to see what went on in this house, but there was nothing they could do to help. My father and mother made the rules, and we were all obliged to follow them.

"No, it's fine. Doesn't sting any longer." A lie, but I'd rather not have Mollie worried. She'd painstakingly applied salve the night before with her gentle fingers.

"What have you come for, then? You'll need to be changed for dinner in a half hour."

"I . . . I found a girl. In the woods. She had a baby, and it was very small and crying. Her mother's dead and buried right there in the yard. I saw the grave." The words tumbled from my mouth. Not at all how I'd planned to propose my idea.

Mollie watched me with more intensity than she had just moments before. "Where, exactly?"

"I'm not sure. We were running in the woods, and there it was. A shack and the girl."

"And a baby? How big?"

I held up my hands to show her. "Tiny."

"A newborn." She said this under her breath, as if she'd forgotten I was in the room. "The mother was dead? Are you certain?"

"Yes, I'm certain." I shuddered, remembering the fresh grave. "The girl said she didn't know what they would eat and that her pa—that's what she called her father—was mean. I heard him shouting."

"You're talking about Sam Quick," Mollie said. "You stay away from there. He's a dangerous man."

My heart sank. "But, Mollie, I thought maybe I could bring them food. I told her. I promised her. I said I'd come tomorrow."

Mollie let out a sigh. "Lad, you shouldn't have done that. You shouldn't make promises about something you can't control."

"You could help me. Think of all the food we throw away." I scrambled to come up with an argument that would win her over to my idea. "I'd just leave it in a basket and never even talk to her. No one will even know we're there. Mollie, please, what will they eat? Winter's going to be hard this year too. Dax said so."

"You're to stay away from there." Her eyes had lost all gentle concern and were now cold and flat as they bored a hole through my heart. This wasn't like Mollie. She was soft and sympathetic to anyone in trouble. The time I'd brought in the injured baby bird that had fallen from the nest, she'd been as concerned as I was. Until I'd been forced to put it back outside.

I pleaded my case as best I could. "If you asked Mrs. Walker to set aside whatever is left over at the end of the day for a family you know, then I could deliver it to them."

"I said no."

"I don't understand. Why not?" I glanced at Dax. He gave me a sympathetic half smile.

"Because this is not your concern," Mollie said. "I'm sorry for the girl, but this is not our business. Lad, I'm trying to keep you from another beating. Your mother will not want you out there. Trust me on this."

I deflated. Atlas lifted his head and licked my boot.

"What is it that's gotten you so worked up?" Mollie asked. "There are other poor families around here."

"I don't know. Something about her. Like I knew her before. She reminded me of that baby bird. She has no one." As hard as my parents were, I had Mollie, Dax, Mrs. Walker, and Lillian. Luci Quick had only a drunkard father and a baby who would not survive without intervention of some kind.

"Luci Quick has a father, and hopefully he'll step up now that his wife's in the grave." Mollie spoke with less alarm in her voice now. "I know it's hard not to have any young people around, but Luci Quick can't be your friend."

Lillian and I weren't allowed to have many friends or go to regular school. Mollie probably thought I was simply desperate for a friend. Latching on to people who didn't belong to me.

Mother barked at us from the doorway. "What does Luci Quick have to do with this family?" She was like the white calla lilies Dax grew in the flower beds, slender and elegant and so very pretty.

I swallowed as I backed into the corner of the room. She hadn't yet changed into evening attire. I could see from her red and puffy eyes that she'd been crying.

I pressed against the wall. If I could have, I would have slipped out the window and run and run. Atlas scrambled to his feet and crossed over to sit next to me. Poor Atlas thought he could protect me from my mother.

What was she doing down here? Usually she sent her maid, Ruth, downstairs with requests or instructions.

"Tell me." Mother entered the room and drew nearer.

"I came upon their shack today. The mother's died, and there's a little baby." For some reason it didn't occur to me to lie. "I was talking to Mollie about taking food out to them." The minute I said the words, I deeply regretted them.

Mother's face contorted, and her skin flushed almost purple. For a second I thought she might strike me. Why? What had I done? However, she rearranged her face into its normal shape and sucked in a shaky breath and held it for a moment, her chest expanding with the effort. Then she let the air from her lungs out slowly, as if extinguishing a flame on a candle. She hated wax on the tablecloths. Once I'd blown too enthusiastically, and droplets of wax had gone everywhere. She'd made sure I never forgot again by plunging my fingers into the hot wax, followed by sending me to Father's study for the strap. "It's kind of you to worry about them, but they're no concern of ours. We can't save everyone. Anyway, what gave you the idea that we owe them anything?"

"Nothing like that," I said. "But they might starve or freeze to death."

She briefly closed her eyes, as if I was both a burden and simpleton. "Your father and I are generous to the local poor, but we cannot save everyone. If Mr. Quick is too lazy or drunk to take care of his own family, then he'll have to reconcile that with God. What if we gave all my money away? Who would take care of you and your sister then?" She put her cold fingers under my chin and lifted my face. "Do you understand?"

"Yes, Mother."

"Good, then we'll think no more of it." She turned to Mollie. "Have you chosen wine for us for tonight?"

"Yes, Mrs. Ford. And I've noted it in the log. They're decanting in the dining room, as you asked."

"Very good. Thank you." Her gaze flickered to Dax for the first time. "The Christmas tree you chose is sparse on one side, but Ruth managed to have its best side facing out from the corner."

"I'm sorry, Mrs. Ford. The tree didn't look that way when I chopped it down."

"Attention to detail, Dax, is what separates the mediocre from the great."

"Yes, ma'am."

She turned to me. "As for you—there's a bath and a suit for you waiting upstairs. Your sister's upstairs practicing her piano. I'm going to get dressed for dinner. Don't disappoint me further by dallying."

"I won't, Mother."

"Have someone bathe that dog," Mother said. "He smells horrendous."

"Of course, Mrs. Ford." Mollie stood up from behind the desk. "I'll take care of that right away."

After Mother had gone, I took in a deep breath, as if my lungs had been temporarily crushed by a boulder. I placed my hand absentmindedly on Atlas's soft yellow head.

"Wesley?" Mollie asked quietly. "You do understand, don't you? Don't go against your mother's wishes."

I nodded, pretending. In fact, I did not understand. Mother's reaction was strange at best. Why would she care in particular about Luci Quick?

I looked up as Dax and Mollie exchanged a look. They knew something I didn't.

All these lies and secrets. Surely at some point in time, they would destroy our household. They lurked in the shadows, ready to jump out and get us when we least expected it.

I was on my way upstairs when Father called out to me. Bracing myself for the worst, I turned around and marched, like a man to his death, into his study.

"Yes, sir?"

Father sat behind a wide mahogany desk. A roaring fire lit the room. Other than the painted portrait of himself, which hung over the fireplace, scientific books on every nonfiction subject one could imagine filled the shelves from floor to ceiling. He spent much of his time writing to booksellers in search of books on one subject or another.

"What's this I hear about you traipsing around the woods and getting involved in things that are none of your concern?" Father was older than Mother by ten years. His gray hair was cropped short. He wore small round glasses that he peered over when he looked at anything but a book. I suspected he would have been considered handsome by those who didn't know him. I couldn't see past the sinister look in his dark-brown eyes or his small mouth, which was pinched closed most of the time.

The fact that he knew the details of my day surprised me. Most of his time was spent locked in his study without seeming to care about Lillian or me. Mother knew the minutiae of our days. She dictated most of it.

"What do you have to say for yourself?" Father leaned back in his chair and placed his hands over his stomach.

How was I supposed to answer? Lillian always advised to say sorry, even if you didn't do it or had no idea what they wanted. "I'm sorry." That apology cost me a few inches of dignity.

His chair creaked as he rose to his feet. I glanced nervously at the riding crop that hung on the rack in the corner. He perched on the edge of the desk and crossed his arms over his chest. "There's something you need to understand. Those people are not like us. We're not to help them, or they'll never help themselves."

I knew better than to argue with him. "Yes, sir."

"I don't want you exposed to that kind of trash."

I bit the inside of my lip to keep from answering.

"I think it's wise for you to stay within the confines of the estate. The girl's father has a reputation in town of being drunk and violent. I don't want you running into trouble." My father had a way of speaking, soft and low but always with a hint of violence just under the surface. I knew that at any moment, his temper could flare. "It upsets your mother when you run all around the countryside like a hick."

"Yes, sir."

"The other thing is—Atlas is no longer young. He shouldn't be running around that way either. If you won't stay home, he won't either. Do you want to be responsible for his demise?"

I didn't think being outside was bad for him, but I bit the other side of my mouth and stayed quiet.

"Go up and change into your dinner clothes." He waved me away as if I were a fly at a meal.

Relieved, I thanked him and slunk out of the study. When I reached the stairs, I took them two at a time.

4

Luci

CHRISTMAS EVE MORNING, I WOKE TO THE WAILS OF MY BABY sister. The light through our dirty windows told me that morning had come. I turned over on my straw mat and lifted up on one elbow to peer into the cradle. Sadie's tiny arms and legs flailed, and her face, red and furious, was scrunched up like she was in pain. Hungry. Again. I didn't know what I would do when we ran out of milk.

Sadie raised the volume of her cries. The wail of hunger. I scrambled upright. I'd been so tired and cold last night that I'd fallen asleep still wearing Mama's old coat and my boots.

Adrenaline pumping now, I opened the door of the wood-stove, praying for a few burning embers. A red-hot log stared back at me. I tossed two pieces of fir into the stove and blew to get them going. Sap from one of the logs sputtered and caught fire.

I poured milk into a pot to warm on the stove. Mrs. Moore from the dairy had told me to heat it no hotter than a person's body temperature and to test it with my finger. Next, I took a cloth diaper from the stack. Last night, I'd washed and hung them to dry on the clothesline I'd strung from one end of the room to the other.

My hands shook from fatigue and hunger as I picked Sadie up from the cradle and set her on the mat to change her. I wiped her clean with a rag and put it in a bucket that I would later take down to the creek to rinse. After that, I'd boil them in another pot on the stove.

Sadie continued to scream. How Pa could sleep through the noise was beyond me. As tired as I was, the moment she started crying, I jerked awake. His snores from the bedroom told me he'd come home sometime after the last feeding around three in the morning.

I poured the now lukewarm milk into the bottle. Finally, I lifted a furious Sadie into my arms. She calmed the moment the makeshift teat was in her mouth. I sank into the rocking chair and watched her eat. Cow's milk couldn't be a proper replacement for Mama's, but what other choice did I have? I didn't know much of anything about babies. Mama had told me that she'd feed Sadie from her breasts. The idea had disgusted me at the time. But that was months ago, back when I was still a girl. Overnight, everything had changed. I had become a mother to this helpless baby and thus no longer a child myself. There was no one else but me to save her. I'd promised Mama. God help us.

I closed my scratchy eyes and rocked. As light as Sadie was, she felt solid and warm in my arms. She was an especially pretty baby. At least she looked that way to me. Did everyone think that about their own babies? I smoothed the fine layer of her white hair, as soft as a down feather. I'd make her a hat from one of Mama's wool socks.

Her eyes fluttered open. She stared up at me with her new eyes.

A wave of love surged through me. "You couldn't help it," I whispered. "You didn't ask to be born or to make Mama sick. But what am I going to do with you?"

After she finished her bottle, I burped her, then put her back in the cradle. Satiated, she closed her eyes and fell asleep. Did she sleep too much? Was she getting enough to eat? I had no idea. *Please, God, guide me. I don't know what I'm doing.*

As advised by the storekeeper, I'd put the beans in a bowl to soak. Now, I peeked under the towel. They'd soaked up most of the water. I hoped that was what they were supposed to do. I dumped all of them into our cast-iron pot and covered them with the last of the boiled drinking water. If I remembered correctly, they'd be done by suppertime. Despite everything, we would go to bed with full stomachs on Christmas Eve.

"Just stay here for a minute without me," I whispered to Sadie, even though she was still sleeping and didn't respond. I grabbed Mama's old coat from the hook and slipped my feet into boots. Holding my breath because of the stench, I took hold of the bucket with the dirty diapers, as well as the empty one for water.

I used the outhouse before setting out for the creek. A thin layer of snow covered the ground and crunched under my feet. My bare fingers hurt from the cold. Overhead, blue sky peeked through the trees. The day would be cold and clear. Pretty but deadly if I didn't keep the house heated. I shivered, thinking of my tiny sister.

Kneeling at the water's edge, I rinsed out the dirty diapers. My hands hurt, but I kept going, squeezing each of the four cloths dry and placing them back in the bucket. I filled the bucket with enough water to cover the diapers and trudged back up the hill to the house. I'd have to make another couple of trips for additional water. Carrying two full buckets was too heavy for me. I needed to grow stronger. How did one do that?

Sadie remained asleep, thankfully. I set the tin bucket on the stove to boil the diapers, then put another piece of wood into the stove. For a minute or two, I warmed my hands before setting out again.

My empty stomach growled as I scooped water into the bucket and trudged back up the hill. *Merry Christmas to me.*

No feeling sorry for yourself, I thought. I had milk and enough flour and beans to last at least a week. Somehow, I'd figure out a way.

Pa and Sadie were still sleeping when I returned. I brought in more firewood and put the bucket of water on to boil. Mama had said it killed whatever could hurt us, as long as we boiled it first. I whipped up a pan of biscuits with the flour and lard and put those in the oven. By the time I was done with all that, Sadie was awake and hungry again.

Here we go. Round two.

THE BOY DIDN'T COME ALL THAT DAY. HE'D PROMISED, AND I knew he'd meant it, but there were circumstances outside of his control. I recognized a kindred spirit. There were demons in his life, just as there were in mine.

Before supper, I stoked the fire to warm our shack. To my surprise, Pa didn't go out that evening. I served us both a bowl of beans and a biscuit. We sat together at the small table to eat. He ate without saying anything other than an occasional grunt. When his bowl was empty, he said, "You did good, girl."

"Thanks, Pa." Pleased by the compliment, I smiled to myself as I finished my own bowl. For a moment, I forgot the direness of our situation or what I'd learned the previous afternoon about Mama. However, when I glanced at Mama's empty chair, it all came rushing back to me. "Have you found any work in town?"

His eyes narrowed as he lifted his face toward me. "I don't need work. I got my poker game. I've been on a winning streak."

"You have?" If that was true, then where were the proceeds?

"Sure. I'd be there now, but the bar's closed on Christmas Eve."

No wonder he was home. I watched him through my lashes. He wore a flannel shirt and brown pants that hid the dirt and grime. His hair had been slicked back and combed; it was greasy enough that it looked like pomade. A stubbly beard covered his face. Small hazel eyes with drooping upper lids peered back at me. "What're you staring at?"

"Nothing." I turned back to my bowl, lifting the last spoonful of beans to my mouth.

"Last night, I had a stroke a bad luck, but I'll get back on top tomorrow," Pa said.

Which was it? A winning streak or a losing one?

"Do you think you could leave a little for me each week to buy food and milk?" I asked. "Maybe after you have a good night?"

"Little girl, you have no idea how the world works, do you?"

"No, sir. I don't." I knew only that one of us needed to make some money, or we wouldn't last until spring.

"I've been thinking we ought to do something with that baby. Sell it to a rich lady or something like that."

My heart thudded to a dead stop. "Pa, no. She's my sister. I promised Mama I'd take care of her."

"She's no kin to me."

I stared into my empty bowl, trying not to cry. *Think,* I told myself. *Come up with a reason to keep her.* What would he see as a benefit to him?

"I turned a blind eye to her comings and goings." Pa

reached into the pocket of his pants and brought out his flask, then took a swig. "But I'm not raising the baby of a whore."

"I'll do it, Pa. You won't have to worry about Sadie. But please, don't make me send her away. I'll do anything you want."

He appeared to ponder this for a moment. "Your mama was always after me for money. Nagging at me to give her what I made. She never understood I couldn't give her what I didn't have. Or that I had to reinvest in the business."

Was there any wonder she'd done what she did? She'd had me to take care of and no one she could turn to for help. I understood then exactly why she'd done what she'd done. She did it for me. I understood a little of that now that Sadie was mine. She would have done anything to keep me safe. Even the unthinkable.

"Listen here, I can't stop playing the game," Pa said. "That's not the way to be a winner. See?"

I didn't see, but it was best to keep that to myself.

"The cards speak to me. They're all I have in this cold world." Pa took another swig from his flask. "I'll tell you what. You can keep it, but that means you're on your own. I'll go my way and you go yours."

"Where will I go?" My voice cracked at the end of the sentence. I pressed my fingernails into the palm of my other hand.

His eyes softened for a split second, as if he remembered I was his daughter. "What I mean is, you can stay here, but I'm not answering to you. I'll come and go as I please."

How was this different than the way he'd lived with Mama?

"You can figure out how to feed that brat and yourself too. You're grown now. I shouldn't have to take care of you."

Grown? Was twelve grown? It seemed the world had been telling me that again and again over the last few days.

"This place was your mama's, so it's only right you stay

here," Pa said, as if he were a generous king bequeathing a home to a peasant. "But you'll have to contribute to the household. You can't get something for nothing. I'll expect you to pay for the food we eat, since I'm letting you keep it." He pointed toward the cradle.

Again, how generous of the benevolent dictator.

I studied the pattern the bean residue had left in my bowl. Was it in the shape of an angel? A hint from above that He would look after us?

Pa shoved away from the table. "Did you hear me?"

Before I could catch up with what was happening, he picked me up out of the chair and tossed me against the wall. I cowered as he lunged toward me. Instead of slapping me, he knocked my forehead with the heel of his hand. The back of my head slammed into the wall. I blinked as stars dotted my vision.

"You say thank you when I give you something, you hear?" Pa asked.

This close, I could smell the whiskey on his breath and the sour smell of his unwashed hair.

"Yes, sir. I'm sorry."

He backed away. "Now that we have an understanding, I'm going to head out for a few hours. Moonshine Mike has a Christmas special for his regular customers."

Moonshine Mike? How many secrets did this town have? Clandestine professions and homemade booze? *Oh, Mama, what did you leave me with?*

I rubbed the back of my head. The sound of me hitting the wall must have woken the baby, because she started fussing in the cradle. Still dazed, I moved slowly to the porch, where I'd stored the milk. From behind me, the floorboards of the porch creaked as Pa lumbered down the steps and into the night.

Angel, if you're there, I could use a little help about now.

5

esley

ON CHRISTMAS EVE, AFTER A MEAL OF ROAST PORK, POTATOES, and carrots, Lillian and I were in the sitting room waiting for Mother and Father. They'd dismissed us from the table but had stayed in the dining room. I wasn't sure why. They'd not said one word during our tense supper. Lillian and I knew better than to speak unless spoken to. The delicious food seemed wasted on us. Mother and Lillian barely ate. I managed to finish mine, but it tasted like chalk in my dry mouth. Father had eaten with his usual gusto, quickly, taking large bites and washing them down with whiskey. He alone seemed oblivious to the chasm that divided our family into three parts: Lillian and me, Mother, and finally Father.

Atlas was asleep in his bed by the fire. Lillian plunked away at the piano, playing "The First Noel." She didn't look up at me, concentrating on the music, her pale face pinched and drawn as her small hands flew up and down the keyboard. Too thin, her shoulder blades seemed without flesh under the fabric of her blue velvet dress.

Lillian's copper-colored hair had been pulled back from her face with a blue bow that matched her dress. Mother said a ginger should never wear red, even though Lillian longed for a red dress. At twelve, she was small for her age and looked even more so hunched over the large piano. Over the last few days, she'd been sick with a bad cold, which had reddened and chapped her nose. Dark half circles under her eyes seemed painted with a deep purple ink. She complained of difficulty sleeping. Fears of the dark and monsters plagued her. I could never understand how the black night was worse than the chaos and uncertainty we faced in our own home. Also, she was so often ill. I feared she was not strong. Lack of sleep didn't help. The strain of trying to please Mother and Father took too much of her energy. There wasn't enough left for herself.

"The music is very pretty," I said.

"Thank you." She spoke softly as her small hands moved over the keyboard.

"How much longer?" I asked. Mother made her practice an hour a day, even on Christmas Eve.

"I've already done my hour practice. Playing makes me feel better." She fumbled on a note and lifted her fingers from the keys, then started back at the beginning of the song. Another rule. She had to start from the top if she made any mistakes.

Atlas lifted his head briefly, as if to check on Lillian. Assured she was fine, he sighed and curled back into a ball. He looked like an old man tonight. The hair around his eyes had grayed, and he seemed thinner than he once was. I looked at him and then back to my sister. My two best friends seemed to be disintegrating right before my eyes.

For our Christmas tree, Dax had cut down an eight-foot fir tree from the property. After trimming off the bottom branches, he'd nailed two crisscrossed boards into its sawed-off trunk so it could stand straight in the corner of the room. Garlands from the extra branches decorated the mantel. We were to decorate the tree after dinner. Now, it stood sparse, waiting. I crossed over to breathe in the spicy scent.

I found it peculiar that Mother had such an affinity for Christmas. Delicate ornaments wrapped in tissue were safely stored in a box and brought down each year. Best of all was Mother's snow globe collection. For the past eight years, Mother had ordered one each autumn from an Austrian company for the coming Christmas. She displayed them on the piano for the entire month of December. They were sentimental scenes: a white-steepled church, Santa with a bag of gifts, a Christmas tree lit with candles, a Ferris wheel, a snowman, Santa's sleigh in the sky pulled by reindeer, tiny figures skating on a frozen pond, and finally my favorite, a cottage. Snow covered the roof, and the windows were painted yellow as if lit from inside. A large decorated tree had presents surrounding it, wrapped red-and-gold packages. The only thing missing was a yellow dog. For some reason, I imagined the cottage perched on a bluff overlooking the sea. I could almost see the ocean from its front room.

I shook the cottage globe gently to encourage the snow to swirl. Staring through the miniature glass, I fell into the world. I was safe there. The snow swirled around us as Atlas and I ran to the edge of the yard to look out to the ocean, gray and foggy on this day before Christmas. We turned back toward the cottage. Atlas and I stood in the stillness and utter silence of the snowy yard and looked through the glass. A woman was at a table, icing gingerbread. She looked up and smiled. Luci, all grown now. Hair the color of wheat glistened, and her green eyes were no longer hungry or fearful. She raised her hand and waved. Another person joined her at the table. My sister. Also grown. No longer thin and brittle. She threw back her head, laughing. A man with floppy brown hair joined them, a bottle of champagne in his hand. He spotted me, watching from the outside, and came to the door, calling out to me. "Wes, it's time to come inside out of the cold." The words were as loud as the notes of Lillian's playing.

Wes. No one had ever called me by the shortened version of my name.

"Wesley." I startled at the sound of Mother's sharp voice and landed squarely back in the real world. I placed the snow globe back into its place on the piano, then turned to face her.

"Yes, Mother?"

She'd dressed for dinner in an elegant eggplant-colored dress and had powdered her face. Her hair had been fixed into an elaborate mound on top of her head. "How many times have I told you to keep your sticky hands off my globes?"

"Sorry, Mother."

I fully expected a punishment, but she walked over to the window instead, looking out as if she expected someone.

My sister began to play "Silent Night."

I went to stand in front of the fire. Knitted stockings hung from nails over the fireplace. Tomorrow they would be filled with candies, an orange, and one other gift.

Mother turned from the window. "The snow's stopped."

I nodded, as if she'd asked a question.

Her heels clicked on the hardwood floor as she crossed over to the box of decorations Dax had brought down from storage. "It's almost eight. I don't know where your father wandered off to, but we might as well begin to decorate the tree." She tapped the top of the piano with her nails. "Lillian, you may stop playing now."

Lillian looked up from the sheet music as she played the last notes of "Silent Night." "Thank you, Mother."

"Yes, fine. Who would like to put the first decoration on the tree?"

Lillian stood up from the piano seat. "I'd like to, please."

Mother settled on the couch. "Wesley, put the box on the table in front of me. I'll unwrap them, and you two can hang them for us."

With care, I lifted the wooden box and set it on the coffee table in front of Mother.

She reached inside and pulled out the first ornament, wrapped in tissue paper. "The angel," she said. "My mother gave me this one for my sixteenth birthday." Made from glass, the ornament was about the size of my mother's small hand. "Here, Wesley, put it near the top."

Ruth, Mother's maid, came in with a tray of drinks—champagne for Mother and Father and juice for us. Ruth had worked for Mother for ten years and was the only one who seemed to know what she needed or wanted at all times. She was the only one who never fell out of favor.

"Thank you, Ruth." Mother gestured toward the liquor cabinet. "Set it there. You may retire for the evening and join the rest of the staff downstairs. I've left gifts for you all with Mollie, and Mrs. Walker's made a wonderful supper."

"Thank you, ma'am. Merry Christmas to you all." Ruth gave us all a warm smile and scuttled out of the room.

"Would you like me to get your glass of champagne?" I asked.

"Yes, please. Thank you." Mother unwrapped another ornament and handed the glass ball to Lillian.

The corner of my eye twitched at the sound of my father's loud footsteps coming down the hall. When he entered the room, I noticed he'd taken off his formal jacket. Wearing only a vest over his shirt, he looked wrong next to Mother's formal gown. I couldn't be certain, but his hair seemed mussed as well. He smelled of cigar smoke.

"Where have you been?" Mother asked.

"I was outside on the back porch. Smoking."

"We didn't wait for you," Mother said.

"Decorating the tree is for women," Pa said, winking at me. "Men don't need such foolishness."

I politely nodded but avoided eye contact. As much as I would have loved to contradict him, I knew it would turn him ugly. No one needed his temper to flare tonight.

We worked in silence for a few minutes. Mother unwrapped the ornaments, and I carried them over to Lillian, who placed them wherever Mother directed.

Father had poured another drink, ignoring the glass of champagne, and prowled around the room. Something had agitated him. Who knew what? We never did.

"Matthew, sit down. You're making me nervous." Mother's back had straightened, and her eyes glittered.

"I'll do as I please in my own home." Father gave Mother a half smile that did nothing to warm his eyes. He stomped over to stand in front of the fire. Atlas woke and raised his head, then lumbered to his feet. His nails clicked on the floor as he headed toward Lillian to sit on his haunches next to her. I was between the couch and the tree and suddenly felt as if I were stranded on an island.

"Here and everywhere else, it seems," Mother said quietly while unwrapping another ornament. "Do as you please, that is."

Please, I thought. Don't provoke him. Not on Christmas Eve. Not with Lillian unwell.

Father rocked back on his heels, watching Mother, an amused lift to his mouth. He placed his drink on the mantel. "The ice queen. What a perfect holiday for you."

She lifted her gaze to him, eyes defiant. She'd changed over the last few days. It seemed she no longer cared whether he was pleased with her. Whatever it was he'd done, she'd hardened. What would happen when she was no longer afraid? The reason we'd all survived this long was that she knew the rules.

As long as she did what he wanted, then all was well. I seemed to be the only one in this house who couldn't bring myself to defer to him. There was still fight in me. But not tonight. This was supposed to be a peaceful occasion.

I glanced at Lillian. She'd frozen by the tree with a glass reindeer in her hand. From downstairs came the sounds of laughter. What would it be like to have dinner and laugh?

"How convenient for you, Matthew. To assign blame where there is none. Married to the ice queen. How sorry I am for you."

He spoke through gritted teeth. "Zelda, have more champagne. Perhaps it will warm you."

"I'm hot. Trust me, I've never been hotter."

"I don't think so." Father crossed the room to the piano and picked up one of the snow globes. "Let's see what this does to you." He hurled the globe against the far wall. It shattered into half a dozen pieces and fell to the floor.

Mother didn't move. Her face placid, she kept her gaze on the fire.

"How about this one?" Father chose the church. Seconds later, it crashed against the wall and broke.

She blinked once but stayed perfectly still with her back to him. Lillian was crying softly, her shoulders hunched forward. Atlas pressed against her legs but seemed to know that to make a move would only make it worse.

One by one, Father pitched the globes into the wall until the only one remaining was the cottage. I held my breath. Would he spare this one?

"Please, Father, stop," Lillian said.

For some reason I couldn't fathom, her plea moved him. "Fine."

"Are you pleased with yourself?" Mother asked, voice flat.

"I always am." Father strode back to the mantel and grabbed his glass of whiskey, before strolling out of the room as if bashing glass globes against the wall was the most ordinary of Christmas activities.

Lillian had stopped crying and sank onto the piano bench. Mother drank the rest of her champagne. "Wesley, would you bring me the other glass?"

"Yes, Mother." I carried the glass of champagne over to her. She took it from me and drank another sip before placing it on the table. "Let's finish what we started." She picked another ornament from the box and unwrapped the tissue paper to reveal a glass bird.

"I'll clean all this up," I said as I headed toward the mess on the far wall.

"Thank you, dear. I'd hate to interrupt the staff from their party." Mother rose from the couch and walked over to the tree. "I'll hang this one, Lillian. May we all be free as birds one day."

THAT NIGHT, AFTER I FINALLY FELL ASLEEP, I HAD A FAMILIAR dream. I was small and sitting on a woman's lap. Someone I knew who smelled of lilacs. "Jonathan, time to go to sleep," she said before singing to me in a soft voice.

Hush, little baby, don't say a word,
Mama's gonna buy you a mockingbird.
And if that mockingbird won't sing,
Mama's gonna buy you a diamond ring.

I woke in the early morning and stared at the wall as the dream slowly faded from my mind. I'd dreamt it often over the years, and always the woman sang and called me Jonathan. When I woke, I had the sensation of having forgotten something important.

Atlas was asleep on the end of my bed. I sat up slowly and brought my knees to my chest. I'd expected to wake thinking of the debacle from the night before, but instead it was the girl and baby who occupied my thoughts. Luci.

It was Christmas Day. Would they have anything to eat? No one should be hungry today, of all days. What were the teachings of Jesus? *Love thy neighbor.*

My thoughts drifted to my parents. We had so much, and yet they managed to make each other miserable.

Atlas stirred, scooting closer and putting his head in my lap. "What do you think, boy? Should we do what's right?"

He let out a soft whine. Atlas was the sympathetic sort if ever there was one. "You're right. We have to. Anyway, we promised."

I dressed quickly, then snuck down to the kitchen without a plan, other than to see what I could find. It was dark and chilly, and I could barely make out the two ovens or the wide sink. The large woodblock island where Mrs. Walker and June worked was scrubbed clean. Overhead, pans hung from a cast-iron rack.

I made my way over to the pantry, where I knew Mrs. Walker kept all the cooking supplies. An icebox in the back held perishables like cheese and milk. I grabbed a hunk of cheese, bread, and a half-gallon jar of milk. Just as I was leaving with my stolen goods tucked into a basket, Mrs. Walker arrived from the hallway.

"Young Wesley, is there something I can do for you?"

"No, Mrs. Walker."

"What do you have there?" Mrs. Walker pointed one pudgy finger toward the basket. Her white hair was stuffed into a cap this morning and made me think of a mushroom. "Are you and Atlas going on a picnic?" Atlas wagged his tail as if we *were* going on a picnic. My partner in crime was a natural. He knew we had more important things to do than flutter around the countryside.

"I'm taking this to someone who needs it." I said it more bravely than I felt at the moment.

Her brow wrinkled. She placed her arms over her ample chest and peered at me with a distinct note of sympathy in her blue eyes. "I see. And who might that be?"

"A girl no older than Lillian." I knew Mrs. Walker had a soft spot for my sister. "And a tiny baby. Their mother died, and their father's a drunk."

"Oh dear."

"Mother doesn't want me to go out there, but I can't understand why."

A glint I couldn't quite place flickered in her eyes. "Right. You told her of your plan?"

"Yes, and she said we couldn't feed the whole world or something like that, even though I know we throw away food."

She seemed to contemplate that for a moment as she gazed up at the ceiling. "I'll tell you what we'll do. If I have anything left at the end of the day, I'll leave it in here." She beckoned me into the pantry and pointed to an empty shelf near the door. "We'll keep this between the two of us, though. I don't want to get in trouble."

"Me neither." I gave her my best grin.

"One more thing." She reached up to an upper shelf and pulled down what looked like a white slug stuffed in a jar. "This is my sourdough starter. If you wait just a moment, I'll put some in a separate jar for you. I can write down the recipe too. You won't be able to take her food forever. This way, she'll be able to make her own bread."

She took the starter to the wood block and transferred some into a pint jar. A foul smell like stinky feet filled my nostrils. "It smells awful."

"That's the yeast, but trust me, she can't go wrong with this." She closed the jar and asked me to wait while she wrote out the recipe. A few minutes later, she tucked it and the jar into my basket. "Be careful. And get back in time for Christmas breakfast. We don't want your father taking the strap to you again this week. Not on Christmas."

"I'll be fast."

"Off with you, then."

Atlas and I walked as quickly as we could. He seemed to know the way, never hesitating as we retraced our steps from two days ago. I'd said I'd come yesterday, but I hadn't. Already I'd let her down. At least they'd have food for Christmas. Mrs. Walker and I had worked out a plan. I smiled to myself. This was a bright spot in my rather dark life. To be of service to another. What could make my burden lighter than that?

When we arrived, I scanned the yard, but the house and yard were quiet. I set the basket down and whispered, "Merry Christmas." Then we headed home.

6

L uci

I'D ALREADY MADE MY SECOND TRIP TO THE CREEK FOR WATER
when I saw the basket. The boy had managed it. Perhaps it had
taken him a day to figure out his plan. I set the bucket near the
front door and looked around. Was he still here? But no, only
quiet met me. I ran to the basket and snatched off the white
cloth that covered the top. Inside, I found a loaf of bread, a
wedge of cheese, and a half-gallon jar of milk. In addition, there
was a canning jar with a lid that contained something cream
colored. I picked it up to inspect it. The label read, *Sourdough
Starter, feed daily with a scoop of flour.* A recipe for sourdough
bread was scrawled on a sheet of paper.

Once inside, I cut a slab of bread and cheese and ate it
standing up by the stove. Sadie had not yet stirred after her
morning bottle. Given her patterns, I probably had an hour to
figure out what to do next. Pa continued to snore from the other

room. He hadn't come home from Moonshine Mike's until the early morning, waking both Sadie and me by crashing into the table.

I cut him a piece of bread and cheese and left it on the table. The rest I left in the basket, which I hid behind the wood-pile. I couldn't trust him not to eat it all at once. In addition, I didn't want him to know about the boy. He was sure to cause trouble. I stacked my arms with a pile of wood and took it inside to the bin next to the stove.

We would have fresh bread for Christmas dinner. There were beans left too. This was a happy Christmas after all. My spirits plummeted when I read the directions. The recipe said to stir flour and the starter together and set them in a cool location for ten or more hours. How strange. Biscuits took minutes but also needed lard, which I was quickly running out of. Never mind—we would have fresh bread for tomorrow. Today, I'd make biscuits instead. Still, we were all right for a few more days. A miracle had surely come our way on this Christmas morning.

 esley

BOTH ATLAS AND I WERE HUNGRY BY THE TIME WE JUMPED OVER the gate to our yard. I was excited to tell Mrs. Walker that we'd managed to leave the basket and were now home. We tore in through the kitchen door. My mother was there with Mrs. Walker, who was in tears.

I came to a halt, as did Atlas. My stomach clenched. I'd gotten Mrs. Walker in trouble.

"Where have you been?" Mother asked.

She already knew, or poor Mrs. Walker wouldn't be crying. "It wasn't Mrs. Walker's fault. She didn't have anything to do with this."

"Instead of marching you upstairs, she sent you off with a basket of our food," Mother said. "That doesn't sound terribly innocent."

"I didn't give her any choice," I said. "I ran out before she could stop me. Isn't that right, Mrs. Walker?" I pleaded with my eyes for her to agree.

Mrs. Walker shook her head as she wiped her eyes. "No, that's not true. I didn't see any harm in helping out a girl and a baby with food we weren't going to eat."

"And you made that decision when it was not your place to do so?" Mother asked.

"Yes, Mrs. Ford." Mrs. Walker lifted her face. "And I'd do it again."

"You may go," Mother said. "Mollie will pay you what we owe you."

"What? No." Tears sprang to my eyes. "This isn't her fault."

"Perhaps you'll remember that next time you disobey me," Mother said.

"But, Mother, Mrs. Walker needs this job."

"She should have thought about that before she helped a criminal."

"It's all right," Mrs. Walker said to me. "I'll be just fine." She took off her apron and set it on the table. "You stay kind, young Wesley. Even when the world isn't."

"I'll try," I said as tears spilled from my eyes.

"Goodbye, then." With that, she grabbed her bag and walked toward the door with her head held high. The door slammed behind her.

"Mother, how could you? Mrs. Walker's been with us for years and years."

Mother turned cold, furious eyes toward me. "Why must you always disobey me?"

"I . . . I don't." This once I had, but it was too important. I had to do what was right. "She's all alone with that baby. Don't you see, Mother? I couldn't let her starve."

"Did you know that girl's mother was the town whore?"

I flinched as if she'd smacked me. *Whore?* I was fairly certain I knew what that meant. A woman who sold her body

49

TESS THOMPSON

for money. "How do you know that?" In hindsight, it wasn't the best question, as it seemed to make her even more furious.

She went perfectly still and looked at me with eyes that bored through my soul. "Your father and I were going to tell you this later today. We're sending you and your sister to boarding school at the beginning of the new year."

The words themselves would not have necessarily been taken, all stacked up in order, as a punishment. But I knew it was. They wanted to send us away. Heat rushed through my body. I shrugged out of my coat and placed it on the table.

"But why?" My throat was as dry as if I'd swallowed a mouthful of sand. "Do you not want us?"

"It has nothing to do with what I *want* but rather what's best for you. I've had enough of your traipsing around the woods like one of these local people. This town isn't what either of you needs. Your sister needs to go to a school where she can learn to be a proper young lady and further study piano. You'll need to meet other young men with whom you can conduct business when you're grown. Families who have the right kind of women for you to marry. Not here in this godforsaken place."

"But Lillian. She's not strong." I had that thought, followed by another. *What about Atlas?* My dog, sensing my dismay, leaned against my leg. "I can't leave Atlas." *What about Luci?* Who would look after her? "Mother, are you doing this to punish me simply because I delivered food to a helpless girl?"

The anger seemed to go out of her then. She placed both hands on the kitchen island and hung her head. "Wesley, don't you agree it would be better for you to leave this house?"

"You mean because of Father?"

She turned her head to look at me. "Yes. How many times can you endure that strap? What about last night? Do you really want to live with a man who would do that on Christmas Eve? Or any night, for that matter. You'll come home for holi-

50

days. It's no good for any of us here. You'll make friends. There will be teachers who will challenge your fine mind."

"What about Atlas?"

She sighed. "He's old, Wesley. You're almost a young man. This is the right thing for you."

"Do you really think Lillian's strong enough?"

"I think this house is making her sick," Mother said.

I stared at her. "You do?"

"He's turned you and your sister into nervous little rabbits. Me as well." She reached out to touch my cheek with the tips of her cold fingers. "This is not a punishment. I want you to have a chance."

Despite the earnestness of her words, there was something more to all this. A thread I couldn't quite find.

"Go upstairs and get changed for breakfast," she said. "We'll try to have a nice day."

I took another hard look at my mother. She looked so sad that my heart ached more for her than for myself and Lillian, perhaps for the first time in my life. Dark circles and bags under her eyes told me she'd cried herself to sleep.

"I'm sorry I disobeyed you, Mother. But what about Mrs. Walker? Can't you ask her back?"

She stiffened and straightened to her full height. "I can't have the staff making decisions that aren't theirs to make. You're a boy. She's a grown woman." She pointed toward the stairs. "Go, please."

I turned to do so but stopped when I saw my father holding his strap. "You're as thickheaded as a mule," Father said. "We couldn't have been clearer."

"It's fine, Mathew. I've handled it."

He raised one eyebrow. "Zelda, I doubt you've handled it as I shall. The boy has to learn." He drew closer, smacking the riding whip's handle against the other hand. "Take off your shirt and lean over the table."

I knew how it went. Two blows to the back. No more, no less. I took off my shirt and held it in front of my chest, shivering despite the warmth of the ovens. For the first time, it occurred to me that June wasn't here. Mother must have sent her upstairs. They didn't like the staff to see what went on behind closed doors.

I put my elbows on the table and braced for the impact. One swift, cruel lick of the strap snapped across my upper back. I yelped in pain. *Remember the snow globe,* I thought. *Go inside. Live there in your mind.* The strap whipped me again, this time on my lower back. He never struck in the same place. Perhaps I should be grateful? The sound of Atlas's growl comforted me and frightened me. I didn't want him hurt because he was protecting me.

Despite my best efforts, tears streamed down my face. I was no longer emotionally hurt. Those days were gone. Now it was simply the physical pain that caused tears.

I pulled my shirt back on as carefully as I could to keep the fabric from touching my stinging flesh.

"Go upstairs and think about what you've done," Father said. "You may come down for lunch but not before."

"It's all right, boy. Come with me," I said to Atlas.

He followed me as I clomped up the stairs, vowing to myself that I would not cry again. Who cared about boarding school? I could go and be lonely there like I was here, except for Atlas. Mother was right. He was old. I'd known all along that his days were numbered. However, I'd wanted him to spend every last bit of his life with me.

My life had been miserable, but I'd had Atlas and Lillian. Now I would be with strangers, possibly cruel strangers.

My back stung as I walked into my bedroom. I closed the door and collapsed onto the braided rug and crossed my legs but didn't lean against the bed. Anything touching my wounds made them sting worse. Atlas sat beside me with his head in my lap.

"They're taking me away from you." I caressed his head and ears. "You remember our good times when I'm gone, all right? Remember how much fun we've had together. Mostly, remember how much I love you and what a good, good dog you've been."

Atlas whined and licked my hand.

"I know, boy. I know. When it's your time, remember it all and be at peace. You'll be up there in heaven chasing rabbits and running in the grass. Someday, I'll be there too."

Atlas's tail thumped.

"Wesley, can I come in?" It was Lillian.

"Yes."

She opened the door slowly, and then seeing me slumped over my dog, she ran to us and collapsed onto the floor. Her braid fell over one shoulder as she leaned close. "Did they tell you? They're sending us away. I don't want to leave you." Lillian started to cry.

I put my arm around her, and she rested her damp cheek on my shoulder. She was so frail and thin.

I had to be brave. She needed to hear the good things about going away to school. "You'll meet friends and get to study more piano with a real teacher. You won't have to tiptoe around wishing you were invisible."

"Do you think the other girls will like me?"

"Of course they will. You'll learn how to be a proper lady, and then you'll marry a prince who will give you a happy-ever-after."

"Is there any such thing?" She sniffed as she pressed the palms of her hands into her eyes. I reached into my pocket to give her my handkerchief. She dabbed her face. "Right now anything happy seems very far away."

"You and I are going to survive. We're going to grow up and live in houses next door to each other."

"By the seaside?"

"Yes, by the seaside. And we'll have Christmas together without any shouting or breaking of things."

She hiccuped. "That sounds nice."

Atlas and Lillian. They were sending me away from my dog and my sister. "He can't break us," I said. "You'll see. We're going to be happy someday, and all this will just be a bad memory."

But that was a lie. I was already broken. He'd already won.

ON THE FIRST DAY OF THE NEW YEAR, I KNELT ON THE LAWN AND gave Atlas one last scratch behind the ears. "You're a good boy."

His tail wagged. He had no idea what was about to happen. I hadn't slept well, as I'd let Atlas sleep right next to me instead of by my feet. If he sensed I was about to leave him, he didn't show it, as he'd slept peacefully. Sometimes in his sleep, his tail wagged. I imagined he was dreaming of chasing a rabbit through the meadow in springtime.

With several feet between them, my mother and father stood at the bottom of the steps. Lillian hung back on the porch, her arms wrapped around a post. Mother was accompanying Lillian on the train ride to her new school. They were to leave tomorrow. My sister and I had already said our goodbyes upstairs, promising to write each other every week.

Mollie had come up earlier to give me a lunch to take on the train, but she hadn't been able to speak because she'd started crying. She'd hugged me before running from the room.

Dax was waiting for me in our wagon. My parents had asked him to take me to the station.

With tears in my eyes, I gave Atlas one last snuggle. "I'll miss you, boy." I reluctantly stood.

I went over to my father and shook his hand. "This will be good for you. Make you a man," he said.

"Yes, sir."

Mother embraced me and whispered in my ear, "Be brave, my boy."

"I will. Goodbye, Mother."

As I turned to walk to the wagon, Atlas followed me, assuming he was to go with me. I patted his head and fought hard against the lump in my throat. "You stay here."

Atlas tilted his head and wagged his tail.

I gave Lillian one last wave and headed toward the wagon. Just as I was about to climb inside, my sister shouted for me to wait and ran across the lawn to hug me. "Don't forget to write."

"I won't." I broke free from her hug and got inside before Atlas could climb in behind me. He sat back on his haunches, looking at me. "You stay here, Atlas." A sob rose up from my belly. "I love you."

"All righty, lad. Stay strong," Dax said under his breath as he clicked for the horses to go. Despite the sound of their hooves on the frozen driveway, I heard Atlas bark. I turned back to look. He chased after us, ears flapping in the wind. I shifted to my knees and put my head out of the wagon. I shouted to him, "Go back, boy. Go back."

But he kept on, running as fast as he could, desperate to catch me until finally the horses outpaced him. I continued to shout at him to go home. When he realized his attempt to catch us was futile, he sat in the middle of the drive, raised his head, and howled. I flopped back into my seat and sobbed as we turned onto the main road.

THE TRAIN STATION BUSTLED WITH PEOPLE. I SAT ON A BENCH with my suitcase at my feet while Dax bought my ticket. This school they were sending me to was half a day away. I'd be there by suppertime. Mother had told me the headmaster was expecting me.

When Dax returned with my ticket, he sat down next to me and patted my knee. "Only a few minutes before it gets here. You know not to talk to strangers and to keep to yourself."

"Yes, all right."

"I know it's hard right now, but this is the best thing for you." The sympathy in his eyes almost got me crying again, but I held my emotions together. I didn't want to cry in a public place.

I nodded, then tucked my chin into my neck.

Dax took off his cap and ran a hand through his salt-and-pepper hair. "She had to send you away for your own good. Your father . . . well, I don't know what to say about what you've had to endure. It's not right."

I nodded again, too miserable to comment.

"You'll meet some good lads. Friends for life. It'll be good to have pals your own age."

"I had you and Mollie. Lillian and Atlas." I choked back a sob.

"We'll be here when you come for holidays."

We sat in silence for a few minutes. A family traveling with two small children plopped onto the bench across from us. The whistle and loud chugging of the steam engine told me the train was near. It was time. A new chapter. Perhaps I was numb or simply too sad to feel anything, but I was ready now. I'd already done the hardest part.

"About the lass and the baby," Dax said. "The missus and I will bring some food and milk to her as best we can. Tell me, now. Where's the girl's house?"

I described how to get there from the meadow. "But you'll be let go like Mrs. Walker."

"Not if I'm stealthy. We have our own cottage. Our own food. We do as we please with it."

My chest swelled with love and gratitude. "They have no one."

"I know." He patted my knee. "A man can't save the whole world, but he can surely save his neighbor."

"I'm sorry about Mrs. Walker. My good intentions got her fired." I cringed, remembering her wet cheeks. I'd done that to her.

"Mollie will get her placed somewhere else. She knows all the other housekeepers in town."

"Write to me and tell me she's all right. And tell her I'm sorry, please? I wanted her to tell Mother it was all my idea, but she wouldn't."

"She's an adult who made her own choice. Anyway, she didn't crumple under pressure. That's a strong woman—the good kind that makes this hard world better. You remember that lesson as you go along."

"I'll try."

He shifted to look at me, then adjusted my cap slightly so he could look into my eyes. "The way it's been for you, that's not how it's supposed to be between parent and child. Don't let it make you hard, lad. Stay pure of heart like the good Lord made you."

I rested my head on his shoulder. "I'll do my best."

"Take it all in. All the learning. Use it for good someday."

"Yes, sir."

The train came to a stop at the station. Soon the doors opened, and people spilled out onto the platform. We both stood. Dax pulled me into an embrace. "You're a fine lad—don't let anyone tell you different. I'll miss you. Write to us when you can."

"Thanks, Dax. For being the one to bring me here." I pressed my forehead against the rough fabric of his tweed coat. "And for always being there. Tell Mollie too."

"It's been my pleasure. Mollie's too."

I stepped back to get one final look at him, hoping to recall the image of his face when I was lonesome. "Will you wait until the train leaves the station?"

"I'll be right here, lad."

I bowed my head, looking at my feet as I held back tears. "Please, take care of Atlas. Don't let him suffer at the end. When it's time, will you be there with him? I don't want him to die alone."

The man who was like a father to me teared up as he placed both hands on my shoulders. "I'll make sure to be there when he leaves this world, don't you worry."

I raised my gaze to meet his. "Tell him I love him at the end. Just so he knows I wouldn't have left him if I could've helped it."

"Don't worry. He already knows. But I'll tell him again."

"Bye, Dax." I broke apart, grabbed my suitcase, and ran toward the train. If I didn't run, I might not be able to go at all.

The attendant took my ticket and pointed to my seat. My parents had paid for a first-class ticket. I'd ride out of here in comfort.

I took my place by the window, storing my suitcase and sack lunch under the seat. The glass was fogged over, so I made a fist and cleared a spot. Dax, as promised, remained on the platform. I waved to him. He couldn't see me, though, so I made a wider swath with my fist and waved again. This time, he waved back. The train began to move, chugging out of the station. I stayed pressed against the window, waving until I could no longer see the platform. Like Atlas, I finally gave up and sat back in the seat. Hot tears leaked from my eyes. I didn't bother to wipe them away. Once again, they'd broken me.

Don't let it make you hard.

At the moment, it seemed as if the hurt would become scar tissue. How could I not become hardened? However, I'd made Dax a promise, and I planned to keep it. Whatever was next, I would do good in the world wherever and whenever I could.

8

Luci

A WEEK WENT BY, BRINGING THE NEW YEAR. EVERY DAY I HOPED for a basket, but none came. Not only did the loneliness stretch out these endless days, but we were almost out of milk and flour. During the early morning, on the first day of the year, I fed Sadie the last of the milk. Although I knew it was fruitless, I stood by the window with the baby in my arms and watched for the boy. I prayed too, begging God to send help. Mama had once said a watched pot never boiled. Was it the same as a watched tree?

After she ate, I put Sadie back in her cradle for her morning nap. I'd already done my water run and brought in the firewood. Too hungry to sleep and too agitated to come up with a plan, I paced around the small room. If only I could crawl out of my skin like a snake, leaving all this behind.

Thoughts of Mama plagued me as I paced. She'd been a

pretty woman, with white-blonde hair and blue eyes. At one time she'd had promise. That's what she'd told me, anyway. "Until I married your pa, that is. Never marry a drinking man."

Despite what I'd learned about how she kept us alive, I still loved her. She'd been good to me, gentle and kind. Now, as I fretted about how to keep my baby sister in milk, I understood how desperate one could become. Women would do anything to keep their children alive.

Pa's snores agitated me further. I imagined putting his nasty pillow over his drunk face and suffocating him. We'd be no worse off without him. Maybe better, given how he'd taken Mama's money for drink.

In the next instant, I was horrified at myself. Would I become a murderer? Was I a monster now, born of desperation and hunger?

I tossed another log into the stove and set the empty bottle in a pot of water. I needed to figure out how to get supplies. Then get on with things. What resources did I have? Did I have anything I could trade? What about my surroundings? Could I trap an animal? With what, though?

I slipped into Mama's old coat in preparation for another trip down to the creek. If only there were fish this time of year. *But wait, what is this? Movement at the edge of the thicket?* I peered through the dirty glass. Not the boy, but a man wearing a newsboy hat and a hunter's jacket appeared. He placed a wooden box near where I'd left the basket.

I ran out of the house, afraid he'd leave before I could talk to him. "Hello, sir?" I must have startled him because he jumped. "Yes, hello there." I recognized an Irish brogue. One of the boys at school had been from Ireland.

"Did the boy send you?"

"He did." Dark-blue eyes peered at me from under the brim of his hat. Lines around his eyes and mouth told me he was older than Pa. His skin had the look of a man who spent a lot of time outdoors. "I'm Dax O'Connelly. My wife, Mollie, and I work for his parents. The lad and his sister—well, we've helped raised them."

"What's happened to him?" I asked, surprised at my boldness.

"His parents sent him away to boarding school. He won't be back for a while."

"What about Atlas?"

A shadow crossed his face. "He's at home. Won't leave the front lawn."

"Waiting for the boy?"

"That's right." The rims of the man's eyes reddened. "He's an old dog. Won't survive to see his boy again."

I hadn't cried when Mama died, even though the grief was a thousand sharp knives to my chest. I'd had too much to do, too many worries over how to live rather than mourn the dead. During the last few trying days, as tired and worried as I was, I hadn't cried. The closest I'd come was when the woman in town had told me the truth about my mother's secret life. However, the thought of that poor dog waiting for his master did me in. Tears blurred my vision.

"Ah, now, lass, don't cry."

"The poor dog." I swiped tears from my cheeks. The air was so cold I was surprised they hadn't become a layer of ice on my skin.

He reached out as if to comfort me but pulled back his hand and shoved it into his coat pocket. "To love someone as much as they love each other is a great gift. Even when parted, the love remains."

I squinted up at him. The winter sun hurt my tired eyes. Was that true? Was some part of Mama still here with me? "He didn't expect to go, did he? Or he wouldn't have promised to bring food."

"That's correct." He smiled. "Wesley's the type to keep his promises if he can."

"Wesley?" *Wesley.* A gentleman's name. Even so, Wesley had understood when I'd told him of my plight. He'd wanted to help. Was it because he knew what it was like to be in a home where you had to have one eye open all the time? Or was it neglect?

"He was sorry he couldn't come himself. Before he left, I told him I'd look after you."

"But why?"

"Wesley and his sister are like our children," Dax said. "We'd do anything for them."

I breathed a sigh of relief. God had answered my prayers. "I'm grateful. I just gave the baby the last of the milk." His eyes were so kind and sympathetic that I felt comfortable enough to share the truth of my troubles. "I didn't know what I was going to do. Pa . . ." I trailed off, unable to bring myself to say what must be obvious.

"Wesley said as much." Dax shuffled his feet in the dry leaves. "Have you thought about telling someone what's happening out here?"

I looked away. A squirrel scampered up a tree and onto a branch. Several pine cones fell to the ground. "I can't. I'm afraid someone will come and take the baby from me. As long as they think Pa's looking after us, no one will get an idea to take her. People want babies, I expect. Not a girl like me. We're in trouble here, but we have to stay together. I promised my mama." All that spilled from my mouth like snow from the sky during a blizzard.

"I see." Dax rubbed his chin with his gloved fingers. "Where's your pa?" His gaze traveled to the house. "Will he harm the baby? Or you?"

"He's in there. Asleep. Drunk." I spit the words out like they tasted bad. "He won't have anything to do with the baby. Mostly, he stays away from us. If he has money to go into town to the bar, that is." I looked down at my numb fingers. "Are Wesley's parents like my pa? Is that why you and Mollie had to raise them?"

"They're not like your pa, exactly. But his father—he's a hard man—a cruel one. Life hasn't been easy for Wesley. Anyway, that's not my business to tell. I've said too much."

He didn't have to say the words. I knew what he meant. The realization stunned me. Even rich people had troubles.

"Tell me, what are your plans to get through the winter?" Dax's gaze now roamed the flat brown yard.

"My biggest trouble is the milk. I have to have it for Sadie, and I have no money to buy it with. I made the sourdough bread. From the starter. I had a little money to buy flour and lard, but it's almost gone."

"During the winter, I'll bring milk for the wee one and flour and cheese and whatever else I can spare for you. But, lass, becoming self-reliant will set you free. A garden is a poor man's savior. Come spring, I'll teach you how to grow vegetables. Potatoes, onions, and carrots you can store for winter. I've seeds to get you started. Again, in the spring, I can repair that chicken coop and bring over a few chicks. That way you'll have eggs before long."

"Why would you do all this for me?" My dull mind couldn't keep up with all that he was saying.

"A man who turns away from his neighbor isn't one I'd like to know."

"Even a neighbor like me?" The daughter of a whore and a drunk?

"In God's eyes, we're all the same." The corners of Dax's eyes creased as he smiled. "I have to get back before anyone notices I'm gone. I'll be back in the next few days. There's a gallon of milk in the box, a loaf of bread, a chunk of cheese, and enough beef stew to eat for a few days. My Mollie made it herself."

My mouth watered. "Thank you." I'd have to hide the box somewhere Pa wouldn't find it.

"This afternoon, bring in more firewood than you think you'll need for the next few days. There's a snowstorm coming."

"There is?" I looked up at the blue sky.

"I can feel it in my left big toe. Always aches before a storm."

"Yes, sir, I can do that."

"You stay safe now," Dax said. "I'll come tomorrow if the weather allows. Otherwise, I'll come after the blizzard rolls through."

I thanked him again as I picked up the wooden box. He took the basket Wesley had left and turned to go. I watched him as he traipsed over the frozen ground and disappeared into the woods.

For the second time that day, I cried. Only this time it was from pure relief.

9

esley

UPON MY ARRIVAL AT SCHOOL, THE HEADMASTER, MR. KANE, welcomed me into his office. One of the staff had picked me up at the station, an older man who introduced himself as Buddy and explained that he was the handyman and chauffeur at the school. After that, the ride to school had been silent. Despite my homesickness, the sight of the large brick building had excited me. Possibilities waited for me. Maybe even a friend.

A roaring fire blazed, warming my face as I sat across from Mr. Kane. The headmaster was middle-aged, somewhere between thirty-five and forty-five, I guessed, with sandy-colored hair sprinkled with white. Kind eyes peered at me through wire-rimmed glasses. The office was long and skinny, with dark walls and an enormous walnut desk. Rows and rows of books lined the shelves. The faint scent of pipe tobacco lingered in the air.

"Wesley, your mother wrote that your enrollment here was somewhat of a surprise to you."

"Yes, sir." Last week I'd been running through the woods with Atlas, saving damsels in distress.

"The first time away from home can be lonely. I've asked one of the boys, Roland Harris, to look after you these first few weeks. He's one of our finest boys, with a heart of gold and a quick mind. He came to us in the fall, so he understands what it's like to be new. I've arranged for you to share a room with him."

"Yes, sir." What would it be like to spend time with a boy my age? Would I be strange to him?

Mr. Kane continued, telling me about the school uniform waiting for me in my room and other details about my classes. "We're only one day into the new term, so you won't be behind. My understanding is that you've been taught at home by your mother and an occasional tutor?"

"That's correct. We had a tutor for math, mostly."

"What's your favorite area of study?"

"English. I love reading."

"What else do you like to do?" He leaned forward slightly, as if genuinely interested.

"I like to build things with wood. That's not really an area of study, I guess." I looked at my hands. My ears burned with embarrassment. I must sound like a simpleton.

"We have a woodshop class and a workshop here on campus, which you may use during your free time. I encourage all the boys to develop practical skills in addition to academics. As a matter of fact, as luck would have it, Roland is also interested in woodwork. You'll have that in common."

A knock on the door drew his gaze from me. "Come in," Mr. Kane said.

I turned to see a scrawny boy with large blue eyes and freckles sprinkled over his nose. He held up his hand in greeting, then hustled across the room to stand in front of the desk. His hair was combed back, but several tufts had escaped and fell over his forehead.

"Roland, this is Wesley Ford." Mr. Kane stood, so I did as well.

Roland stuck out his hand and grinned at me. "Nice to meet you." He wore blue trousers and a white shirt paired with a red tie. The uniform.

"You too." My ears continued to burn.

"I'll have Roland take you to your room. You can get acquainted before our evening meal. Dinner's always at six. Lights out at ten."

"Breakfast at seven." Roland had a slow way of speaking, drawing out vowels to make them sound like two syllables. "Then we have class until three."

"Exercise in the late afternoon," Mr. Kane said. "We have several sports you can participate in, including cross-country running, which your mother said you have aptitude for."

I bit back a smile, not wanting to seem too eager in front of Roland. "Running is a sport?"

"Yes, indeed it is," Mr. Kane said. "We have paths through the woods." He gestured toward the windows behind him.

"I'll show you tomorrow," Roland said. "If you don't mind running in the rain."

"As long as I can run, I don't care what's falling from the sky." My spirits lifted. So far, this new life here at school seemed much better than the one at home. I wouldn't have to hear my parents fighting or endure Father's strap. Roland could be a friend. They had a woodworking shop and running paths through the woods. But no Atlas. I put that aside. *Be present in the immediate.*

"I hung both sets of your uniform in the wardrobe in your room, plus your exercise clothes." Roland's gaze moved to my suitcase. "I hope you didn't bring much, because there's not much space. The uniforms aren't too bad, except for the tie. Chokes a fellow if you're not careful."

"Not much, no," I said.

"Off you go," Mr. Kane said, giving us a gentle smile. "I've work to do."

"Yes, sir," we said at the same time.

I nodded at Mr. Kane, then picked up my suitcase and followed Roland out of the room. We walked down a wooden hallway past empty classrooms. "That's where we have school, obviously." He pointed to a double door. "There's the dining hall. They keep the doors closed until it's mealtime." I caught a whiff of food that smelled like beef gravy, and my stomach growled. I'd been too upset to eat my lunch and had mistakenly left it under the seat on the train. I thought of Mollie, how she'd made it with love just this morning. That seemed like a thousand years ago now.

A wave of homesickness cramped my stomach. *Don't think of it,* I told myself. *This is your new life.*

We climbed a flight of stairs. Doors about a dozen feet apart lined both sides of a long hallway. "This is where we all sleep. I've been the only one without a roommate. I'm awfully glad you're here." We walked all the way to the end before he stopped and pulled a key from his pocket. "I always lock up since some of the others like to prank. I don't take kindly to anyone messing with my things. There's a key for you too." He opened the door, and I followed him into a small room with two tall twin beds that looked as if they were built on stilts. Each had a desk underneath with identical stacks of books. "I got your books today so you'd be ready for tomorrow."

We each had a skinny wardrobe at the foot of the beds. "You can put your things in there," Roland said. "They give us each half a dozen hangers."

As I unpacked, he told me a little about himself. He was from North Carolina and the oldest of five. "I have four younger sisters. They're a lot of trouble." His warm tone belied his words. "Do you have siblings?"

"I have one sister. Lillian. She's two years younger."

"Will you miss her?" Roland plopped onto his bed and tucked his arms behind his head. "Because I miss mine, even though it's a lot quieter now."

"I will." How much I wouldn't say. I didn't want to look like a baby. I tugged off my shirt to put on the school uniform.

Roland gasped. "What happened to your back?"

I'd forgotten the red marks would still be there. Over the years, there had been so many I didn't think about it much. They eventually faded. "That's from my father."

"He whips you?" Roland sounded flabbergasted by the idea.

"Only me. Not my sister." *Thank God.* If he had ever laid a hand on her, I don't know what I would have done.

"Are you all right?"

"Sure. I'm used to it. And now I'm here, so he can't hurt me." I tugged the uniform shirt over my head.

"My parents would never strike us, even if we'd done something bad."

I sat on the edge of my bed. No wonder he was positive and grateful. He had a loving family.

"What did you do to get those?" Roland asked.

"I took a basket of food to a poor family in the woods." I explained to him about Luci and the baby and how Atlas had found them. "Atlas can sniff trouble or when someone needs help. He led me right there."

"Why'd he beat you for that? Being charitable is in the Bible. The Good Samaritan and everything."

I shrugged. "He likes punishing me. It makes him happy, I think." Saying the words I'd never said to anyone was a relief. Speaking the truth lessened the sting.

"What about your mother?"

"She has to go along with whatever he wants. We all do."

"I'd say it's good you're here."

"That's what my mother thought. They're sending Lillian away too. If I can help it, I'm only going back for holidays. Do they have summer term here?"

"No, but some boys stay if they don't have anyone to go home to. They do summer work, like polishing floors and working outside. I plan to stay for most of the summer to earn some money."

"Then I will too. If they don't call me home, which I don't think they will."

"You can come home with me," Roland said. "My family's door is always open." His forehead wrinkled. "But what about the girl and the baby? Will they be all right?"

I told him about Dax and Mollie. "He promised to take care of them for me."

His face relaxed. "Good. If it were one of my sisters, I'd hope there was someone good like you out there looking after them."

THAT NIGHT, WE LAY IN OUR TWIN BEDS. ALTHOUGH WE STILL HAD thirty minutes before lights out, we'd blown out the lamp and gotten into bed. The room was drafty and cold, but I was warm under the quilt. Rain pattered against our one small window in a comforting rhythm. Dinner in the dining hall had been loud and chaotic. Yet, I'd enjoyed myself. Eating in peace with no fear of Father's sudden temper or Mother's withering look of disappointment at my mere existence had made for a relaxing meal.

The other boys at our table had been friendly for the most part and curious about me. Most of them had been together for a couple of years, having all started together at thirteen. Roland and I were the outliers.

"How you doing?" Roland asked from the dark. "I

remember the first night I had this ache in my stomach," Roland said. "I wanted to cry my eyes out, but it goes away after a few days."

"I miss my dog and my sister." I scrunched my eyes closed, hoping to stop myself from crying. The image of Atlas on the road flashed before me. *Please forgive me, boy. I didn't want to leave you.* "But besides that, no."

"When I first came here, I couldn't sleep because it was so quiet. When I'd go to bed at home, I could hear all my sisters giggling and talking in the other room. I never thought I'd miss them so much. At the time, I just wished they'd be quiet so I could sleep."

"Why'd you come here?"

"That's just pure luck, if you want to know the dang truth. My folks don't have much and could never afford a place like this. You won't believe it, but someone paid for me to come here. We don't know who."

"A benefactor?"

"Sure thing. Can you believe how lucky I am? My mama says I was born that way. Good things always happen to me."

I had the feeling that Roland was the type to make his own luck. Being around him was like having sun on your shoulders. Roland Harris would teach me a thing or two about how to be grateful.

"Do you like it here?" I asked.

Roland's chuckle reminded me of corn popping. "Sure. What's not to love? Books, sports, all the food you can eat. Did Mr. Kane tell you about the wood room? You can build anything you want in there. Someday I want to build my own house."

I smiled in the darkness. "I think about that sometimes too."

"Really?"

"Yes. One time I went to this place by the ocean, and I

thought I'd like to build a cottage that looked out over the water. I thought how peaceful it would be. I'd stay there forever and never have to go back home."

"We'll do it one day," Roland said. "We can build cottages a short distance apart. Once they're built, we'll find wives and bring them home with us. They'll be best friends, and we'll be best friends. We'll all sit on our porches and watch the waves roll in."

I thought of Luci. Her small, pale face and those giant eyes that portrayed fear and courage at the same time. *Keep her safe,* I prayed silently. *Until I can come back for her.*

"You can marry my sister," I said. "Then everything would be just right."

Roland laughed quietly. "I should probably meet her first."

"You will. Someday." Tomorrow I would write to her and tell her about Roland. Not too soon to plant the seed. I smiled and rolled onto my side to face the wall. "Night, Roland."

"Night, Wes."

Wes. No one had ever called me that. *Wes* was a fresh start. Someone new without the burdens of the past. I would become a man here. I'd emerge triumphant, no longer a frightened, whipped boy. With that thought, I fell asleep.

That first night in my new bed, I had the dream of the woman who called me Jonathan. When I woke, the words of the lullaby still echoed through my mind. *If that mockingbird don't sing, Mama's gonna buy you a diamond ring.*

PART II

SUMMER 1910

10

esley

THE NEWS OF MY FATHER'S DEATH CAME IN THE FORM OF A
telegram from my sister.

FATHER DEAD. HEART FAILURE. MOTHER IN FLORIDA.
ARRIVED LAST NIGHT. PLEASE COME HOME. BRING ROLAND.

My father was dead. It didn't seem possible that the devil
had perished. I couldn't imagine the world without him,
actually.

We'd been discussing what to make for our bachelor dinner
later that night when a knock on the front door had drawn our
attention.

Now, I let the paper flutter to the floor as I turned to look at
my friend, who had one knee on the window seat and one eye
pressed against the spyglass. Dressed casually in a shirt that
stretched across his wide shoulders, he hardly resembled the

scrawny boy he'd been when we'd first met at school. Building our cottages had made us strong.

"Who was at the door?" Roland asked, still looking through the spyglass. With light-brown hair perpetually tousled over his forehead, he appeared careless and irresponsible, but this was not the truth of his character. In truth, he was steady, even-tempered, and strong as an ox, both in spirit and body.

"Telegraph. My father's dead. Heart failure."

Roland jerked away from the spyglass and turned to look at me. "What?" He shoved his hands into the pockets of his trousers. His sympathetic eyes matched the sea outside the window. "*I'm sorry* doesn't seem like the right thing to say."

"Lillian says Mother's in Florida." I sat down, heavy, on the bench. "I don't know if she'll come back for his burial or not." I turned back to my beloved sea. A fishing boat was anchored not far from shore. "She says for me to bring you." Despite the news and my tumbling thoughts, I smiled. "Not surprisingly, of course."

Roland sucked in his cheeks as he sat down on the window seat. "You know, then?"

"No man loves the post office as much as you." He and my sister wrote to each other every week. Every Friday morning, he drove into town and came back smiling. I could easily imagine him ripping open the envelope and reading it slouched against the side of the building.

He grimaced. "I couldn't stop myself. The months we all spent together last summer—well, I was done for."

"Why haven't you said anything?"

"I wasn't sure how you'd feel. She's your sister. And young."

My decent, decent friend. "Not too young for you."

"Yes, but look at me. What do I have to offer? No profession. Living on her brother's land."

I moved to the window to stand beside him. The skies were blue over the ocean as white-capped waves crashed to shore.

"None of that matters if she loves you," I said.

"What do you think? About her and me."

"I think it's fine. Very fine. If you love her, that's all that matters to me. I know the man you are."

"It's easy for you to think that way. You're rich."

True enough. I couldn't argue with him. I hadn't been at school a month when I received news of two deaths. Dax wrote to me that Atlas had passed peacefully in his bed by the fire. I'd already mourned him so much by then, but still, it hit me hard. Roland had been sympathetic and had not ridiculed me for crying.

The other news came a month later and changed the trajectory of my life. My mother's father had died. To everyone's surprise, he'd left the bulk of his fortune to me. I couldn't understand why. I'd never met the man. Mother had not spoken to him since her marriage to my father. Apparently, he wanted to keep his wealth in the family.

"Regardless of wealth, certain souls are meant to be together," I said.

"My heartbeat changed the moment I met her and has never been the same." He looked over at me. "Do I have your blessing?"

I brushed away his question with a brusque retort. "We're already brothers. What more could I ask for?"

"You're growing soft in your old age."

I laughed. "True enough."

Roland shifted slightly, tucking one foot around his opposite ankle. The sunlight through the windows spilled into the room. "Are you sure you want to go home? It's been almost six years, and you're all the better for it. Maybe let them bury him and say good riddance."

"I would, but Lillian needs me. Us."

He smiled faintly. "She really did ask for me?"

I didn't answer, simply rolled my eyes.

Father had forbidden me to come home during my years at school. I was happy to stay away, even though I missed Dax and Mollie. Holidays I spent with Roland's family. We'd spent summers working on campus doing janitorial and outdoor tasks. One summer, we'd aided the shop teacher in making new desks and repairing classrooms that had suffered from a broken pipe during a cold snap. Our woodworking skills had improved so much that summer that our teacher had humbly declared we had surpassed his ability to teach us. Of all the things we learned in school, our carpentry and finishing skills might have been the most important.

Once a term, Mother had taken the train to see me. During her first visit, she'd admitted that she and Father were living apart. They'd decided to keep the estate and staff but made sure to never be there at the same time. Mother, oddly enough, had gone down to Florida to visit friends and decided to stay part of the year. She'd purchased a bungalow near the beach.

Last summer, after we'd finished Roland's house, I'd sent for Lillian, having spoken to Mother about her staying with me until it was time to return to school. She'd stayed for almost three months. Pale, sickly Lillian was no longer. She'd become strong and beautiful at school, growing in confidence and soaking up praise from the music teacher.

We'd all spent a lot of time together during her visit, but the two of them had managed to sneak off alone for walks down at the beach or to sit on Roland's sun porch to watch the sunset. I suppose, if truth were told, they were not sneaking, since I purposely left them alone. Roland was too fine a man to take advantage of my sister. I knew his intentions were pure. He wanted to make her his wife. I'd assumed they'd be engaged by summer's end.

She'd been about to set out when Father died.

"Do you think she'll like it here?" Roland asked. "I mean, if she decides I'm for her. The winters, you know."

"She'll be warm wherever you are."

When we were seventeen, Roland and I had taken a train trip up to Maine to visit another of our classmates. We'd both been entranced by the blue of the ocean and the crispness of the air. Our classmate had taught us how to boil lobsters and crack open their shells for the succulent meat.

We'd made a pact. When we left school, I would buy land near the little town of Castaway. Together, we would build cottages for each of us. The moment we graduated from school, we headed out together. A twenty-acre piece of land on a bluff over the ocean was available for purchase. I didn't hesitate.

As planned, Roland and I had used our carpentry skills and built a cottage. After a long winter, we built a second one for him. They were not large or fancy but cozy and comfortable. We loved every inch of them.

Now that we'd built our homes, we were pondering different business ideas. Roland wanted to open a new kind of shop in Castaway, one that sold produce and meats in addition to the traditional dry goods. "One place for everything," he said when he'd told me the plan. Anyone else he told the idea to immediately dismissed it as reckless and almost scandalous. How outrageous for a young man to be so bold. However, I believed in him completely and had offered him a loan. So far, he'd refused. As good-natured and generous as he was to others, he was equally stubborn. He refused to take a loan, saying that the property and his cottage had been enough of a gift. Thus, we were at a stalemate.

My father was dead. I thought I should feel something more, but the truth was, when I'd left home, I'd put him away inside a locked box in my mind.

"Do you ever think about the girl? Luci?"

Roland watched me with the eyes of a discerning man who knew me much too well.

"Sometimes."

"Tempted to visit her while we're there?" Roland asked.

"That would make me ridiculous, wouldn't it?"

Roland grinned. "You're the one who believes in soul mates."

"I was so certain that her destiny and mine were intertwined." I chuckled. "But I was a kid back then. An overly romantic one at that. And we'd only met that one time." I'd thought of her often in the years since I'd been away. I could recall the exact color of her eyes that had peered back at me. The jolt of it, the feeling that I was meant to be with her, was there too. Dax hadn't mentioned her in his letters unless I asked. He'd always written back with a brief line or two that they seemed to be doing well. Like he was in person, Dax was a succinct communicator. No wasted words.

"Dax *has* written that she's done well and what a clever girl she is. He taught her how to plant and care for a vegetable garden. Doesn't know how she grows anything in that hard dirt, but she manages." I watched a speck of dust dance in the sunlight. "I might drop by to say hello."

"If I were a betting man, which I'm not, I'd guess she'd like to thank you for sending Dax over there to help. Who knows what might have happened to them had you not done so? Maybe it's God's way of getting you back there."

"Now who's being romantic?"

"You've influenced me over the years, which I find irritating." Roland stood. "If we're going today, we best get packed and on our way. Are we driving or taking the train?"

"We'll take the motorcar."

"I'll be ready in half an hour."

"Don't hurry on my account." I smiled.

"Very funny."

LATE THE NEXT AFTERNOON, ROLAND AND I ARRIVED AT MY family's estate. Nothing appeared to have changed. The grass was green, and flowers bloomed in the front beds.

I parked and got out of the car. My long legs had cramped during the drive. Roland did the same, stretching his arms over his head. The front door flew open, and Lillian came running out and across the lawn. "You're here, thank goodness."

She threw herself into my arms. I held her tightly for a moment before stepping away and taking her hands. She wore a cream-colored dress with a sailor collar and a dropped waist, which had become so popular. Her thick ginger hair was arranged at the base of her neck.

She stepped toward Roland, hazel eyes shining. "Hi, you." My sister was petite and looked even more so next to my tall friend.

"Hello, you." He snatched his hat from his head and held it against his chest, staring at her as if he'd forgotten my existence.

She ducked her head as her cheeks reddened. "I've waited so long to see you, and now I don't know what to say."

Roland flashed his infectious smile. "Not to worry. I do. You're beautiful. Even more so than the last time I saw you."

"Thank you. You're looking well yourself." She turned to me. "Are you ready for this?"

"How's it been?" I asked. My sister had been home a few times over the years, but only when Mother was home.

"This house of horrors keeps on in its usual manner." Lillian frowned as she clutched the sailor collar of her dress and looked from one of us to the other. "Mother sent a telegram that she won't arrive for at least a week. She said to bury him without her."

Roland and I exchanged a glance.

"We'll take care of it, then," I said. "And then we'll be on our way."

"I'm so worried about Dax and Mollie," Lillian said. "Mother says she's selling the house. And June—what will she do? Plus, there's the cook. She's French and seems temperamental. Mollie's been beside herself waiting for you, Wesley. Dax too, even though he didn't say as much."

"Selling the place?" This surprised me. "I thought she'd want to stay since he's gone for good."

"She said she'd explain everything when she gets here. It was very mysterious." Lillian gestured toward the house. "You must be thirsty from your long drive. We've put Father in the parlor, which is ghastly. I've never known anyone to die before, and I'm sure I've bungled everything."

Roland reached into his jacket pocket and pulled out his handkerchief, which he pressed into Lillian's hand. "We're here now."

"I'm so glad you boys came." Lillian wiped at her eyes. "Now, come inside. Mollie had Etta, the new cook, make up sandwiches and lemonade for us. Mollie says she has a terrible temper and hates to make meals at odd times, so I hope they'll be fit to eat."

With a pang, I thought of Mrs. Walker. However, as Dax had assured me, she'd come out just fine after her abrupt dismissal. Mollie had found her a position with one of the other wealthy families, where she remained to this day. On the other hand, our house had gone through three cooks since Mrs. Walker's dismissal. From what Mollie had told us, Father always found some fault with them. One of them, he'd accused of trying to poison him.

We grabbed our bags from the car and then walked with Lillian across the front lawn to the screened porch and through the front door. My eyes took a moment to adjust to the dim hallway. Same white wainscoting and dark wood paneling. The parlor was to the right. I couldn't help myself. I had to look. Heaps of roses were draped over a closed coffin.

"Closed?" I asked.

"Yes. It's best. He'd gotten all red and puffy. Poor Mollie, she was the one to find him. She said he was slumped over the desk with his face in a piece of berry pie. At first she thought it was blood. Isn't that awful?"

A shiver went up my spine. There were too many bad memories lurking here.

"Anyway, come along to the sitting room. I have a surprise for you."

We followed her down the hallway. The sitting room had always been my favorite room in the house. It was less formal than the parlor, with tall windows that let in light all times of the year. My sister's baby grand piano still took up one corner of the room, shiny and black in the sunlight. Shelves filled with books lined one wall.

My heart leapt into my throat at the sight of a dog who looked remarkably like Atlas had as a puppy. "Whose is this?"

"Mollie said Gus appeared the morning Father died," Lillian said. "She thinks someone dropped him here, hoping we'd give him a good home. Doesn't he look just like Atlas?"

"He does," I said.

Currently, Gus napped in a spot of sunlight. As I drew closer, he raised his head and stared at me for a moment, then leapt to his feet, tail wagging. I knelt to pet him and looked into those sweet brown eyes. I swear it seemed as if no time had passed and this was my Atlas.

"Hello, Gus. Pleased to meet you." He was so excited his entire body shook. I petted him and scratched behind his ears like Atlas had loved. Apparently, Gus did too. Or was it Atlas in a new, young body? *Don't be ridiculous,* I thought.

Gus licked my face. "Is it you, old boy?" I whispered. He barked and wagged his tail harder. "Did you come back for me?" He sat on his haunches and offered his paw for a shake. "How'd you know how to do that, you clever pup?"

"Ah, it's my lad come home."

I turned toward the voice of the man I'd missed for nearly six years. My chest ached with love as I rose to greet him. He wore his usual gardening attire and held his hat in his hand. The years had been kind to him. He looked no older than the last time I'd seen him.

Dax's eyes shone with tears as he pulled me into a quick embrace. "You look good. All grown. Taller than me."

"Yes, sir. I've brought my best friend, Roland Harris." I introduced them, and they shook hands.

"Welcome, Roland. Lillian has been telling us all about you now, hasn't she?" Dax asked.

"Dax, don't go telling all my secrets," Lillian said. "A proper young lady doesn't speak of such things."

Roland laughed. "I'm glad to be a subject of conversation when it's coming from your mouth."

"Well then, you'll be quite glad," Dax said, teasing. "She hasn't stopped speaking of you."

"Dax, you're terrible." Lillian's cheeks glowed pink. She was happy, I thought. This was my sister, glowing and in love. The frail little girl she'd once been seemed only a ghost of a very distant past.

Gus had caught sight of his tail and did three circles in pursuit.

"Do you see how he resembles Atlas?"

"I do. How did you find him?" I asked.

"That's a long story," Dax said. "Which Mollie will want to tell you."

As if summoned, Mollie entered the room with her usual hard-heeled gait. She started to cry at the sight of me. "Oh, dearie, you're home at last."

I embraced her. She smelled of lavender, as she always had. "Mollie, don't cry. We're back together now." Her black hair had more white, but like her husband she had aged well. She was as plump and pink and robust as she'd always been.

Her eyes narrowed as she inspected me from head to toe. "You've grown very handsome." She patted my shoulders. "Such muscles. Your eyes are as pretty as ever. I hope your outer beauty hasn't gone to your head."

I grinned over at Roland. "I have my friend here to make sure I stay humble."

She let go of me to greet Roland. "And this is Roland. Goodness me, aren't you a large one?"

"Nice to meet you," Roland said, eyes twinkling. "I've heard many Mollie stories over the years."

Mollie tutted. "I'm sure highly exaggerated by Wesley. He was always overly romantic with his view of the world."

"One of his many charms," Roland said.

"Please, lads, sit down," Mollie said. "I'll pour us lemonades."

Gus followed me over to one of the chairs. As I settled in, he lay next to me with his chin on my foot. My eyes stung, remembering how Atlas had done the same.

"I told you," Lillian said to Mollie as she sat on one end of the couch. "We're right."

"Right about what?" I asked.

"It's only a fanciful idea." Mollie took the seat next to Lillian.

"Do tell." Roland took the chair nearest Lillian.

I leaned over to give Gus's ears another scratch as I waited for Mollie to begin.

"First, I have to tell you about Atlas. Brace yourself, because it's very sad."

"Go ahead."

I exchanged a glance with Dax, who had not chosen to sit, and instead stood near the piano.

"Atlas sat in the front yard every day for almost a month

waiting for you to come back." Mollie retrieved a handkerchief tucked inside the sleeve of her blouse and dabbed her eyes. "He'd only come in at night to sleep in his bed. Next morning, right back out there. Saddest sight I've ever seen."

My chest ached, imagining him doing so. I wanted to shout for her to stop. That I couldn't bear to hear the details.

Dax sank onto the piano seat. "One day I went out there and we had a little talk. I told him he had to get on with things and that it would make you sad to see him waiting for you. I asked him to keep me company in my workshop because I missed you too. He must have understood, because he followed me out there and slept under my bench for the rest of the day. That evening, I took him to our cottage. I'd brought his bed from the big house. He curled up in there. I petted him and reminded him of the good times he'd had with his favorite boy. He licked my hand and then closed his eyes."

"Forever." Mollie pressed the handkerchief against the base of her throat. "But he didn't suffer, Wesley."

Thinking of him peaceful in their cottage cheered me somewhat but not enough to erase the image of him waiting on the front lawn for a boy who never came home. "It wasn't right to rip us apart."

"You had to leave here," Mollie said. "Living that way. With that man. Who knows how long before it worsened or you were big enough to fight back."

"Tell Wesley the rest," Lillian said softly.

Mollie nodded. "Now, this next part you wouldn't believe if you weren't here to see it with your own eyes. The morning after I found your father, I was dusting the parlor to get it ready for the coffin and something on the front lawn caught my eye. It was Gus here, sitting in the exact same place Atlas had all those days, looking down the driveway as if waiting for you."

"It's like Atlas in a new body," Lillian said, interrupting, like an excited child.

"God forgive me for saying so, but it makes a person wonder," Mollie said.

"I'm not wondering," Lillian said.

Gus thumped his tail and resumed his position on my foot.

"What a thing," Roland said.

"Isn't it?" Lillian asked as they smiled at each other.

Mollie waved her hands in a dismissive gesture. "All that's well and good, but we need to talk about the next few days. We've arranged to bury your father tomorrow morning."

"Father left directions. There's a plot in the cemetery." Lillian's voice wavered. She pressed Roland's handkerchief to her mouth before continuing. "What happens to a soul no one mourns?"

"That's not our concern," Mollie said. "God works it all out."

"How is it that all I feel is relief?" Lillian asked. "Does that make me a bad person?"

"He was a hard, mean man who sent his children away," Mollie said flatly. "What else would you feel?"

"You two came out just fine anyway," Dax said with a proud lilt in his voice. "Look at the two of you."

"Thank you, Dax." Lillian's expression lightened. "That's only because we had you and Mollie. We must have been such trouble to you."

Dax shook his head and smiled. "Oh now, lass, we love you like our own. 'Tis no trouble."

"We had some good times, didn't we?" Mollie asked. "I have to believe that, or some days I'm not sure I can get out of bed. The guilt, you know."

"You have nothing to be guilty over," I said.

No one said anything for a moment until Mollie spoke. "Now that you've finished school, Lillian, do you plan on going with Wesley?"

"That's been our plan," Lillian said. "I was finishing up the last term, which happened to coincide nicely with Father's death." A giggle escaped. "I'm sorry. I didn't mean it to sound that way."

"It's all right, lass," Dax said. "We want you to go where you'll be happy."

"We suspect your mother's planning on selling the estate," Mollie said.

"Where will you go?" Lillian asked.

"We're not sure yet," Mollie said. "Things are rather discombobulated at the moment. All the changes at once are troubling to a person like me."

"You'll come with us," Lillian said. "Right, Wesley?"

I looked over at Roland. He gave me a slight nod. "We've built two cottages," I said. "I don't see why we couldn't build another."

I described our property and how the bluff had room for multiple residences.

"No, lad, we can't let you do anything of the sort," Dax said.

"We don't have to decide anything now," I said. "Once Mother arrives, we'll know more about her plans."

"Quite right," Mollie said. "For now, we'll focus on getting the dead buried."

As Roland had said, good riddance.

11

L uci

THAT AFTERNOON, THE CREEK RAN THICK WITH TROUT. INSECTS hovered just above the surface, tempting them to rise up from the cold depths with their pointy mouths to snatch their breakfast. Occasionally they jumped, creating a splash and ripple of water, their silver scales sparkling in the sun.

I stood in the water about knee-deep with my skirt pulled up and tucked into the waist of my bloomers. When a fish came near, I attempted to stab it with a stick I'd sharpened into a spear. Some days I'd managed to get one. Today, I'd had no luck. The only reward for my efforts were a sweaty brow and an empty stomach.

"Sadie, I can't get one." I wiped my face with the sleeve of my blouse as I trudged out of the water.

Sadie was squatting on a grassy knoll a few feet way. She

made a satisfied grunt as she plucked a mushroom from the soft dirt. Because of her fair skin, I always insisted she wear a straw hat to protect her from the dappled sunlight that filtered through the trees. A white-blonde braid hung down her back. "Sister, should I try?" She brushed the mushroom clean, then dropped it into a bowl. This time of year, we found a lot of mushrooms. I worried we'd stumble upon a poisonous one, but Sadie claimed she could smell the difference. So far, she'd been right.

"No, we'll come back later. Maybe when it's cooler, more will swim into the shallow parts." I sat next to her, careful not to sit on any mushrooms, and spread my legs out to dry. Blue sky poked through the lush maples and firs. Blackberries ripened on the bushes a short distance up the creek. When they were ready, Sadie and I would pick as many as we could before the birds took them. Life here was a battle between us and nature. I was a soldier already. Sadie was quickly becoming one.

We both had our strengths. I was calculating and innovative, often able to make the most use of whatever the elements offered. I'd built traps made from tree branches to catch rabbits. When Dax had gifted me with seeds that first spring, he had erected a log fence around the garden to keep out the deer and rabbits, who were quite happy to eat the fruits and vegetables of my labor.

We'd chosen a spot as close to the creek as possible, where the dirt was moister. Also, the closer it was to the creek, the less distance and time it took to haul buckets of water up the slope. However, I'd wanted a sunny spot, so I'd had no choice but to plant the garden in the clearing.

Sadie had a keen sense of smell and taste. She could tell if something was off by the scent. I felt certain she'd saved us from poisoning more than once.

"I need a fishing pole," I said to Sadie.

What I needed was a fly connected to a hook. I'd heard men

talking about fishing the last time I'd gone into town. They'd said the year was particularly good for trout and a man was a fool if he couldn't catch one.

What about a young woman? Was I a fool? Because I sure couldn't catch one without a hook.

Last month when Dax had come with tomato starters for my garden, I'd told him about my idea.

"I need a fake fly," I said. "Attached to a hook and a long string. When they come up to bite, the hook would catch them and I could pull them in."

We'd been talking at the edge of the chicken coop, watching the chicks peck the ground. No longer the size of my palm, they were about six weeks old and growing fast. My older hens were inside in their nests.

Dax took off his straw hat and slicked his damp hair off his forehead. "Yes indeed. You're speaking of fly-fishing."

"It has a name?"

"Been around for centuries. But you need a special kind of line made from silk or horsehair and a bamboo rod. I shouldn't think we could find them around here. Not that we could afford, anyway."

But I couldn't let the idea go. Every time I saw those fish swimming through the stream, I ached with ambition. A few of them needed to be in my frying pan. What if I found a branch or twig similar to a bamboo pole? I could use part of a feather that looked like a bug and tie to the end, then dangle it over the water. But without a hook, how would I catch them? I'd have to think that through later.

"Do you have enough mushrooms?" My legs were dry, so I rose to my feet and let my skirt fall back around my ankles. I didn't wear boots much in the warm months, saving them for winter. Calluses on the bottoms of my feet were shields against rocks and roots.

"Yes, enough for today." She scrambled to her feet. "I'll wash them."

While she did so, I scooped water into my bucket upstream of where she knelt. "I'll fry them and a few green tomatoes up with some lard. That'll have to do for today." I said this more to myself than Sadie. When she'd been a baby, I'd gotten into the habit of telling her everything I was doing or asking her questions as if she understood. This had two outcomes. One was that she didn't feel the need to answer me. Two, she spoke with the ease of one much older. The way she described the world around her often amazed me. This was why I was hell-bent on getting her in school. If I hadn't been able to go before she was born, where would we be? I could read and add up numbers. Although, too often the number was zero.

Enough time had passed that people in town had stopped looking at me with disdain and distrust. Sadie could start school without anyone calling her the daughter of a whore. Folks might not care about us and most pretended we didn't exist, but at least they left me alone. I'd survived without doing what my mama had done. I'd kept us fed and clothed, even though my father was a drunk and a gambler.

But still, I couldn't grow complacent. Always, around every corner or shadow, darkness waited to destroy us. This constant diligence had made me weary and old before my time. What was I to do differently? Survival was the only choice. This was my life, and I would make the most of it however I could.

When we'd completed our tasks, I started up the hill. Sadie, with a gait as graceful and quiet as a deer, followed behind me.

I stopped at the garden. After I set down my bucket, I opened the gate to the log fence Dax had helped me build. Without it, I wouldn't have a chance of a crop. Again, the game between the elements and me was a fierce one.

Sadie and I plucked a few of the largest green tomatoes from the vines and added them to her bowl.

My vegetable garden, thanks to Dax's seeds and solid tutelage, would serve us well this summer. We'd enjoyed carrots and lettuce in the spring. Next month, my beans, tomatoes, and squash would start to produce. By fall, I could dig up the potatoes.

Sadie had turned five last winter. The fifth anniversary of our mama's death. I could hardly remember the time before Mama died. The last days of my childhood had blurred into extinction. Sometimes at night before I fell into an exhausted sleep, I thought about the days after Mama died. I considered how Wesley had appeared out of nowhere, as if fated to help us, and wondered about the mysteries of the universe that I so desperately wanted to understand. Then, how Dax had stepped in to do what Wesley couldn't.

Was there such a thing as fate? Or were we at the mercy of the innate kindness of others? Or did kindness make the difference in all aspects of our lives? Without it, would we be anything more than the animals that wanted to eat my vegetables? All I knew without doubt was that Sadie—and probably me too—would not have survived without that first act of kindness from Wesley. I wanted to be of service to others at some time in my life. But right now and for the foreseeable future, I could only do what needed to be done for my sister and me.

Once in a blue moon, I asked Dax about Wesley. I mentioned him casually, so as not to clue Dax in on the wild fantasies that plagued my mind during the night when I was awakened by Pa stumbling through the front door. Wesley had saved us from certain starvation, of course, and I was grateful. But there was this other feeling too—the one that had me convinced we were intertwined somehow. Two lost souls meant for each other.

The latest I knew of Wesley was that he was no longer at school. He'd graduated with honors and had moved to the seaside. My heart had hurt a little. He hadn't come back for me.

Dax, perhaps noticing my disappointment, had quickly added that as long as his father was here, Wesley would not be coming home. I understood. If I could've gotten away from Pa, I wouldn't risk entrapment by returning.

I'd have liked to ask Dax if he had the post information so that I might write to Wesley, but I was too shy. What a fool he'd think me. A girl like me asking for a rich boy's address?

When we reached the house, Pa was sitting on the porch wearing his dirty pants and a ragged flannel shirt. He held a bowl in one hand and scooped whatever was in it into his mouth with his fingers. What had I left in the house instead of hiding it in my secret spot behind the woodpile? As we drew nearer, I could see that it was the last of the rice I'd made the night before to go with my pan of beans. I'd traded Mrs. Adams some fresh lettuce and half a dozen eggs for a few cups of rice. Strangely enough, Mrs. Adams had become a friend to me. As a woman who lived alone, I doubted she needed as many eggs as I'd traded for flour, rice, and lard over the years.

"Sadie, what do you have in your bucket?" Pa leered at her. The way he looked at her worried me. If he touched her, I would kill him with my bare hands. I kept her close at all times, never letting her out of my sight. I'd found a sharp rock at the creek last summer and slept with it near our mat on the floor. If he came sniffing around her, I would bash in his face.

"Bring it to me," Pa said.

Sadie's gaze flickered to mine. She stepped closer to me.

"No, that's for our supper," I said. "Mushrooms that I'll fry up with some eggs."

"Do it now," he said.

"Supper's in a few hours." If I served our main meal now, we'd all go to bed hungry. Not that Pa was usually here for supper anyway.

He got up from the porch, unsteady on his feet, and staggered toward me. Before I could escape, he grabbed me by the hair and pulled me close. His breath reeked of stale whiskey. "You'll make me supper now."

I struggled to get away, but his other hand wrapped around my neck. He pressed against my windpipe.

"When I ask for a meal, I want it now." With one hand still around my neck, he slammed the heel of his other hand into my cheek. He removed his hand from my throat and pushed me to the ground.

Black dots danced before me. Tears leaked from my eyes. I covered my face with my arms and waited for the next blow. Despite the pounding between my ears, I heard Sadie's small, frightened voice. "There's fresh bread in the box. You can have all of it."

Pa cursed. "Why didn't you say so?"

I lifted my face to look at him. He swayed slightly and then lumbered back toward the steps and up to the porch. Seconds later, the door slammed shut.

Sadie sank to the ground next to me. "Sister, how bad does it hurt? Did he break a bone?" She caressed my upper arm and peered at me with her light eyes.

"I'm all right." My cheek throbbed, but I didn't want to alarm her further. "It'll just be a bruise."

"We'll go down to the creek, and I'll soak a rag to put on your face."

Sadly, we'd been through this enough times that my five-year-old sister knew what to do for blows to the face. I nodded and rose up from the ground like an injured bird shoved from the nest.

Sadie took my hand and led me toward the creek. I wondered, not for the first time, who was saving whom. At the moment, this tiny girl appeared to be in the lead.

THE BRUISE ON MY CHEEK HAD LESSENED TO A DULL ACHE BY THE time I fried up our tomatoes and mushrooms for supper. As I worked at the stove, it occurred to me that Dax hadn't come by in at least a week. He often came by on a Sunday to check on us and bring milk and cheese. I hoped all was well. Lately, I'd noticed his gait had slowed. I knew he worked hard at the Fords'. Was it too much for him?

I put our supper onto tin plates and set them on the table. Sadie had been playing on the floor with her doll I'd made out of the material from the old pouch. I'd cut and sewn the back and front pieces, then stuffed it with the leftover fabric. Buttons made the eyes, red yarn a mouth. The poor thing had no nose, but Sadie didn't care. She loved her baby and had named it Sugar. Where she came up with that I had no idea, since we hardly ever had any of it in our house.

We sat at the table and bowed our heads. I said a quick prayer of thanks, and then we tackled our food. Along with our vegetables, I'd thrown together some biscuits to take the place of the bread Pa had taken. We were eating well this summer, but even so, I worried about the winter. Would my potatoes be rotten when I dug them up? Or would they have failed to grow? Nothing was assured.

"Sister, why did you sigh?"

"Did I?" I looked across the table at her sweet face. What would I do without her? The summer days were long and required no candlelight. Outside the windows, evening faded into tranquility. In moments such as this it was hard to remember the cold, bitter winters. "I was thinking about my potatoes." I pushed away my empty plate and folded my hands together on the table.

Sadie patted my hands. "Don't worry. You always figure out how to make everything nice and keep my tummy full."

I glanced around the tidy room. Dishes were washed and floors swept clean every night after supper. In the mornings, we folded our bedding into a neat pile and stored it on the rocking chair to keep the spiders from crawling inside and surprising us. The woven mats we slept on were rolled up and placed in one corner. Still, nothing could hide our poverty. Floorboards had rotted and loosened. Each of our curtainless windows had at least one crack that I feared would worsen with the next frost. The wood-burning cookstove needed blackening.

No one but a girl who'd grown up as Sadie had would think this was nice. She didn't see the room as it truly was. This was her home. I was her family.

"Sister, if Pa isn't my real pa, who is?"

I started. We'd never talked about any of the details of her lineage. She knew, of course, that Mama had died and that I was her sister. The rest of it, I'd left out of the story. If she wanted to know more when she was grown, I would tell her. Until then I would keep quiet. "How did you know about Pa?"

"He told me."

"When?" When had he been alone with her?

"The other night when you were using the outhouse, he came home. I was sitting on my mat talking to Sugar. He sat next to me and whispered in my ear that I should come to him later. That I could sleep in his bed with him. That there was nothing wrong with it because I wasn't his kid." Her bottom lip trembled. "He said not to tell you. He scared me, Sister."

My dinner threatened to come right back up. I set my fork on my plate, trying to conjure the right words. Rage blinded me. Perspiration dampened the palms of my hands. "I'm very glad you told me this. It's wrong for a little girl to sleep in a man's bed, no matter if he's her father or not. Do you understand?"

"Yes." She nodded, her big blue eyes never leaving my face.

"From now on, you stay with me. If I go to the outhouse, you come with me."

"All right."

"You tell me everything. Don't worry. I'll never be mad at you."

"He said you would call me a liar."

I clasped my hands together under the table and tried to steady my breath. The pulse at my neck quickened. "Did he touch you?"

She shook her head. "You came back, and he got up quick and went to the bedroom."

"When was this?"

"Last night."

"Why didn't you tell me this morning?"

"I forgot."

I studied her. She didn't lie. There was never any reason to. She *had* forgotten. I'd done similar things when I was her age. I hadn't remembered Mama's comings and goings in the middle of the night. It wasn't until I learned the truth that memories piled on top of one another into the full truth. "Do you mean you put it aside, like locked it in a box?"

"I think so."

"Have there been any other times you forgot?"

"I don't think so." Tears traveled down her thin face.

I took in another breath to gather myself. Every nerve in my body burned. I wanted to run into town and haul him out of the bar and slit his throat. For Sadie's sake, I needed to remain calm. Otherwise, I'd scare her. "Come here, baby." I held out my arms.

She came around the table and crawled onto my lap. I was a tall woman, and she was petite and too thin, so she fit just as nicely as she always had. I could still remember the pleasant heaviness of the baby she'd been. "Listen to me, baby girl. I'm here. I'll always figure out a way to keep you safe. I always have, and I always will. You hear me?"

"I hear you." The flutter of her eyelashes tickled my neck as she nodded her head.

"If we have to leave here to do it, we will." Even as I said it, I wondered how on earth I would manage that.

I did the only thing I knew to do. The only thing that had ever worked. I prayed.

12

esley

DEW SPARKLED ON THE GRASS AS I CROSSED THE LAWN TO THE vegetable gardens. Gus ran ahead of me, leaving tracks. I hadn't had a chance to talk to Dax alone and wanted to ask him about Luci. Although I was embarrassed, my need to know outweighed my reluctance to seem a fool. I found him in the fenced-off vegetable beds watering his tomato plants. Spring vegetables were ready to harvest, including clumps of lettuce, carrots with tall tops, and peas that crawled up wooden spikes.

He straightened at my approach and looped his thumbs through the straps of his overalls. "Good morning. What a sight for sore eyes you are."

"You too." I adjusted my hat to get a better look at him. Gus walked along one row, sniffing as he went.

"You sleep all right?"

"Not really." I'd tossed and turned in my old bed. It was too short for me now, so my feet dangled over the end. Unwanted memories had been my bedfellows.

"He's gone, lad. We'll put him in the ground, and you can go on with your life."

"Have you and Mollie talked about coming with us?"

"A tad, yes." He scratched under the collar of his shirt. "She's proud, you know."

"I know."

"But how she feels about you and your sister might win over the old pride. I can't yet tell."

A fat robin fluttered over and landed on a fence post. Gus barked, and the bird flew away as quickly as it had landed. "The invitation is open. Whenever she decides."

"Will you stay and wait to see your mother?"

"Yes, I'd like to. Lillian wants to as well. So we'll be here a few weeks, anyway."

"Good, good. Mollie will want to stay and do whatever needs doing for Mrs. Ford. Perhaps after everything's settled and sold, she'll see that this change could be good for us."

I nodded as I shifted my weight from one foot to the other.

"Something you want to ask me?" Dax's eyes twinkled.

"What? No. I mean, not really."

"You want to know how Luci's getting on?"

"Well, yes. How is she?"

"She's done fine. Just fine." He smiled, pride in his eyes. "Hardest-working girl you'd ever meet in your life. Clever too."

I nodded and looked up at the sky, already a deep blue despite the early hour. "I'm glad to hear." Gus flopped down in the middle of the row between beans and squash and rested his head on his paws.

"She asks about you," Dax said, almost as if it were an afterthought. I knew better.

"Yes?" My shoulders rose and fell. I wanted to beg him to tell me every detail, but I refrained. Although Dax would never mock me, I felt embarrassed over my schoolboy hopefulness that I'd remained in her thoughts as she'd remained in mine. "How, exactly?"

"Similarly to you—as if it didn't matter one way or another when I know sure as anything that it's the opposite."

I shrugged my shoulders and grimaced as I turned my gaze toward the direction of the woods. "These feelings might just be a romantic notion."

"Might be. Might not be. I knew the minute I set eyes upon my Mollie. She was the one for me."

"I've thought about her more than I should."

"How much is *should*? Can we measure it?"

I chuckled. "You think I should call on her?"

Dax adjusted the brim of his hat. "Well, now, how else will you know?"

"I suppose."

"They'll be wanting you inside," Dax said. "To go out to the cemetery."

"Right, yes." I hesitated, wishing I could remain here with Dax and the scent of tomatoes ripening on their vines. It occurred to me that he wasn't dressed for a burial. "Aren't you coming with us?"

Dax shook his head. "No, lad. I can't watch them lower him in the ground and not spit on his coffin."

I stared at him, aghast.

"When I think of all that went on in this house." Dax stuck his hands in the pockets of his overalls. "To you, especially. I cannot pretend. I'm happy he's gone and hope he burns in hell."

"He can't hurt me any longer."

"That's right. You can bury all the memories with the man, lad, and never think of him again."

I called for Gus. He rose from the warm ground and shook himself clean. As I crossed the lawn toward the house, an image of Father's face when he reached for the strap told me that no amount of time would erase my memories. I could only use them to shape the man I wanted to be. Isn't that the only thing we can do after someone has harmed us? Ensure that something good comes from our suffering?

What would my good be? Only time would tell.

WE WERE HOME BY LUNCH. THE BURIAL HAD BEEN A PALTRY gathering of five. After the preacher tossed the first handful of dirt over the coffin, he said a few prayers and took our money, and we returned to our cars. There were no mourners to invite back to the house. After a meal, Roland and Lillian went out to the back porch to play chess. I wanted to be alone and wandered restlessly around the sitting room.

Finally, not making a decision so much as my feet leading me in that direction, I went into Father's study. My gaze lifted immediately to the painting of him that hung over the fireplace. I did not look at the strap, but I felt it there as if it were a poisonous snake ready to strike. I stared at the painting. The artist had captured him well. His cold eyes stared back at me. I shivered as the sounds of the strap against my skin echoed between my ears.

Gus bounded in through the open door. He leaned against my leg and barked at the painting.

"You remember him, old boy?"

He growled.

"Don't worry. He can't hurt me now." I reached down to touch Gus's head.

"You didn't take everything from me," I whispered to the painting. "Your cruelty made me stronger. Better." A man had emerged from my broken pieces.

Perhaps I'd not been fully free until now. No longer confined by his presence, I could soar. Was it time?

Time to find Luci?

IN THE LATE AFTERNOON WHILE LILLIAN AND ROLAND ROCKED ON the front porch swing together, I took Gus out for a walk. I'd left my jacket and tie at the house and rolled up my sleeves. A straw hat provided shade for my eyes.

Gus, as Atlas had done, took the lead. Wildflowers were in full bloom in the meadow. Tall grasses swayed in the breeze. When we reached the woods that led to Luci's house, I hesitated. It had been years since I'd roamed these woods. Would I get hopelessly lost?

Gus barked and twisted his head to show me which way to go.

"You know the way?"

He barked as an answer that could only be interpreted as yes.

The pine needles crunched under my feet as I wove through trees, making sure not to twist an ankle on roots, rocks, and dips in the ground. Fifteen minutes later, Gus had led us right there.

I stopped just outside the clearing. The shack looked better than the last time I'd been here. New boards had replaced the rotted ones. A log enclosure that I assumed was a vegetable garden had been built on the flat parcel of land before it angled downward toward the creek. *Smart,* I thought. Less distance to carry water than if she'd set it nearer the house. Chickens pecked in the grass outside a repaired henhouse. Bedsheets flapped in the breeze on a clothesline hung between the house and coop.

Dax, I thought. This was all Dax. My heart ached with love for the man who surely hadn't needed more work than he already had. I imagined him here during his days off, helping a stranger because I'd asked him to.

I heard a rustle of leaves and looked over to see a young woman emerge from behind the garden structure. She carried two buckets. A little girl with hair so fair it was almost white trailed behind her. The baby, I presumed, now a girl.

Despite her shabby clothes, Luci had grown into a great beauty—tall, slender, and straight-backed. Shiny honey-colored tresses had been gathered into a bun at the back of her long neck.

From inside the shack, a man in a dark hat, dirty trousers, and a gray shirt that had once been white stumbled onto the porch. He held a flask in his left hand.

"Luci, where's my dinner?" He had the gravelly voice of a man who smoked and drank to excess.

Luci set the buckets on the bottom step of the porch. The little girl hid behind her skirts. "We've nothing left. When I take the sheets to Mrs. Webb, she'll pay me and I'll go into town to get supplies."

"What happened to last week's money?" He took a long swig from his flask.

"You spent it on booze. I know you took it from my hiding place." Her tone was cold and brittle. "And now we have nothing left but flour and lard."

"Well you best get on with it. I'm hungry." He sat weakly on the steps. "Come here, Sadie girl. Let me look at you."

"Sadie, go play," Luci said.

Sadie. She'd named the baby Sadie.

Sadie ran away to the side of the house and plopped onto the ground, drawing her knees to her chest and burying her face. Hardly a game, I thought. The leering way he'd looked after her chilled my blood.

"You have no need to look at her," Luci said.

"I like pretty things," he said, slurring his words.

"You stay away from her, you hear me?" Luci drew closer to him.

He waved his hand as if she were a fly bothering him. "Be quiet now. I've got an aching head."

Luci called to her sister. "Come on, Sadie. We'll go see if we can catch a fish."

Sadie rose from her position and took Luci's outstretched hand. They walked back to where they'd just come from. To the creek, I presumed.

Gus and I waited until her father went back into the house. Then, careful to stay in the woods rather than the clearing, we headed toward the creek.

13

Luci

I BREATHED A SIGH OF RELIEF WHEN WE REACHED THE CREEK. IF we stayed away for a few hours, Pa would probably have disappeared into town or over to Moonshine Mike's.

"I'm hot," Sadie said. "Can I wade into the water?"

"Yes, just be sure to hike up your dress so it doesn't get wet." I answered absentmindedly because I was focused once more on my idea for a fly. I'd found a wild goose feather in the yard that morning. It was a sign, I told myself. Now, I took it from my pocket and sat on a rock near the water. I tucked my skirt up around my knees and placed my feet in the cool water. As if to taunt me, a silvery-scaled fish jumped out in the middle of the creek. If only I had a hook. I'd racked my brain but couldn't come up with an idea of how to make one from anything I had around the house.

I heard a crack of a twig and turned to look, expecting to see

Pa and already coming up with ways to get rid of him. But it wasn't Pa. My heart thumped an extra beat at the sight before me. A man and a yellow dog stood near a fallen rotted tree. His eyes. They were familiar. I'd once seen them in a boy's face, under a cap. Wesley? The boy grown into a man?

He was a giant of a man, tall with wide shoulders and dressed in impeccable gray tweed trousers and a white shirt with the sleeves rolled up. A straw hat made a dappled pattern on his cheeks and chin. Next to him, a yellow dog with friendly eyes wagged his tail. He looked like Atlas, only he was a puppy, young and vibrant.

Aware that my bare feet and calves were exposed, I tugged my skirt back into place and rose to my feet. "Is it you?"

"Hi, Luci. I'm back." He remained by the fallen log.

"Is it really you?" I inched toward him, sure I was seeing things that were not there.

"Yes, Wesley Ford. Is it really you, Luci Quick?"

I nodded, too shocked to speak.

Out of the corner of my eye, I saw Sadie splashing through the water toward me. By the time she reached me, her wet skirt clung to her bare legs. She pressed against my hip, nearly knocking me off my feet.

He took off his hat and held it against his chest. Dark-blue eyes sparkled in the morning sun as he stared back at me. "I'm sorry if I've startled you."

"You most certainly have. I've been waiting for your return for almost six years." The flirtatious lilt in my voice made me sound like a different woman. One accustomed to handsome men appearing out of the woods.

"I was detained." His full mouth lifted in a smile. "My father didn't want me home, or I would have been here sooner."

"Oh my, it really *is* you." My hands flew to my mouth. What a sight I must be. Hatless and wearing no shoes—hair a mess and my dress hardly better than a rag. He'd come back a sophisticated and elegant man. He had a strong jaw and high cheekbones. His features were no longer pinched and nervous. "I can't believe you're here. I've thought so many times about this moment." I hadn't meant to be so forthcoming. There was something so easy between us.

He stepped closer, still holding his hat to his chest. "As have I. Even though you've changed from a girl, I would know you anywhere."

"Your eyes are the same. I knew them right away." If only he knew how often I saw them when I closed my eyes at night.

What did we look like to him? Did he pity us? I smoothed my free hand over my cotton dress, worn so thin I feared he could see right through the fabric. I had no corset, only an undergarment I'd made from a flour sack. Sadie wore a simple dress made from burlap.

"I was nervous to come, but I wanted to see you." Words rushed from his mouth, making me forget my concerns about my appearance. "Dax said it would be all right. I hope I haven't scared you."

"No, no. I'm surprised but so very happy to see you."

"Sister?" Sadie tugged on my skirt. "Who is it?"

I turned to Sadie. Goodness, I'd almost forgotten she was there. "Honey, this is Wesley. The boy who sent Dax to help us."

She smiled up at the broad-shouldered man. "Hi, Wesley."

He smiled back at her. "Hello, Sadie." His hat dangled from one hand. The yellow dog reclined on his haunches. "This is Gus."

"He's cute," Sadie said. "May I pet him?" I'd taught her good manners. Even if we were poor, we could still behave like proper young ladies.

"You may."

"Hi, Gus." Sadie knelt in the grass. Gus flopped onto his stomach and rested his chin on his front paws. "Are you a nice dog?"

Gus wagged his tail.

"Sister says I can't pet dogs I don't know."

"It's all right," I said. "Gus is a gentle dog."

Sadie petted his head before looking up at Wesley. "His fur is soft."

"Isn't it, though?" Wesley shook his head as if astounded. "But, Sadie, you were no bigger than my shoe the last time I saw you. Now here you are all grown up."

Sadie beamed. "I was only a few days old, right, Sister?" She squinted into the late sun that had slid between trees as she looked over at me.

"That's right." I swallowed against the ache at the back of my throat. Seeing him brought back the fear of those days. We would not have made it without him. "We can't ever thank you enough. Dax helped us." I waved toward the hill. "He did everything. All that first winter, he brought milk for Sadie and food for me. Come spring, he came out here with his saw and a hammer and repaired the chicken coop and built garden walls. Then he brought chicks for us. By fall we had eggs. He taught me how to grow vegetables."

"You've done well," he said.

"It's all Dax."

"Not according to him. He says he can't believe what you've done. Growing vegetables in hard dirt."

"Why are you here? Have you moved back?" The questions spilled from my mouth without heed.

"My father died. I came to bury him."

I watched him carefully for clues. Was he sad? Or relieved, as I would be? "I'm sorry?" It came out as a question.

"I'm not mourning him. No reason in the world I would." His expression sobered. "What happened to your cheek there?"

I touched my fingers to the bruise. "Pa. Don't worry, it's nothing."

He looked up at the sky, then back to me. "Are you safe here?"

I hesitated. How could I answer that?

"Tell me the truth," he said softly.

"Safe enough."

For a long moment, he was silent, as if thinking through what to say next. "I know about what it's like to be hit. Only my father used a strap. I have the scars on my back as proof."

My eyes filled with tears. I could see the little boy he'd been the last time I'd seen him so clearly just then. Such kind eyes and a sweet smile. He knew what it was like to be hurt by a person who was supposed to look after you.

"That's one of the reasons I was sent away to school. Mother thought it best if I was no longer living with them. She was right. Even though I didn't want to leave Atlas or my sister."

"I'm sorry about Atlas. Dax told me he waited for you on the lawn." My voice cracked. "It makes me sad to think of him."

His eyes clouded over for a few seconds before he shrugged. "All a long time ago." He glanced over at Gus, who was currently lapping water from the creek. "Dax said Gus showed up at the house the day Father died. Mollie spotted him on the lawn in the exact same place Atlas used to wait for me."

I thought about that for a moment. Was it possible? "Maybe special dogs come back?"

"Maybe they do."

Our eyes locked. We stood there, gawking at each other.

"You're beautiful, Luci. Do you know that?"

I flushed with pleasure at his words. "I never think of it one way or the other."

"I've never forgotten you. All this time, I imagined what it would be like to see you again." He reached toward me as if he was going to brush a strand of hair from my cheek, but he pulled back at the last moment. "I told you back then that I'd come back. I couldn't then, but I can now. If you'd like."

"To do what?" I asked.

"To court you."

"How could you possibly?" I tugged on the front of my ratty dress. "Look at this."

"I don't care about your dress." He placed his hat back over his curls. I missed them immediately. "I'd like a chance to see if I'm right," he said.

"About what?"

"If you and I are meant to be. I know it sounds overly romantic, but I have a feeling."

I wanted to say I did as well, but I held back the words. How could we possibly be right together when our circumstances were so different? "You're rich, Wesley, and I'm poor as dirt. Do you see this?" I waved toward the creek. "When you came here, I was sitting on that rock trying to figure out how to make a hook so I could catch a fish for our dinner."

"I could bring you a hook."

I laughed, despite my twisted thoughts, which alternated between elation and terror. "That was an example of how far apart we are, not a plea."

"But you need a hook?"

"And a pole, for that matter."

"I see. Well, let me see what I can do." He called out to Gus. "Come on, boy. Time to go home." He turned back to me. "What time should I come by tomorrow?"

"I don't know. Do rich people sleep late?"

He grinned down at me. "Maybe some do. Not me. I'm up with the sun every morning. Too much to learn and do to sleep away the day."

"All right, then. Come tomorrow afternoon."

"Why not tomorrow morning? I could bring breakfast."

I turned toward the water just as another fish jumped. The mischievous devils were taunting me. "That's kind of you, but I have chores that take up most of the morning."

"Fine. I'll come in the afternoon."

"Meet me here in case Pa's home."

"Of course." He tipped his hat. "I'll see you then." Gus was now at his side, as Sadie was by mine. "Goodbye, Sadie."

Sadie giggled. "Bye, Wesley."

I watched him gracefully bound up the hill and disappear over the other side. *What just happened?* "What was that?" I mumbled under my breath.

"That was Wesley and Gus," Sadie said.

Yes, it was indeed.

THE NEXT AFTERNOON, SADIE AND I WAITED DOWN BY THE CREEK for Wesley. At the sound of twigs snapping, my stomach fluttered with nerves. Gus barked as he clambered down the hill toward Sadie. Wesley strode behind him, carrying a long pole and a net.

Sadie straightened from where she'd been washing her feet in the stream and shouted out first to Wesley and then Gus.

The dog barked once more and licked Sadie's face when she knelt to hug him.

"Hello there," Wesley said to me. "I've brought you something." He held the pole out for me. "Made of bamboo. And this is to scoop them out of the water when you've hooked them." He made a swishing movement with the net. "I've got several hooks too."

"Where did you get this?" I ran my fingers up and down the smooth wood.

"In town. I had to ask around, but I found a man who makes these and sells them to sporting types. He assured me this will catch a fish." He pulled a small bag from inside his jacket pocket. "Hooks and twine to tie to the end."

"I've got feathers," I said.

"Feathers?"

"Yes. See, I have this idea." I told him about how the fish came up for the bugs. "I thought if I had something that seemed like a bug they would be tricked, and I could hook them. Then Dax told me this kind of fishing is called fly-fishing and rich people do it for fun." I reached for the feather I'd been carrying around in my apron pocket. "Do you think we could get this onto the hook?"

He took it from me. "Yes, but it would have to be much smaller to seem like a bug."

"That's what I thought too."

"I have a pocketknife. I'll see what I can do." He shrugged out of his jacket and placed it over a maple tree branch. Next, he rolled up his sleeves and sat on the rock where I so often perched. "Here now, let's see what I can do." He snapped open the blade and cut the softest part of the feather from the rest. "I'll tie it on here if I can."

He cut a small piece from the roll of twine. "Will you hold the hook for me?"

I nodded and sat down beside him. He handed me the metal hook, and I held it between my thumb and index finger. My hand shook, so I wrapped my other hand around my wrist to steady it.

"Good. Keep holding it still if you can."

This close, I caught the glorious scent of him. I took in a deep breath, light-headed. With deft movements, he tied the stiff part of the feather around the front of the hook.

"There. I think it's done." He twisted to gaze directly at me and gave me a triumphant smile. "Shall we tie it to a line?"

"Yes, please." Reluctantly I stood, wishing I could stay seated by his side for a little longer, and followed him to the water's edge.

"And lastly, he told me to tie a cork to a spot right above the hook so that it will float and not sink." He reached into his pocket and pulled out a strangely shaped object that I'd never seen before. "This is a champagne cork that I took from the house. Dax drilled a hole in it for us." He strung the twine through the hole, then attached the hook.

"I asked him about fly-fishing, and he said the sportsmen use silk line, which he didn't have. He said to use worms and forget this nonsense about fly-fishing. If this doesn't work, don't worry. I'll dig you up some worms and we'll try those."

"Trout don't like worms," I said. "They like bugs."

Wesley tied the hook with its feather to the end of the line. "I hope they like feathers pretending to be a bug," he said as he tied the other end of the twine to the skinny end of the bamboo. "He made a little notch here where the string goes so that it won't slide off."

When he was done, he handed it to me. "Would you like to try?"

I nodded. "Sadie, move a little farther from us. I don't want to hook you."

Sadie giggled as she and Gus moved farther up the creek. "Is this far enough?"

"That'll do," Wesley said, clearly amused by my sister. "Wait, let me take off my shoes so I'm ready to wade in with the net."

"You're so sure I'll catch something?" I asked.

"We must always imagine the best possible outcome."

I tried not to watch too closely, as I'd never seen a man's bare feet except for Pa's, but my eyes wouldn't obey. He sat back on the rock and slid out of his shoes, then tugged off his socks. His feet were shaped as nicely as the rest of him. He rolled up the cuffs of his pants. His calves were muscular and covered lightly with hair. Seeing a part of him that was usually covered gave me a strange sensation inside my tummy. I didn't know what exactly, but I felt like lightning had struck me and I was lit from within.

He looked up and caught me staring at him. I flushed and turned away, pretending to be interested in the pole.

"I'm ready now," he said. Then he yelped as he walked across the rocky ground. "Ouch, my poor feet."

Sadie giggled again. She and Gus had settled against a log with his head in her lap.

I'd imagined what I would do with my line many times before now. I thought that if I could swirl the line in the air above the water, imitating a bug before letting it settle on the surface, it would surely convince a trout to bite. I lifted my arm, but the twine was too heavy. It did not swirl but plunked into the water. However, the cork kept all but the hook above the surface. I shook the pole, hoping to make the feather quiver like a fly.

To my utter amazement, seconds later I had a bite. "I've got one." The pole bent from the weight of the fish. My palms dampened, but I held on as I stepped backward, pulling my catch toward shore.

Sadie shouted with glee, followed by Gus's bark.

"I'll get him." Wesley sounded as excited as I felt as he waded out a few feet with the net in one hand. He scooped under the water and came up with a wriggling fish caught in the netting. "He's a big one."

"You did it, Sister. You caught a fish!" Gus barked and circled around Sadie.

Wesley came out of the water holding the net out in front of him. The speckled trout flopped and gasped, but I couldn't soften to the poor creature. I'd caught supper.

"You were right, clever Luci." Wesley placed the net down on the grass. "The feather looked like a fly."

I knelt and took hold of the slippery fish to withdraw the hook from where it had lodged in its mouth. The feather was now wet and limp. I'd have to tie another onto the hook.

Wesley sat back on the grass. When I looked over at him, he

was watching me with a smile on his face. "You're quite something, Luci girl."

Sadie sat next to Wesley. "Is that what you're going to call Sister? Luci girl?"

"I suppose so," Wesley said.

"What will you call me?" Sadie asked, looking up at him with adoring eyes. It seemed I wasn't the only one taken with Wesley Ford.

He tapped his temple and squinted his eyes as if thinking hard. "What shall I call Sadie? How about Sadie Bug?"

Sadie giggled. "I'm not a bug."

"You're cute like a ladybug," he said. "Which rhymes with Sadie Bug."

If I hadn't been in love with him before, I certainly was now.

14

esley

THAT EVENING, I PACED ABOUT THE SITTING ROOM, RESTLESS AND unsettled. Lillian was at the piano playing a waltz. Roland had the newspaper open on the coffee table.

"Shall we go into town?" I asked.

"To do what?" Lillian continued to play.

"Look around?"

Lillian graciously declined, saying she'd rather stay in and go to bed early. "These last few days have tired me. But you go, Roland. Sow wild oats, or whatever the saying is."

Roland laughed as he got up from the couch to stand beside her. He lifted her hand to his mouth. "I'd rather stay with you, but I should keep your brother company and out of trouble."

We donned our hats and went out the front door. Gus followed and ran out to the lawn. As we were about to climb into the car, he came rushing up with a stick in his mouth. He dropped it at my feet. I tossed it out to the lawn. Gus barked, then leapt after it. He was glorious. Young and nimble, so full of life and zeal. Did we all have rebirth to look forward to at the end of our days? To come back again to chase dreams and sticks, youthfulness restored?

Lillian had come out to the porch. "Come here, Gus. I'll toss your stick. You boys have fun."

I thanked her with a wave, and we climbed into the car. A moment later, we were headed down the dirt driveway. The evening was pleasant and warm. The scent of honeysuckle wafted into the open car.

The engine was loud, preventing us from talking. When we arrived in town, I parked near the saloon. "What should we do?" I asked.

"Let's take a walk," Roland said. "I've something I want to talk to you about."

We headed toward the center of town. The main street of Devon had brick buildings with the usual types of businesses for a small town: dry goods, butcher, feed store. A church with a tall steeple stood in the middle of town, with a park and a gazebo next door. With the warm weather, couples were out for evening strolls in the park. Women strutted about in their pretty dresses. *Luci should have a pretty dress,* I thought. *I'd like to give her one.* At the thought, I smiled to myself. She preferred a fishing pole to a dress. For now, anyway.

Roland was quiet until we reached the park. "Can we sit?" He pointed to a bench.

"What is it?" I asked. "Are you all right?"

"I want to talk about Lillian. To state my intentions and ask your permission to propose to her."

I was a great actor, I thought as I nodded calmly. "If she'll have you, then you have my permission."

"There's another thing." His voice sounded tight, as if the

words were hard to say. I supposed they were, for a man like Roland. "I'd like to take you up on your offer of a loan."

I wanted to shout for joy, but I kept it in check. "Excellent," I said casually. "We'll go into Rochester tomorrow to draw up papers. Do you want the corner lot?" I owned several of the empty lots in Castaway. The one on the corner of Main and First would be the best location.

"Not so fast. We need to talk terms." Roland laid out what he figured it would cost to build and stock the store. "If you cover the up-front costs, I'll give you fifty percent of the store, plus pay you back with interest for the original loan."

I took a moment to come up with a counterargument. A couple near the gazebo had stopped to share a kiss. "No interest. Ten percent ownership."

"Unacceptable. That's a pity loan." He put up a hand. "Now wait, I have a proposal. I've been thinking this through for a while, playing with the numbers, and I have an idea. The way to make money as shop owners is through expansion. True profit comes from having multiple stores in multiple towns. We open the first in Castaway, and the following year, if things have gone well, we'll open another one in another town. This is a way for you to continue acquiring wealth, in addition to the property you've bought. Something to leave to our sons, should we have any."

"Or daughters."

Roland chuckled. "Right, or daughters."

I warmed to the idea without hesitation. He was right that building on my current wealth was necessary for my children and grandchildren. I needed to ensure a future for them. If all went as we hoped, Luci would be a part of my life. There was Sadie to think of too, and God willing, other children as well. "Whatever success we have with the first one, we'll replicate."

"My thought too," Roland said. "You're in agreement, then?"

"Yes, we'll go to Rochester tomorrow and make it legal.

Regardless, this doesn't change the fact that you're a stubborn goat."

"That I am," Roland said, sounding pleased with himself. He shifted to stare up at the sky. I did the same. A sliver of moon hung just over the large fir tree in the corner of the park. Darkness had come, bringing with it the appearance of twinkling fireflies over the grass.

"My only aim in life is to take care of Lillian," Roland said. "She'll want fine things. What if I can't provide them?"

"She'll have the finest man. That will be enough."

Roland picked up a flat stone someone had left on the bench and rubbed it between his thumb and forefinger. "I hope she won't regret taking a chance on a fellow like me." He turned the stone over and over in the palm of his hand. "This plan of mine better work."

"Don't think like that. Our plan will work. We're partners now. Together, we can conquer the world, or at least open a few shops. All Lillian wants is to be cherished by the man she loves and to live in a peaceful home. Anyway, money isn't the only factor in a happy marriage. Look no farther than my family to know the truth of that."

"My parents are poor but happy," Roland said. "Still, it would be nice if things were easier for my mother."

"Yet another reason to build an empire." I nudged his ribs with my elbow. "Enough of this worry. We have much to look forward to."

Again, we were quiet for a few minutes, watching the dance of the fireflies. "Do you remember that first night we ever shared a room?" I asked. "I said then you would marry my sister."

"You did not."

"I did. I swear. I could see it all then."

"I think you've reinvented history, but even so, I don't care. As long as she says yes, I'll be the happiest man on earth."

"She'll say yes."

"I want to marry before we leave here," Roland said. "That way I can take her home as my bride."

"Whatever you want, I'll help," I said as we shook hands. "We'll be brothers. Like I've always wanted us to be."

"We've been brothers from the first."

How right he was.

"What happened when you went out to see Luci?" Roland asked.

"How did you know I went out there?"

"Because I know you."

I told him as briefly as I could about our encounter and my return with the fishing pole.

"I know it sounds strange, but she's the one," I said. "I'm as sure of it as I am about our partnership."

"As a man in love, I can only say that it's true what my father told me. 'When you know, you know.'"

"Look at us. No longer bachelors."

"For tonight, we are," Roland said. "Let's go get a drink at the bar."

"One last night out before we're tied down forever."

THE BAR WAS LOCATED ON A BACK STREET NOT FAR FROM THE park. As we approached on foot, I heard the sounds of men's voices and laughter coming from inside the building. "You sure about this?" I asked.

"Why not? If it's rough, we'll leave."

I opened the door, and we walked inside to a long, narrow room with a bar that ran the entire length of one wall. Men leaned against the counter, talking in small groups. Others played poker at tables.

I spotted Sam Quick almost immediately, as if I'd known he

would be there. In hindsight, I'm not sure how I hadn't antici-
pated his presence, given what I knew about his daily habits.
And there he was, grimy and skinny and playing poker with
money Luci had earned and needed. A hatred for the man
flooded me. I was not a violent person. In fact, I shied away
from it because of my father. Anything not to be like him. But
Quick evoked a beast from inside me. I would have gladly
pummeled him, given half the chance.

"That's Quick," I said under my breath. "There in the dirty
newsboy cap."

"We should've figured he'd be here."

I nodded. "True enough."

We ordered a whiskey from a barkeep named Wade.

"You fellas interested in a game?" Wade threw a towel across
his shoulder. "They're always looking for fresh blood."

"Sure, we'll play a round or two," Roland said. "We've never
much played, though."

That was a lie. We'd spend many clandestine evenings at
school playing poker with the other boys as a way to pass the
time. We never played for money, using marbles instead.
Regardless, I'd learned how to read people for clues to the
hands they held.

Wade led us over to a table with four other men. "You have
room for two more?"

Four sets of eyes fixed upon us. Two of the men were young,
probably no older than Roland and me, and were well dressed
and clean-shaven. The third was an older man with white hair
and a handlebar mustache. Their fourth companion, Sam
Quick, had a scraggly beard and unwashed clothes. A cigar
hung out of one corner of his mouth.

The man with the handlebar mustache spoke first. "Sure
thing. I'm Harry."

The young ones introduced themselves as Rob and Jim.

"Sam Quick." Beady eyes lifted from his drink and fixed on

my face. Scowling, he nodded slightly. "You two ain't from around here?"

"No, sir," Roland said. "Visiting friends."

"Have a seat, then," Rob said. "We're about to start a new round."

I took a seat across from Quick. Roland sat between Rob and Jim. If I couldn't pummel him, at least I could take his money and give it to Luci.

"Can we buy you boys a round?" I asked.

"Sure thing," Quick said, brightening.

I gestured to the barkeep. "Can we get a bottle of whiskey?" I asked.

Roland shot me a worried look.

In seconds, a whiskey bottle was on the table. With everyone's drink freshened, we began to play. We played one round, which I won. Rob dealt another round. I picked up my cards, pleased to see I had two queens.

"Mr. Quick," I said as I poured him another three-finger whiskey. "What do you do for a living?"

"This here's it." He let out a phlegmy laugh.

I seethed, knowing he must have taken whatever Luci had made from her laundry delivery to be here for a poker game. I had to get them out of there.

We continued to play. I quickly figured out Quick's facial tics. When he had a good hand, the left corner of his mouth lifted into a half smile. If the hand was no good and he was bluffing, he jiggled his leg.

Quick won a few rounds and then lost to me five times in a row. Unless he had a stash in his pocket, his money was gone.

Quick hung his head. His jaw muscles clenched and unclenched. "Hey now. I need a chance to get that back. I got an eighteen-year-old daughter. Real pretty. How about we go all or nothing." He gestured toward my pile of money. "If I win, I'll take that off your hands. I lose, you can have Luci for whatever purpose you want."

I stared at him, stunned. "You're putting your daughter up for collateral?"

"Sure. She's real pretty. Right, boys?"

None of the other men looked up from whatever had suddenly fascinated them on the tabletop. Rob mumbled something about getting a beer at the bar. Except for Roland, the others followed him.

I took a moment to think through his offer. My initial reaction had been horror and disgust. Who did this donkey's ass think he was? His daughter was not his property to give away in a poker game. However, as I thought through the different scenarios, I warmed to the idea. If I lost to him, there was no chance he was taking the money home to Luci. The money would be used for whiskey and poker. Probably gone by the end of the night. Nevertheless, if I won, I could use his inhumane offer as further proof that she and Sadie should come away with me. Even if she wasn't ready to agree that I should bring her home as my wife, the least I could do was give her the pot of money. Winning was certainly the better outcome.

"Wesley, we should probably go." Roland shifted in his chair and nodded toward the door.

"No, I think I'll take him up on his offer," I said, keeping my voice casual. "But I want it in writing before we start." The entire bar had grown quiet, their attention on us. I motioned to the barkeep. "You have a piece of paper and a pen back there?"

"It's a book where I write down who owes me what, but I could tear a piece out for you." He disappeared under the counter for a moment before popping back up with a crude tablet.

Roland got up to get the paper and pen. When he returned, he set the sheet of paper in front of me. "Do you know what you're doing?" Roland asked under his breath.

I smiled at him. "Pen, please."

He set it in my hand.

"I'll write it for you," I said to Quick, all pleasant as could be. As if I didn't want to take him out back and beat him.

Quick nodded, then took another swig from his glass.

I wrote in my best penmanship:

This note serves as proof that I, Sam Quick, lost my daughter, Luci Quick, in a poker game to Wesley Ford on June 22, 1910. Mr. Ford now has the right to do with her whatever he wishes.

"Let's have someone deal for us, to make sure neither of us cheat," I said. "Rob, how about you?"

Rob, with a wary expression that told me exactly how much he wished he'd chosen somewhere else to be that night, agreed with a nod. He came back to the table and sat between us. I pushed the worn and grimy deck of cards toward him. After shuffling three times, he cut them in half and then again. "Five-card draw again?"

"That's right." We'd each get five cards and then have the chance to trade in three of them. I took a moment to say a silent prayer. *Lord, I'm sure you don't approve of gambling, but could you make an exception just this once and have it go my way? I promise to do good with it.*

The cards made a flapping sound as Rob dealt them one by one. When he finished, I looked at mine: two aces, a five, a seven, and a queen.

Quick put three of his cards down to exchange for fresh ones. Rob took three from the top of his pile and slid them over to my opponent. Quick lifted the corners of each. His half smile appeared.

My stomach clenched from nerves. He had a good hand. I needed a better one.

I kept the aces and the queen and asked for two replacements. I held my breath as Rob slid three new cards my way.

God blessed me with two more aces. Roland fidgeted in his chair.

"Put them down, boys," Rob said.

I went first, laying them down all at once. Quick's face crumpled into that of a bulldog, all wrinkled and sagging. With a disgusted grunt, he tossed his cards on the table. He had a full house. Three tens and two eights. A good hand, but not as good as mine.

I pushed the paper and pen across the table. "Sign it."

Without so much as a twitch, Sam Quick signed his name. Roland snatched it up and put it in his pocket.

My head swam with what this meant. Not only did I keep the pile of cash, which I could give to Luci, but I could use the note to further my cause. She should be my wife and not fall victim to the whims of her father. What if I'd been a man who intended harm? There were men in this very room who would easily have taken the note quite literally. The longer she lived with Quick, the more likely harm would befall her and Sadie.

But what would be the good in that? Wouldn't it only hurt her to know that her father had so easily offered her up? No, not Luci. She was too pragmatic. He couldn't hurt her emotionally. His fists were the problem.

I scooped up my winnings from the table and put them in my pockets. Roland got up from the table, shooting me a look. Time to go before we ended up dead.

"Take her," Quick said. "The little one too. Less mouths to feed."

As if he was the one feeding them. I balled my hands into fists, imagining the satisfaction it would give me to knock him to the floor.

"Wes, let's go," Roland said.

I nodded. "Good evening, gentlemen."

I followed Roland out the door, hoping I wasn't about to get popped in the back. It wasn't until we were safely in my car headed down the road that I could breathe easily.

When we arrived home, I killed the engine and turned to Roland. "Now what am I supposed to do?"

"What do you want to do?"

"I want to get them out of there."

"That man," Roland said, sputtering. "I've never been more appalled by a man in my life. I mean, what kind of father offers his child up in a poker game? A daughter, no less. When I think of my sisters and how precious they are, I want to string that man up by his toenails. I'm in. Whatever it takes, we're getting them out of there."

For the second time that night, we shook hands.

15

Luci

THE SUMMER MORNING AFTER MY FIRST FISHING EXPEDITION smelled of honeysuckle. Grass tickled my bare feet as I hung Mrs. Reed's wet sheets on the line. I'd tossed my hat on the grass, and the late-morning sun warmed the top of my head. Resting in the shade of an oak, Sadie hummed a tune under her breath as she traced the letters I'd made for her on my old slate. I wanted her to be ahead of the other children when she went to school in the fall. From inside, Pa's snores assured me we were safe for now. He'd come home late last night very drunk, falling once and knocking a tin bowl to the floor. I'd pretended to stay asleep, drawing Sadie closer to me.

He hadn't bothered us, though, stumbling into the bedroom. The reassuring squeak of the bed frame as he fell onto the mattress had assured me that he would not bother us the rest of the night. I'd fallen back to sleep, thinking of Wesley.

I fastened the last sheet. When I rounded the side, I squeaked in surprise. Wesley and Gus were crossing the yard from the direction of the road.

"Sister, Wesley and Gus are here," Sadie said, as if I couldn't see that for myself.

"Good morning, ladies. I'm sorry to come so early." He removed his hat and nodded at Sadie and then me. "But I have an urgent matter to discuss." He sounded stiff and formal, unlike the carefree man of yesterday.

"Is something wrong?" I asked.

He played with his hat, turning it around in his hands. "Sadie Bug, would you take Gus down to the creek for a drink of water?"

"Sure." Sadie jumped to her feet. "Come on, Gus."

The two of them tore across the grass.

When they were out of sight, he turned back to me. "I ran into your father last night at the saloon. My friend Roland and I joined him in a poker game." He put up a hand. "Which I don't normally do. Gamble. So please do not worry about that."

My heart sank. Pa had done something awful. Of that I was certain. Had it brought Wesley to his senses? Did he now understand that he wanted nothing to do with the Quick family, including me? "What did he do? I'm afraid to know. Did he steal from you?" Or threaten him?

"Not exactly, no." His eyes glittered with anger. "He lost all his money to me. In a last effort to win it back, he offered you up as collateral. All or nothing. The pot or you, depending on which of us won."

"Offered me up?" The bruise on my cheek throbbed to life. I touched my fingers to the sore spot. "I don't understand what you're saying."

Wesley's gaze flickered to my cheek. His jaw clenched before he continued. "If I were to win, he told me I could take you—to do with you as I wish." He grimaced as he pulled a piece of paper from the pocket of his trousers. "Here's the agreement."

With a shaking hand, I took the paper. The script was tidy and remarkably straight, other than a small ink stain in the right-hand corner.

This note serves as proof that I, Sam Quick, lost my daughter, Luci Quick, in a poker game to Wesley Ford on June 22, 1910. Mr. Ford now has the right to do with her whatever he wishes.

The letter was signed by my father. I'd know Pa's handwriting anywhere. Even for Pa, this was a new low. What did this mean? "I'm not property. Am I?" I didn't actually know. Could my father use me like money?

"No, you're not anyone's property. Not his or mine or any man's. Come away with me. You and Sadie. Living with a man who thinks he can give you away in a poker game is criminal. I can't leave you here. What if he did it again and the man was not of good character? Can you imagine what would happen?"

The breeze ruffled the damp sheet. It would dry fast in the sun. Would I be here to fold it into a neat square?

"Come away with you? To where?"

"To my home. I want you to marry me."

My mouth dropped open. Too stunned to answer, I simply stared at him. I must have heard him incorrectly. Marry him? A man I didn't know? Women had done such things for centuries, I reminded myself. We were nothing more than property exchanged between men. Then again, this was Wesley. He was not a stranger to me. Not really. It might seem so on the surface because of our limited time spent together. But I knew differently.

"Please, Luci, say yes. I'll take you away from all this."

"I have vegetables growing. And the chickens." Even to me the words sounded absurd compared to what he was offering.

"I'll provide everything you and Sadie will ever need. I'll

give you a good life and treat you with respect and kindness. And love."

No one had ever wanted me. Except, for some reason I couldn't fathom, Wesley Ford.

"How could I possibly be your wife? I don't know how to live in a nice house or with fancy people." I knew enough to know there were rules, conventions, and that I understood nothing of his world.

Wesley's eyes softened as he gazed down at me. "I'm not fancy."

"Just rich?"

He put his hands in his pants pockets and glanced downward. "Yes, I'm rich. But money doesn't make the man. What's in his heart and how he treats people less fortunate than himself—those are the measures of a man. I want to be a good man. For you."

My legs weakened. I was afraid I might topple over in shock. *For you.* He could have his pick of debutantes from New York City or Boston. I finally squeaked out the ultimate question. "But you could have anyone. Why me?"

"I think you know the answer to that. You feel it too, don't you? The inevitability of us."

"Yes," I whispered. "I've daydreamed that it was true. But I never thought you'd ever come back."

"I knew it the moment I saw you again. There's no reason we shouldn't be together. We can make a life and a family. I have a cottage in Maine that overlooks the ocean. The air smells of salt and sea. You won't have to spend every waking moment working to make sure you and Sadie have enough to eat."

I laughed, tickled by his pleas and arguments. "I wouldn't follow you because of your cottage or any of the rest of your worldly goods. I would come because I want you."

"I don't care about the reason, only that you're willing. Please, Luci, say yes."

Who would look after Pa? As much as I feared and loathed him, he was still my father. "Would it be wrong to leave Pa here alone?"

"He made the choice when he offered you up in a poker game. You owe him nothing."

He was right. My own father had sold me for the chance to win a game. A game he'd lost, as he always did, with money he'd stolen from me in the first place.

There was the other thing too. The worry about Sadie.

Another reason to take Wesley Ford's offer of marriage.

Yet, all those compelling reasons were not why I would go. I would say yes because I wanted to be with Wesley. As poor and desperate as I'd been for nearly six years, my romantic heart still believed in love. I wanted to marry for love.

Marriage. I'd have to give him my body. He would come to me at night and touch me. I glanced at his hands. Long fingers. Clean fingernails. Those fingers would caress my bare skin. I stifled a shudder. Aghast at myself, I realized I'd welcome him into my bed gladly. I craved him. How was that possible?

"What is it you're thinking? I can't read your thoughts. I'll be able to someday but not yet."

I looked up at him, squinting slightly because of the sun behind his head. "I was thinking about what it means to be married. I'm an innocent. I know nothing."

He smiled as he took my hand and brushed his lips across my knuckles. "We shall learn together."

"What if you're simply kind, Wesley? What if I'm not at all what you want?"

"I know my own mind."

"Will you be embarrassed of my clothes?"

"Nothing about you would ever embarrass me. However, it

would please me to buy you a new wardrobe. Whatever you want. My sister will help."

"I've just learned to fish." What would it be like to have food without effort?

"There are streams where we're going," he said.

I gestured toward the sheets hanging on the line. "I have to deliver these to Mrs. Reed later. She's expecting them. I can't let her down."

"I'll send a new set to her." He sounded amused. "Are there any other impediments?"

"I guess not."

"Good, then. I'll ask again." He dropped to one knee. "Forgive me for the lack of a ring. We'll take care of that right away. Luci, will you marry me?"

"Yes." Would I soon wake to find myself on the floor with nothing but my mat to cushion me? And then there was the other kind of dream—the ones of wishes and hopes. They were dangerous. Having them meant one could be crushed when they didn't come true.

"Is this all real? Or a dream?" I asked.

"If it's a dream, I hope we stay in it together."

Just like that, he'd understood my thoughts.

"I know this seems like madness," he said. "But what if it's simply fate? What if we're more than our circumstances? Souls adrift until we find each other?"

"Only a rich man could have such thoughts." I smiled so he would know I meant no unkindness.

He rose to his feet. "May I kiss your hand?"

I swallowed, nervous. "Yes."

He took my left hand and ran his thumb over the tops of my fingers. "I'll get you a ring as soon as possible."

"I shall like to wear one."

He brushed his thumb just under my bruise. "I'll keep you safe from harm."

I believed him with all my heart. "I'll do my best to do the same for you."

"Gather whatever you want to bring. My motorcar is on the road."

"We're going now?"

"Yes, the sooner the better, don't you agree?" Wesley gestured toward the house.

As if transfixed, I nodded. "Would you go down and get Sadie and Gus while I pull a few things together?"

"Yes. Do hurry, before your father wakes."

"I will, yes." I scurried across the grass and inside the shack. Pa continued to snore from the bedroom. I scanned the room. Our woodstove was cold this time of day, so no need to put out a fire. Besides the rickety table and two chairs, the rocking chair my grandfather had made for my mama was our only piece of furniture. Sadie's cradle had broken one night when Pa had crashed it against the wall.

I grabbed Sugar for Sadie and shoved my feet into my old boots.

"Luci?" Sadie stood by the door.

I crossed over to her and knelt on my knees and spoke just above a whisper. All we needed was for Pa to wake. "We're going with Wesley."

"How come?"

"We're getting married."

Her face lit up. "You are?"

"Yes, and he's going to take us to his cottage by the sea, where we'll live."

"The ocean?" Sadie's eyes widened. "We've never been to the ocean. And I'm to come too?"

"Yes, no one will ever take you from me."

"I'm a little scared."

"Me too." I hugged her close, with Sugar between us. "But we're braver than we are scared. We can do this. Now put on your shoes. As fast as you can."

"All right." She took Sugar from me and did as I asked.

I smoothed the front of my dress. Braver than we were scared? What a lie that was. I was terrified. Yet there was a calm assuredness too. This was right. For me and Sadie.

Hand in hand, we slipped out the door. Wesley and Gus were waiting for us near the path toward the dirt road. Without a word, we followed them through the trees to the road. Sadie gasped at the sight of the shiny black motorcar.

"Wesley, is this yours?" Sadie asked.

"Yes, Sadie, it is."

Sadie beamed up at him. "And I get to ride in it?"

"Anytime you wish."

The Cadillac name in swirly cursive gave me a shiver down the back of my spine. Two lights like the eyes of a creature adorned the front. Black tires with spokes of dark wood were as big around as our old table. I started shaking anew. I'd never ridden in a motorcar or even a wagon or carriage. The noise of their engines scared me. I'd heard of people getting hurt from cranking the lever.

"Come on, then. No time to waste." Wesley smiled at me, and my legs weakened. My fingers twitched; I wished I could run them along his jawline.

We stepped closer. "In the back with you, young lady," he said to Sadie as he lifted her into the car.

Gus followed Sadie into the car and sat beside her.

He guided me to the other side of the car. "You'll sit here." I took his hand and he helped me into the front seat.

"I'm afraid."

"Of what?" Wesley asked.

"Will it be loud? What if I fall out? There's no door."

"I'll drive slowly."

"What about a ditch? I could bounce out."

"I'll be careful to avoid ditches." Wesley's mouth twitched.

"It's not funny." I couldn't help but laugh.

"Sister, don't be scared." Sadie leaned forward. "We're having an adventure."

"Yes, fine." The seat was surprisingly soft. He went around to the front of the car and turned the lever. I held my breath, steeling myself against the roar of the engine. But it was not too loud, more like the purr of a large cat. "It's not bad," I said as I turned back to look at Sadie.

She bounced on the seat and clapped her hands. "It's good."

So many shiny parts too. I put my hands under my legs to keep from trailing them along the glimmering surfaces.

Seconds later, Wesley sat behind the steering wheel. He pulled a pair of leather gloves over his hands. "Ladies, are we ready?"

"Yes!" Sadie shouted from the back.

Gus barked. I looked back to see that he sat on the seat like a person.

Then we lurched away, leaving a cloud of dust behind us.

WESLEY KILLED THE ENGINE IN FRONT OF HIS FAMILY'S ESTATE. I'D only seen it from town, looking up to the hill. Up close the brick house seemed even finer, with large windows framed in white trim. The garden was full of blooming roses, foxgloves, lilies, and green scrubs. A rolling lawn went all the way around both sides of the house.

He smacked both hands against the steering wheel. "This is going to come as a shock to my sister. As well as Roland."

"What does that mean?"

"It means that I didn't announce my intentions before I did it." He cut himself off. "Sadie, do you see that swing there on the tree?"

"Yes, sir."

"Would you like to play on it?"

Sadie nodded. "Yes, please."

"Great." He got out of the car and, instead of opening the door, lifted a squealing Sadie from the back seat. Gus jumped out of his own accord and waited for Sadie, wagging his tail.

I watched in amazement as she ran toward the swing with Gus on her heels.

He offered his hand to me and helped me out of the car. I'd never been more aware of the calluses on my hands.

We strolled over to stand before a flower bed. Bees buzzed happily from flower to flower. He picked a daisy from a clump that grew at the edge of the flower garden and offered it to me.

"I'm afraid I may be in a dream." I took the flower from his outstretched hand. "I often wondered if I'd made you up."

He brushed the daisy petals under my chin. "I'm real."

I closed my eyes, enjoying the sensation of the flower on my skin. I'd not felt safe in the world since Sadie had come. I was a protector, not the protected. With him, I felt as if I was melting into a softer version of myself.

"I'm going to need a moment to explain all this to Lillian and Roland. Would you mind terribly sitting on the front porch? Just for a few minutes?"

"Yes, that's fine."

Sadie was happily playing on the swing. I wandered up to the porch and sat in one of the rocking chairs that looked out over the valley below. So this was what it was like to look down instead of up.

16

esley

I STOOD IN FRONT OF THE FIREPLACE FACING LILLIAN AND MOLLIE, who took up either end of the couch. Near the piano, Dax shifted restlessly from one foot to the other. Roland sat in the chair next to Lillian.

"What's so important?" Lillian asked lightly. "You've interrupted our game of chess."

"I was about to beat her anyway," Roland said.

"What do you need, dearie?" Mollie asked. "I've a thousand things to do this afternoon."

Roland crossed one leg over the other. "Has someone been murdered and we're all the suspects?"

Lillian laughed and pointed a finger at Dax. "Isn't it always the gardener?"

"Never the gardener," Mollie said. "But sometimes the housekeeper."

"As humorous as you all are, I've called you together because I have something to tell you." I paused, searching for the words. They all stared at me, waiting. "Last night Roland and I were at the saloon and we got into a poker game with some men."

"Why must you do such things?" Mollie asked. "Gambling and drinking in town with the ruffians will only lead to trouble."

"Yes, well, that proved to be true," I said, looking over at Roland for help, but he simply stared back at me with a slight smirk on his face. "One of the men in our poker game was Sam Quick. Luci's father."

"Luci? *The* Luci?" Lillian asked.

"The same, yes." I shoved my hands into the pockets of my trousers. "After a few hands, I'd beaten Sam Quick out of all his money. That was when he challenged me to an all-or-nothing game in which he put up Luci as currency."

"He used his daughter as the bet?" Lillian had flushed pink. "She's not his property, for heaven's sake."

"Yes, right. Of course she's not." I cleared my throat. "I won, as you might have guessed. This morning I went out to see her and asked her to be my wife."

Everyone spoke at once, except Dax.

"Your wife?" Lillian asked.

"What did she say?" Roland asked.

"Lord have mercy," Mollie said.

"After spending the afternoon with her yesterday, I'm more than certain she's the woman made just for me." I was on a roll now, and the words spilled from me. "She's agreed to marry me. I've brought her and Sadie here. I'd like to get them both new wardrobes before we leave for Castaway. We'll wait for Mother to arrive, as I'd like her to meet my bride." I spoke with more confidence than I felt, given the way Mollie was staring at me as if I'd suddenly grown horns.

"Dear Lord, have you lost your mind?" Mollie stood abruptly, knocking over a vase on the table. "This is all too fast."

Dax reached down to rescue the vase, which had not broken, thanks to the thick rug.

"I do believe I *have* lost my mind." I rocked back on my heels. "But for all the right reasons."

"Did you bring them here against their will?" Mollie asked.

I cringed at the look of horror on her face. "Of course not. I didn't pick her up and haul her into the car with brute force."

"Who in their right mind would get into the car of a stranger?" Mollie asked. "A man, no less."

"He hurts her," I said. "The bruise on her cheek will tell you that."

Mollie continued as if she hadn't heard me. "And what about the child? Are you really prepared to take in a five-year-old girl? You'll have to be her father." She plopped back onto the couch, as if my announcement was such a great burden that she couldn't possibly stand another moment.

"I understand the swiftness of my decision is troubling," I said to Mollie. "However, getting her out of there before her father harmed her or Sadie further was utmost in my mind."

Dax nodded, his blue eyes thoughtful. "The wee one has been on my mind lately. Something's not right about that man."

"He gave her away in a poker game," I said to Mollie, hoping to appeal to her sense of justice. "What sort of father does that?"

"The same kind who took a strap to his son for bringing a poor family a basket of food?" Lillian asked dryly.

"That her father is violent may well be true, but I don't see how that's your problem to solve." Mollie's dark-blue eyes glittered. "I'm not being unreasonable. This is highly unusual behavior from an educated man."

"That has nothing to do with anything." I'd been patient,

but my irritation toward Mollie was growing strong. "She and I belong together. Whatever hurts her, hurts me."

"You've only observed her like one might a painting or sculpture," Mollie said. "Just because she's pretty to look at doesn't mean you love her."

"I fell in love with you at first sight," Dax said. "Right there in front of the schoolhouse."

Mollie shook her head crossly. "No one wants to hear that old story again."

"I might," I said. "Because it's exactly how I feel about Luci."

Dax flashed his gentle smile. "The loveliest lass in all the land she was."

"For pity's sake." Mollie crossed her arms across her bosom and glared at me. "I don't know what's wrong with the two of you. You're both hopeless romantics."

"The world needs romantics," Dax said.

"I agree," Roland said. "And Wes is the best one of all."

"And you'll all live happily ever after, I suppose?" Mollie asked. "The prince and his pauper?"

"Mollie," Dax said quietly. "Be kind."

"Wesley, you've been bringing injured birds to me since you were old enough to talk," Mollie said. "This is no different. Just be careful, love. Pretty birds can sing and sing, but we don't know who they are behind the song."

"Were any of my injured birds ever any trouble?" I asked.

Mollie closed her eyes and let out a long-suffering sigh. "Well, no. They were birds."

I laughed. "Well, then, your metaphor's not working."

"What about their father?" Mollie asked. "Will he give you trouble?"

"Give him money," Lillian said. "That'll keep him away."

"No, then he'll always come back for more," Roland said. "You'll never get rid of a man like that."

"Do you know what her mother was?" The words came out of Mollie's mouth like bullets from a gun.

"What do you mean?" Lillian asked.

"Her mother was . . . the oldest profession in the world," Mollie said.

Roland coughed and looked down at his lap.

"They're the daughters of—" Mollie pressed her lips together. "Well, you know."

A dart of surprise pierced my chest. I hadn't realized Mollie knew. "How do you know that?"

"Everyone in town knew," Mollie said.

I ached for Luci. How hard it must have been for her in a town where she was shunned.

"You don't know enough about her." Mollie slapped the couch cushion. "That's all there is to it."

"I know her," Dax said. "There's no one finer."

I nodded as I shot him a grateful smile. "She kept an infant alive when she was a child herself, with no one to help except for Dax."

"Toughest little thing I've ever known," Dax said. "Never once complained. Worked that hard piece of land like a man."

"I can't imagine how she did it," Lillian said. "I would've just walked out into the cold with the baby and let us both freeze to death."

"Lillian, you would not have done that," Roland said.

"Mettle untested." Lillian looked over at Roland and raised her eyebrows. "Perhaps I'll be useless as a wife and mother."

"Not a chance." Roland reached over to give my sister's hand a squeeze.

Mollie rolled her eyes. "We'll simply have to pray this doesn't ruin us all." She tented her hands as if she was going to begin praying immediately.

"This will *not* ruin us," I said.

"You're a grown man. I suppose I'll have to trust you know

your own mind." Mollie pushed away a curl that had loosened from her bun.

"Lillian, will you arrange for a seamstress to come? They're in desperate need of new dresses."

"Yes, yes. It'll be a rush if we're to get them ready to meet Mother." Lillian glanced over at Mollie. "We can do it, though."

"I'll tell June to get rooms ready for them," Mollie said.

"The question is, where are they?" Roland asked.

"She's outside on the porch, and Sadie's enjoying the swing." I grimaced as I scratched the back of my neck. "I asked Luci to give us a few minutes to talk."

Lillian stood and smoothed her skirt. "I'll send June down to fetch the dressmaker." She turned to me. "Wesley, would you like to introduce Roland and me to Luci?"

Roland and I exchanged a quick glance before following Lillian from the room. When we reached the hallway, my sister whispered, "I hope you know what you're doing."

"I most certainly do not." I grinned down at her. "But it's going to be all right. You'll soon see for yourself."

17

L uci

NOT ACCUSTOMED TO SITTING DURING THE DAY, I'D GROWN sleepy on the covered porch. Sadie was happily swinging with Sugar on her lap. The leaves of the wide oak rustled, and the combination with the happy buzz of bees as they flew from one rhododendron blossom to another provided a soothing lullaby. I startled awake when the front door of the house opened and Wesley appeared with a young woman. I stood and clasped my hands together. Sadie ran from the swing and up the stairs to stand beside me.

"This is my sister, Lillian," Wesley said to me. "And my best friend, Roland."

"Pleased to meet you," Roland said. "And you too, Miss Sadie."

"So happy to make your acquaintance." Lillian's white organza dress contrasted with her neatly pinned ginger hair.

Pretty hazel eyes sparkled at me as she took both my hands. "Welcome to the family." A waft of her perfume smelled of roses and wealth. I hadn't known a person could smell rich, but Lillian was proof.

I croaked out a thank-you, as my throat had gone dry. My ugly dress and old boots were suddenly all I could think of as I took in her beauty.

She dropped my hands and turned to Sadie. "And this angel must be Sadie."

Sadie nodded but didn't speak, clearly as enchanted by her as I.

"If you ladies will excuse us," Wesley said. "Roland and I have business to attend to in town, but we'll be back later."

"Yes, we'll leave you ladies to get acquainted." Roland kissed Lillian's hand. "Behave yourself until my return."

"How boring," Lillian said.

Her gaze followed him as he went down the stairs and into the yard.

I see, I thought. *They're in love.* Perhaps I would get more of the particulars from Lillian? Is that what women did? Talk about love? I didn't know how to be friends with anyone but Sadie.

Lillian turned back to Sadie. "Can you believe that old swing was mine when I was your age? Sometimes Wesley would push me. Shall I do the same for you now?"

Sadie bounced on the tips of her toes. "Yes, yes. I can give you a turn too."

"Do you think it will hold me?" Lillian asked as the two of them walked down the stairs.

Wesley drew closer and brushed a wisp of hair away from my eyes before whispering in my ear, "Will you be all right without me?"

"I think so." My breath hitched. I yearned to put my arms

around his neck and press close, even to feel his mouth upon my own. Was this what it was to be in love?

"I'll only be gone a few hours. Lillian will look after you."

"All right."

He grazed my unbruised cheek with his knuckle. "Don't look sad. I'll always come back to you."

"I'll see you later, then." My voice trembled. Was I attached to him already?

He gave me one last smile before turning and bouncing down the steps. "Goodbye, young ladies. We'll be home soon."

"Goodbye, Wesley," Sadie called out from the swing, where she flew high with her legs straight out in front of her. She was a little girl just then, not scrounging for mushrooms in the dirt or helping me to bring in wood for the stove. With Wesley she might have a chance for a real childhood.

I wrapped an arm around a post and watched him crank the shaft of the Cadillac. After the motor roared to life, he got in, giving one last wave before the car lurched forward, spewing gravel. I steadied myself for what might come next. Would Lillian be unkind now that he was gone? My experience with women in town told me to expect as much. I crossed over to the large oak to stand near her. Gus had wandered over to a flower bed and was currently digging under a rosebush.

"Are you hungry?" Lillian asked me. "We can have lunch whenever you're ready."

"Whenever is fine," I said, unsure of the proper response.

During the backswing, Lillian wrapped her arms around Sadie's waist to stop the momentum. "Let's go now, then."

Sadie hopped from the swing onto the grass. "I'm always ready for lunch."

Lillian laughed. "I'm so glad to hear that, because Etta makes the most heavenly cucumber-and-ham sandwiches."

"Who's Etta?" Sadie asked as we started across the lawn toward the porch.

"She's Mother's cook. Etta comes from France and makes the most delicious cakes. Do you like cake, Sadie?"

"Oh yes." Sadie tromped up the stairs next to Lillian. "We never have cake except on my birthday. Sister makes a small one just for me. Don't you, Sister?"

"I do." Every year I worried I wouldn't have enough for the cup of sugar. Somehow, I'd always managed.

"Aren't you lucky to have such a good sister?" Lillian asked.

"I know." Sadie smiled sweetly. "She's given me everything I've ever needed."

Lillian halted at the top of the stairs. "We'll have lunch first. Then, when you've had your fill, we'll show you your rooms. You might enjoy a nice rest this afternoon? I'll have June prepare a hot bath for you, if you like?"

"A bath? Do you have a creek like Sister and me?" Sadie asked.

I inwardly cringed, embarrassed. On the hot afternoons during the summer, Sadie and I bathed in the cold water of the creek. During cold months, I hauled water up from the creek and heated it for sponge baths from a bucket. She wouldn't understand that people had actual tubs inside bathrooms with running water. That led to my next question. Did we smell bad? I knew we did not give off the scent of roses as Lillian did.

"Wesley asked if I might help enhance your wardrobes," Lillian said. "I would simply loan you a dress while yours are being made, but we're not at all the same size." Indeed, I was at least five inches taller than petite Lillian. She continued without a pause for a breath. "I'll have the dressmaker from town come to show us fabric and take your measurements. You'll need day dresses and a few for evening. One for church, of course." She turned toward Sadie, smiling. "For you too, little miss."

Sadie beamed up at her. Who could blame her? Lillian was like sunshine after a long cloudy spell.

"Will you mind if I help you choose?" Lillian asked. "Fashion is my obsession."

"I suppose not." I clutched the collar of my shabby dress. A wave of heat rushed over me. Despite her kind ways, Lillian must see us as pitiful. Poor trash who lived on the mercy of the creek and the kindness of strangers.

Lillian's eyes widened as she sucked in her bottom lip. "I've offended you. I'm sorry. It's just that being silly myself and in love with clothes, I thought you might be as well." Her tiny ears reddened. "Do I seem frivolous to you? I'm sure I must. I've been spoiled my whole life. The very last thing I want is to hurt you in any way. I want so very much to be friends."

"No, no, it's not that." Touched at her honesty, I allowed myself the same generosity. "I'm embarrassed by how we might appear to *you*. Not the other way around."

Lillian gave me a long, hard look. "Do you want to know what I see when I look at you?" She didn't wait for me to answer. "I see grit, determination, and courage. In all truth, I feel diminished in your presence."

"Diminished?" Sadie asked. "What does that mean?"

"Like I'm not good enough to be in your company," Lillian said. "Because I've never done one thing to aid in my own survival, while your sister here has done that and taken care of you too."

I warmed again, but this time because I was pleased, not shamed. "That's kind of you to say. Thank you."

"We shall agree to a mutual admiration, then?" Lillian asked. She looked at me and then Sadie. "And leave our feelings of inadequacy out here from here on?" She took one of my hands between hers and gave it a good squeeze. "We're to be sisters, after all."

"Yes, agreed," I said.

"We've never had a bath in a house," Sadie said. "But I want to."

Lillian smiled down at Sadie. "Darling, you'll feel like a fresh daisy afterward."

That made Sadie giggle, and so we were laughing as we entered the house. Gus, whom I'd completely forgotten about, slipped in behind us.

My eyes took a moment to adjust to the dim light of the foyer. When I could see clearly, I almost gasped at the splendor of the dark wood trim and whitewashed walls. A crystal chandelier hung from a high ceiling. To our right, a stairway led up to another floor.

We walked down the hallway past the formal parlor and toward the back of the house. I stole a peek into the stately and formal room, intimidated once more by the ornate furniture and burgundy velvet couches.

With Gus in the lead, we continued down the hallway until we reached double doors that led out to a screened porch. A table covered with a white cloth was set for three. I stared out to the rolling lawns, flower beds, and a pond that reflected the blue sky. Several ducks floated on the water, occasionally bobbing under the water to eat a bug, their feathery bottoms the only part left to wriggle hello. The scent of flowers and the sound of a bird singing added to the charm. What was it like to have this every day? To never wonder if the next meal was coming or not?

A fat gray cat rose from his place in a spot of sun and stretched before catching sight of Gus. He wagged his tail and came close, as if greeting a friend. The feline had other ideas. He hissed at Gus, who ran behind Lillian, then sauntered over to Sadie. He meowed and looked up at her with large green eyes. Sadie clapped her hands together, clearly delighted. "Sister, isn't he pretty?" At these words of encouragement, he fell onto his back and showed her his belly.

"He's a she," Lillian said. "We call her Shadow because you can't see her until she's right in front of you. She lives mostly outside and catches awful little creatures for food. The beastly thing won't set foot in the house. On the coldest and warmest of days, she'll acquiesce to the screened porch here. Pet her with caution. She's been known to turn on a person for no reason."

Sadie giggled as Shadow pressed against her calves. "She tickles."

"There's Dax out in his vegetable garden." Lillian pointed toward a vegetable garden at the far end of the yard where Dax, wearing a wide-brimmed straw hat, was bent over a row of tomato plants. I could see the red fruit from here. My stomach growled.

"Is that all yours?" Sadie asked. "All those vegetables?"

"They are. Would you like to say hello to Dax before lunch?" Lillian asked.

I hadn't thought about Dax until this very moment. What would he think of Wesley and me? He knew me. Understood how we lived. Would he approve? "Does he know we're here and why?"

"Yes, he was with us earlier when Wesley made his proclamation," Lillian said. "He thinks a lot of you. I'm already terribly jealous."

"You are?" I squeezed one hand around the other, causing a knuckle to crack.

Lillian laughed. "Now don't look like that. I'm only teasing."

We walked out across the lawn toward the fenced vegetable garden. Gus, seeming to have forgotten his run-in with Shadow, ran ahead. When we reached the gate, Lillian lifted the latch and let us pass through before following. Dax straightened at the sound of the gate shutting. "Ah now, it's Luci and Sadie."

Sadie ran up to him. "Dax, we're here to stay with you."

He peered down at her. "Isn't it fine?" He turned to me. "Luci, good to see you, lass."

I fought tears at the sight of his dear face under the brim of his straw hat. "You too." To avoid eye contact, I looked around at the garden. Fat tomatoes ripened on the vines. Pea plants crawled up a trellis, with plump pods ready for picking. My garden wasn't as robust as this. The soil was hard and rocky. A pang of homesickness washed over me. As ridiculous as the thought was considering where we were, those vegetables were mine. Some days they were my only source of pride. They'd perish within days without water. And what of Pa? Had I assured his death?

"We're about to have lunch," Lillian said. "We wanted to say hello first."

"Yes, off with you now," Dax said. "I've rows to hoe."

Lillian took Sadie by the hand, and they set off toward the porch. I smiled at Dax and then turned to follow, but he stopped me with a touch on my shoulder. "Lass, one moment."

"Yes?"

"Is this what you want? Wesley?"

"He didn't force me. I came because I wanted to."

"Is it only because of what he can offer you? He cares for you."

I understood then that he was not asking out of concern for me but for Wesley. He didn't want Wesley to be in an unhappy marriage or taken advantage of because of his wealth. Shy, I looked down at the soft dirt under my boots. "I think I could love him very much."

"I see." He put both hands around his hoe and leaned against it, watching me.

"Do you disapprove?" I asked. "Because you know how we've lived?"

"Not that, lass. Our Wesley's a sensitive soul. Romantic. I'd not care for him to get hurt."

"I've not had much love in my life. I know its value."

His face crinkled into one of his warm smiles. "All right then. Very good."

"My vegetables will all die." I looked up, squinting into the sun. "I just left them there."

"Sometimes you have to let go of one thing to seize the next."

"All that work wasted."

A second or two passed before he spoke again. "He's right to take you out of there. Remember that truth."

"Yes." My cheeks flamed, remembering the way Pa had looked at Sadie. I couldn't say that out loud, not to gentle Dax, who probably couldn't fathom such a thing. As close as we'd been through the years, I'd never told him of the violence or my fear for Sadie. Perhaps he knew? "Thank you, Dax."

"Go on and have your lunch."

I bade him farewell and walked down the dirt row and out the gate. From here, I could see Lillian and Sadie already seated at the table. I hurried across the lawn to meet them.

Along the side of the porch, climbing roses bloomed pink. Lush beds spilled over with flowers of every color, none of which I knew by name. I walked up the stairs and through the screened door.

Silverware sparkled in the filtered light. A pitcher of lemonade sweated onto a doily in the middle of the table.

"Sit, please," Lillian said. "I'll pour us a drink while we wait for our sandwiches."

I sat in the empty chair next to my sister.

"Do you like lemonade?" Lillian asked Sadie.

"I've never had it before," Sadie said. "One time they were selling it at the Fourth of July parade, but we didn't have any because we have to save our pennies for supplies."

I flushed, both guilty and ashamed. I'd have given a lot for her to have had a glass that day, but as she said, that was not possible.

Lillian lifted her glass and took a dainty sip, then puckered her lips. "It's a little sour."

"May I drink, Sister?"

"Yes, go ahead," I said.

Sadie took her glass in two hands and brought it to her mouth. Her eyes flew open wide at the first taste. "It's like drinking sunshine."

Lillian laughed. "Yes, a little."

I drank from my own glass. If it tasted sour to Lillian, I could only marvel at its sweetness.

"You must be thirsty after the ride in that dreadful car. Doesn't it make the most awful noise?"

"Motorcars scare me," I said.

"Me too. Wesley thinks it's silly. I suppose it is, but I'm quite sure I'll fall out one of these days and be killed by those hideous tires."

The woman who must be Mollie appeared with a tray of sandwiches, cut into squares and piled on top of one another. In addition, a bowl of perfectly red strawberries, hulled and cut in halves. A small pitcher held cream.

I was curious to get a good look at Mollie, as I'd never met her, only heard Dax talk about her. Plump and pretty, she wore a black skirt, a white blouse, and a full apron, as well as a cap over her black-and-white curls.

"Mollie, thank you," Lillian said.

"You're welcome, Miss Lillian." She peered at me with dark-blue eyes.

"This is Luci and Sadie," Lillian said.

"Welcome," Mollie said. "I'll be happy to show you to your rooms after lunch."

I thanked her and prompted Sadie to as well with a tap of my boot against hers.

Sadie's eyes hadn't left the plate of sandwiches. "Thank you."

"The child's hungry," Mollie said. "Enjoy your lunch. I'll be back later." She hustled away, disappearing into the house.

I helped Sadie to two sandwiches and took two for myself. Lillian scooped a generous portion of hulled strawberries into one of the smaller bowls and poured cream over them, then set it in front of Sadie. "Mollie says strawberries will make our cheeks pink."

Was that true? A smaller version of the ones in front of me grew wild in the forest. Only a few times had I come upon them before the birds had eaten them up and left only the stems as evidence.

"Use your spoon," I said to Sadie, afraid she'd grab a strawberry from the bowl with her hands.

She nodded and picked up the small spoon and carefully placed it under a strawberry slice. "They smell good." She placed the berry in her mouth and chewed. "It . . . it tastes like love."

Lillian laughed. "I've never thought about what love tastes like, but I know strawberries and cream are one of my favorite combinations."

Aware of my roughened hands next to Lillian's smooth, white ones, I lifted a sandwich to my mouth and took as refined a bite as I could muster. My stomach was so empty I could have gorged on the entire mound.

Lillian had taken one square for herself and several strawberries.

We ate in silence for a few minutes. I had to agree with Sadie that the strawberries and cream tasted like love or heaven.

Sadie polished off both sandwiches, as well as her strawberries. She put her hand over her stomach. "It's so full in there."

"Good." Lillian poked her fork into a slice of strawberry.

"Will we truly stay in there?" Sadie pointed at the house.

"For a few weeks," Lillian said. "Then you'll go to live by the sea."

"Will you come too?" Sadie asked.

"I'd like to, but I'm waiting for something." Lillian's lively eyes dulled.

"For what?" Sadie asked.

"For Roland Harris to ask to marry me."

Sadie blinked and looked over at me, then back at Lillian. "Will he?"

"I'm not sure. He hasn't much money, and he's afraid I wouldn't be happy."

Sadie wrinkled her nose. "But you want to marry him."

"That's correct, Miss Sadie," Lillian said. "Would you like to run over to the pond and look for the swans? There are a pair who take a swim every afternoon around this time." She pointed toward the water. "Oh yes, do you see them there coming out from behind the bush?"

Indeed there was a pair of elegant white swans, swimming in tandem.

"May I, Sister?"

"Yes, but don't go in the water." I felt the need to say this, given that at home she swam or waded in the creek whenever she wanted.

"I won't." Sadie got up from the table and ran toward the pond.

"Does Wesley know of your feelings for Roland?"

"Yes, he's encouraging of the relationship. The two of them built identical cottages on Wesley's property. He's told me in confidence that he'd like me to return with them as Roland's wife. Which is all I want. Roland loves me, but he's not sure he's enough. He insists he cannot marry me without having a more secure future."

"You're certain of him, though?"

"Yes, he's hardworking and clever. I have no doubt he'll provide a good life for me. Perhaps not opulent like this one, but I don't care. I'd follow Roland around the earth if he asked." Lillian rested her chin in one hand and stared out toward the pond. "He doesn't understand that I'd rather be poor and married to him than rich and married to anyone else. My brother has offered him a loan so that he can open a shop in Castaway, but he refuses. Who am I to question him? I have nothing to offer to the marriage. My father didn't leave me anything in his will. I'm penniless and without one worthy skill. For heaven's sake, I don't even know how to make a cup of tea."

"It's not hard. All you need is boiled water and some tea leaves."

A faint smile lifted her mouth. "If I marry Roland, you'll have to instruct me in all household matters."

"If I can be of service to you, I'd be happy to." I said this with humility, as I wasn't sure I was familiar with the ways of the elite when it came to running households.

"Do you think I'm silly? To assume that love is more important than security?"

"Will he provide you a home and enough to eat?" I asked.

"Yes. I have no doubt."

"And you're willing to sacrifice if you have to?"

"I believe so, yes."

"If it hadn't been for Wesley finding us and asking Dax to help, I'm certain Sadie would have perished. If I'd lost her too, I would have lost the will to fight. In the end, love is the only thing that keeps us from succumbing to the hardness of life. As long as there's a person we love, there's a reason to keep fighting."

18

 esley

"Where are we going?" Roland asked as I turned onto the main road.

"We're going over to Rochester to see about a ring and to have a business agreement put together by my attorney and then to the bank to set up an account for you."

"A ring for Luci?"

"And a ring for my sister."

Roland sighed and lifted his face to the sky. "Wes, I don't know."

"It'll be rolled into the loan. Do you really want to propose to Lillian without a ring?"

"I don't, no."

"If we leave here next week without her, both of your hearts will be broken. I won't have it. And if I give a ring to Luci, you have to do the same."

Roland didn't talk for the rest of the drive, staring out at the scenery with a brooding expression on his face. The car was too loud to talk on the road anyway. I hoped he'd come to his senses by the time we reached Rochester.

I parked in the lot behind a jewelry store that I'd been to once before to buy a trinket for my sister's sweet sixteen birthday. After killing the engine, I turned to him. "What will it be?"

"Your sister told me she'd rather be married to me than to anyone else, rich or poor."

"What's the problem, then?"

"My pride."

"Listen here. Through nothing but luck, I'm rich," I said. "The same goes for your circumstances. Or Luci's or Lillian's, for that matter. We can't control these things. What we can do, however, is take opportunities that are presented to us. I'm offering you a chance to change the course of your life. You'd be a fool not to accept."

"I already told you I'd take the loan. But a ring? I don't know, it's such a personal thing. To take money from the brother of the woman I want to marry seems wrong."

"Please, Roland. Do it for her. Imagine her face when you ask her."

He closed his eyes and let out a long sigh. "All right, fine."

I punched his shoulder. "Good man."

LATER THAT AFTERNOON, I EMERGED FROM DAX'S SHOP WITH A child-size table and two chairs. When we'd arrived home from Rochester, I'd spotted Sadie playing under one of the oaks with two of Lillian's old dolls and the homemade one she called Sugar. She'd had a blanket spread out with the dolls propped up against the trunk of the tree.

I'd remembered a child's table that had once been in

Lillian's room. June had found it, as well as a child's tea set, and had brought them down for me. I spent an hour or so cleaning them up and then set them under the tree. Gus was asleep on the blanket, and I'd just placed the child's tea set on the table when Mollie came marching across the lawn carrying a plate of cookies. "Have you gone soft?" She set the cookies on the table.

"I'm hoping to win her heart." I placed each of the dolls in a chair.

"I don't think there's any question of that." Mollie folded her arms across her chest and glared at me with a mixture of indulgence and impatience. "You'll be a good father to her, but careful not to spoil her."

"Thank you, Mollie. I'll try. I have Dax to model myself after."

"She's a sweet little girl. Didn't even fuss when I combed out her tangles. They've had it hard."

"Those days are over." I took the box with the ring out of my jacket pocket to show Mollie. The diamond sparkled in the sun.

"It's nice," Mollie said and looked away, but not before I saw the glisten of tears in her eyes.

"I'm going to give it to her tonight. Roland has one for Lillian."

"You'll have her marrying Roland, then?"

"That's what they both want."

She gestured toward the vegetable gardens, where Dax was kneeling over beans. "Do you really think Lillian can be a poor man's wife? She doesn't know the first thing about how to live."

"They won't be poor. I'll make sure of it. I've got plans for the future. Roland will prosper."

"Just because you want something doesn't mean it will happen. There's God and free will to contend with."

"I'm not worried." I grinned at her. "Love will win in the end."

"What's your plan? Are you going to leave before your

mother's return?" The strain in her voice caused me to look at her more carefully. Was it nervousness I saw in her eyes?

"Why do you ask?"

"It would be best if you did."

"Mollie, I don't care if she approves of my choice of a wife, and she has no hold over Lillian either. What business is it of hers?"

She unfolded her arms and looked out toward the pond. "There are things you don't know. Things that passed between your mother and father. As much as it pains me, I think it's best if you go before she arrives."

I tilted my head, studying her. "What's this really about?"

She sniffed and ran her hands down the front of her apron. "I've only just gotten you all back, and now you're going to leave."

"You just said you wanted me to go."

"Only because of your mother."

"Mollie, come with us. I'll build you and Dax a cottage near ours. You can help with the babies that will surely come. You can make sure Lillian keeps her family fed. Dax can make a garden and sell his vegetables in town."

"You have it all worked out, don't you?"

"I do. Will you bring up some champagne from the cellar? We're going to celebrate tonight."

She made a harumph sound and turned on her heel and stomped across the yard. The back door slammed behind her.

"Come on, Gus. Let's find Sadie."

He jumped to his feet and headed toward the side of the house. The dog knew where she was without a search. Such a clever pooch. I found Sadie on the swing, holding on to the rope with both hands while lying back with her face toward the sky and her skinny legs dangling. She had on a new dress and shoes. Her hair was fixed in two braids. A straw hat hung from a string around her neck, nearly touching the ground.

"Sadie Bug," I said. "What're you doing?"

She straightened. The hat fell behind her shoulders. "Hi, Wesley. I was counting the leaves of the tree."

"How many are there?"

"I only got to eleven and then I had to start over because that's as far as I can count. Sister hasn't taught me what comes next."

I crossed over to the swing. Dax had put this up for Lillian and me years ago. He'd cut a hole on each side of a wide piece of wood and strung rope through them and then looped it up and over a thick branch. "Would you like a push?"

"Yes, please. I can't get very far on my own."

"Hold on tight. I don't want you falling off and breaking an arm. Your sister wouldn't like that."

She squeezed her hands around both ends of the rope. I gave the swing a gentle nudge. She squealed as she crested upward and then back to me. I gave her a more robust push the second time around. We continued this for a few minutes. Above us a bird chirped as if happy to see a child swinging on his or her favorite tree.

After a few minutes of this, I told her I had a surprise for her in the back. "Would you like to see it?"

"Yes."

I chuckled at the enthusiasm in her voice and took hold of the swing to stop any further momentum and waited for her to hop to the ground.

"We'll head around the side of the house. Mollie doesn't like it when we come in from outside only to run right back out again." I gestured toward the pathway made of flat rocks that led to the backyard. "Stay on the stone pathway so we don't hurt any of Dax's flowers." Batches of daisies, lilies, and foxglove grew on either side.

"I already know that. Dax told me himself."

She ran across the grass until she reached the stone pathway, then turned back toward me, gesturing impatiently for me to follow. "Come on, Wesley. I'll show you what to do."

To do? I jogged over to her. "Are we playing a game?"

Her eyebrows rose slightly, as if it should be obvious. "Yes. You can't step on any of the cracks. Otherwise, a wicked witch will come and snatch you away."

"Lead the way."

Sadie jumped from one stepping-stone to another, careful not to land on any of the cracks. The thyme that grew between the rocks would be grateful, I supposed, not to be trampled upon. The flowers rustled from the breeze made by her swirling skirt.

I stepped carefully as instructed, amused as she leapt over the last rock and into the grass. The moment she spotted the table, she screamed and ran toward the tree.

I quickly followed. "Do you like it? It used to be Lillian's, and I had June bring it down from the attic."

"Wesley, I love it." She hurled herself against my legs, wrapping her arms around me. "Thank you."

"You're welcome." I blinked to keep my eyes dry.

She looked up at me. "I don't want to go back home. What will we have to do to stay with you?"

"What do you mean?"

"No one ever gave us anything that Sister didn't have to work for."

"Not this time."

She sucked her bottom lip under the top one and watched me with those big blue eyes. "Will Pa come find us?"

"No. He doesn't know where you are."

She appeared to contemplate this for a moment, and satisfied with the answer, she moved on to the next topic. "Will you come to a tea party with me and the dolls?"

"I've never been to a doll tea party."

She slipped her hand into mine and smiled up at me. "I hadn't either. Until you brought me here."

"Show me the way."

Still holding my hand, she led me over to the table. "You'll have to sit on the ground. But the dolls don't mind."

I did as she asked, stretching my long legs out to one side. "Would you like a cookie?" I asked.

"Am I allowed?"

"Mollie brought them for you. She likes for children to have a cookie in the afternoons." I offered her one from the plate.

She took the smallest one. "I'll save the bigger one for you." She bit into her sugar cookie. "It's like eating a cloud."

I tried one for myself. The buttery-sweet cookie melted in my mouth. "Etta knows how to make a cookie. French, you know."

Sadie didn't answer, too busy eating.

I ate the rest of my cookie, then reclined on my elbows with my legs stretched out in front of me.

She let out a joyful sigh and plopped near me, imitating my stance. "My stomach feels so good here."

"Mine too. Roland and I have been bachelors, and neither one of us can cook." I yawned. The warm afternoon made me sleepy. I lay on my back. Leaves fluttered from their branches, reminding me of the counting lesson. "After eleven comes twelve, then thirteen. Can you remember those?"

"What do they look like?" She lay on her back and looked up too.

"Like ten, only with a two instead of a zero and a three instead of a zero."

She pointed up at one of the branches and began counting under her breath. "One, two, three." When she reached number thirteen, she asked what was next.

"Fourteen," I said sleepily. "Then fifteen."

19

L uci

FOR THE FIRST TIME IN NEARLY SIX YEARS, I WAS SPENDING THE afternoon without my sister. Mollie had whisked her away after lunch, promising to show Sadie the room where she was to sleep and to supervise a bath. To my surprise, Sadie had gone without a fuss, excited to see her room and to have a bath. As for me, I was in the hands of Lillian.

First she showed me into a bedroom on the second floor of the house. A bed larger than I'd ever seen took up much of the room. The dresser had a washbasin and jug set on top of an oval doily.

Now, Lillian gestured about the room. "Will this do for you?"

"Oh yes. Thank you." I thought of our crude mats at home. What would it feel like to sleep on a real bed? And what about Sadie? Would she want to sleep by herself in a strange room?

How would I handle that when I was sleeping in a marriage bed with Wesley? I put that thought aside. One moment at a time.

A young woman wearing a plain gray skirt and a white blouse covered with a pinafore arrived in the room. She didn't look much older than Lillian and me. However, the quick and determined way she moved told me she had efficiency and practicality on her mind at all times. A cap partially hid her dark hair. Green eyes framed with thick lashes and a round face made her look almost like a doll. The sleeves of her blouse were rolled up, showing arms ropey with muscles. She was small in stature with a sturdy figure, and I had a feeling there wasn't much she couldn't do. In another circumstance, perhaps I would have found a kinship with her. Instead, I was to sleep in a bedroom with a bed large enough for a queen. Soon I would marry Wesley. Would I ever feel right in a room such as this?

"June, this is Luci."

"Nice to meet you, Miss Luci." June bobbed her head in deference. If she thought any less of me because of my shabby attire, it did not show in her expression. "Please let me know if you need anything at all." June went to the wardrobe and opened one door. "There's a skirt and blouse here for you. I made this for one of the other maids who was about your height. She only lasted a day after she tripped and broke several pieces of china. Mollie was having none of that."

"June can sew faster than anyone," Lillian said. "She has six younger brothers and sisters."

"Thank you, Miss Lillian," June said. "I've sewn a lot of clothes in my life for the younger ones."

June took the skirt and blouse out of the closet and laid them on the bed. "This is just to wear until we get your fine dresses made." The skirt was in the same light-gray color as June's.

"It's lovely," I said. "I've never had a new skirt and blouse before."

"Thank you, Miss Luci," June said. "I've run your bath. There are undergarments in the chest there." She pointed to a chest with six drawers.

Six! How many clothes did these people own?

"Is there anything else you need?"

"I can't think of anything." An indoor bath. Running water? My mind could hardly keep up with all this new information.

"Would you like help getting dressed?" June asked. "Miss Lillian's modern and prefers to do it all herself, but I'm happy to help."

I shook my head. Help me get dressed? What did that mean?

"June's wonderful with hair," Lillian said. "She did mine this morning. I hate this awful red color, but she makes it better."

June beamed. "You have pretty hair, Miss Lillian."

"It's not true. I don't know where I got it either. No one in our family has red hair. Why was I cursed?"

"I like your hair," I said shyly.

"You're both sweet, but I shall remain bitter over my fate." Lillian grinned, looking not at all sorry for her situation. "Roland loves it, though, so who am I to complain? Beauty's in the eye of the beholder, and all that."

"You have such thick, pretty hair, Miss Luci," June said. "I'd be pleased to fix it for you."

I thanked her, unsure what else to say. Was my hair pretty? Prior to this, I'd not thought a lot about my appearance. We'd had only a small, cracked mirror. Whenever I'd looked into it, my face had contorted into a misshapen monster. Sometimes when I went into town, I caught a glimpse of myself in the window of a shop, but I never stopped to stare at my reflection.

There was no time to worry over my appearance. How I looked had no bearing on my life.

Now, in this new world I'd fallen into, there would be new dresses, mirrors, and strawberries and cream. And family. Sadie and I would no longer be isolated. The burden of our subsistence would not be mine alone.

IN THE CLAW-FOOT BATH, I SCRUBBED MY HAIR TWICE AND MY body three times with soap that smelled of flowers and felt like silk under my fingers. When the water grew tepid, I climbed out and dried off with the towel June had left for me. A small round rug provided a soft cushion for my feet.

I drew closer to the mirror that hung over the sink. What I saw did not please me. I looked like a skeleton with skin barely covering my bones. My collarbones were hard, skinny snakes and my shoulders sharp points.

I glanced down at my stomach. Flat. No hips to speak of. I held my breasts in my hands and turned back to look in the mirror. They were no bigger than the crab apples I picked from a tree just off the dirt road. What would Wesley think of me? Would I feel like bones under his hands? I thought of his long fingers. Goose bumps rose on my arms. I should be more afraid of the wedding night than I was. What kind of woman was I? If only I had someone to ask about how exactly things worked.

I used a brush on my hair, wincing as I worked through tangles. It hung down my back, frayed and dry at the ends. When I'd finished, I noticed another brush, smaller than the one from the tub, along with a small bowl with a powder. For my teeth, I realized. At home I made brushes from sticks, fraying one end and making the other into a point. They were rough at best, often causing our gums to bleed. However, my mother had taught me to take care of my teeth if I possibly could. I'd taught the same to Sadie.

I dipped my finger into the powder and spread it over the brush. It didn't taste like much of anything and bubbled on my teeth. When I was done, I rinsed the fancy brush and set it back on the sink. Was that where I should leave it? What if it was improper? Again, I wished there was someone to ask these questions. Maybe June? She would understand that I didn't know.

Thankfully, she'd told me about the undergarments she'd left, or I might not have known they were for me. Now, I pulled the undergarment over my head. The material was surprisingly soft, not like the one I'd made from a flour sack. I pulled on the bloomers next, glad to see the opening between the legs for easier access to the toilet. Would they make me wear a corset once the dresses were made?

A knock on the door, followed by Lillian's voice, stole my attention from examining myself further.

"Darling, do you need anything?"

"I'm not yet dressed," I said.

"June will meet you in your room once you're ready. The dressmaker comes in an hour."

"All right. Thank you." I waited until I no longer heard her footsteps before stepping into the linen skirt. *Get on with it,* I told myself. I couldn't hide in here forever.

THE REST OF THE AFTERNOON PASSED BY IN A FLURRY OF ACTIVITY. June cut inches off my hair to even up the ends and fixed my newly shorn locks into a knot at the base of my neck. After that, the dressmaker came and took Sadie's and my measurements. With Lillian's help, we picked out fabrics from a book filled with samples. For me, there were to be day dresses, evening dresses, three hats, undergarments, stockings, gloves, new boots, shoes, and a corset. For winter, a wool coat and yet another hat. Sadie was to have a smaller wardrobe, since she would be growing. By the time it was all over, I felt as if I'd worked all day.

Sadie, however, seemed to be thriving in our new environment. Her eyes shone as she examined the different fabrics and took advice from Lillian about which to choose and why. Sparkling clean, she wore a sailor dress that had once been Lillian's and looked like a different little girl than the one I'd brought here. In fact, she seemed like a girl who belonged in a house like this one. I couldn't think about it too much or I would weep.

Lillian, perhaps taking pity on me, suggested a rest before dinner. I didn't argue. Sadie asked if she could play in her room. "I'm not tired at all, Sister."

I consented, although I would have preferred she stay with me. I wasn't used to being apart from her for such long periods.

I'd peeked into Sadie's room earlier. They'd put her in what had once been the nursery. Mollie had brought down dolls and a wooden rocking horse from the attic. She'd never had anything but Sugar. That she wanted to play rather than nap was no surprise.

"Sister, did you know I had a tea party with Wesley?"

"You did?"

"And he pushed me on the swing. Then he fell asleep under the tree."

Sadie held my hand as we climbed the stairs, weary. I left her to play and went into my room. I lay down on the bed but found it strangely soft. It was only when I moved to the floor and sprawled out on the braided rug that I fell asleep.

20

esley

ROLAND AND I WERE IN THE SITTING ROOM DISCUSSING BUSINESS when Mollie bustled in carrying a tray with a champagne bottle in an ice bucket and four flutes.

"Etta's making a special supper for the four of you," Mollie said as she set the tray down on the table near the liquor cabinet. "I'm going to take Sadie downstairs to eat and then put her to bed so that Luci can enjoy her evening."

"Thank you, Mollie," I said.

Sadie came bounding into the room with Gus at her heels. "Where's Sister?"

"She's upstairs getting ready for dinner," Mollie said. "You're going to eat with us downstairs."

"How come?" Sadie's bottom lip trembled. "I've never eaten dinner without her before."

"It's much more fun down there with Mollie and Dax," I

said. "That's where Lillian and I often ate when we were your age. You and Gus will have more fun down there than up here having to sit still for the whole dinner."

Sadie nodded as her eyes darted between Mollie and me. Gus pressed against Sadie's legs and licked her hand. She smiled and patted his head. "If Gus is there, I won't be scared."

"What's your favorite supper, Sadie?" Mollie asked.

"Most anything will do. Sister always finds something to feed me, even if she has to make stone soup."

"Stone soup?" Mollie frowned.

"It isn't really made of a stone, but Sister calls it that when we have nothing much around to eat. She told me a story about a town that made soup from a stone. Everyone added something to the pot until it was soup instead of hot water and a stone. Sister says when people come together, no one goes hungry. She says Dax was the person who helped us and that he's a blessing."

I exchanged a look with Roland. The sympathy in his eyes reminded me why he was my best friend.

"We're going to have stew for our supper," Mollie said to Sadie. "Come on now, give me your hand, love. We'll leave the adults to their champagne."

"Yes, ma'am. Bye, Wesley. Bye, Roland."

I watched as she and Gus trotted behind Mollie.

"There's something so precious about that little one," I said to Roland after they left.

"Breaks my heart," Roland said. "Thinking about them with that man."

"Agreed." I wandered to the open window, which brought the scent of freshly cut grass into the room. Outside, birds sang their evening song.

"Shall I open our champagne?" Roland asked.

"Yes, please." A hummingbird flew close to the window and hovered for a moment before darting away to suck the nectar from a hibiscus. Behind me, Roland popped the cork on the champagne.

As I turned away from the window, Luci and Lillian walked into the sitting room.

My breath caught at the sight of Luci. Her hair, which had been in a simple bun on top of her head earlier, had been arranged into an attractive bump at the back of her long neck. Her skin glowed. Although she wore only a plain gray skirt and white blouse, she looked as elegant as any New York debutante hoped to be. My sister had given her a pair of gloves to wear over her slender arms and small hands.

"You're lovely." I took her gloved hand and barely brushed my lips against her knuckles.

She flushed pink. "Thank you."

Roland boldly kissed my sister's gloved hand and whispered something in her ear that made her giggle.

"Would either of you care for champagne?" Roland asked.

"Champagne? How scandalous." Lillian guided Luci over to the couch. "Yes, please."

Roland poured, and I delivered a glass to each of the ladies.

Luci took a timid sip. She scrunched up her face, then swallowed. "It tickles."

"That's the bubbles." Lillian took a dainty tug at hers. "You'll get used to them, but never ever have more than two glasses or your head will throb. I made that mistake at my graduation party. The next morning, I actually prayed for God to take me to heaven right then and there. I've never been more miserable."

"Perhaps you need me to look out for you," Roland said.

"Isn't that obvious?" Lillian smiled over at him.

"Tell me, ladies." Roland's eyes glittered. "In regard to marriage, if you could choose between true love and money, which would it be?"

Lillian looked into her champagne glass as she answered.

"Wesley and I have had so little of love that we know it's much better than wealth."

"But would you marry a poor man?" Roland asked. "Now that you know your future, would you rather have a rich one?"

"I'd choose love," Luci said softly. "I've had little of both, but love is much preferred, even with an empty stomach. My Sadie has been the best part of my life. Without love, what good would money be? What would be the reason for anything? Everyone needs someone to fight for. A reason to be."

"I think you know my answer." Lillian's cheeks had flushed, and she gave Roland a shy smile. I was reminded of what she'd looked like as a little girl.

"Do I?" Roland asked, still deadly serious. "Tell me exactly."

"Of all the men in the world, rich or poor, I'd choose you every time." Lillian lifted her gaze to meet his with eyes glassy from unshed tears. "Don't you know that by now?"

"I wanted to hear the words," Roland said.

"And now you have." Lillian dabbed at her eyes. "The question is, what will you do about it?"

I TUCKED LUCI'S ARM INTO MINE AS I LED THE WAY TO THE DINING room. She trembled at the sight of the table, which had been set for a formal dinner with sparkling silver and a white tablecloth. Heavy burgundy curtains had been pulled back so that we might enjoy the view of Dax's roses. These summer days were long, and the sun was yet to set, spilling orange over the gardens.

Roland escorted Lillian to her seat on one end of the rectangular table.

Luci took her arm from mine and looked around the room, clearly uncertain as to what to do next. I went to the chair nearest mine at the other end of the table and pulled it out for her. "Luci, would you care to sit here?"

She nodded and moved over to me. I waited until she was settled before helping her to scoot closer to the table.

As Roland and I sat, Luci kept her gaze on Lillian. When Lillian placed her napkin on her lap, Luci followed. She wouldn't know anything about formal etiquette. Rules that Lillian and I took for granted, having followed them all our lives, would cause her to stumble.

Our first course arrived, oysters on the half shell, brought up from the kitchen by June. They'd been carefully shucked.

"I can't believe it," Lillian said. "How did Etta find them?"

"She's French," I said. "She has her ways."

I looked over at Luci. Her bottom lip trembled as if she was trying hard not to cry.

"Luci, darling, what's the matter?" Lillian asked.

Luci, with a stricken expression, turned toward Lillian. "It's the forks. There are so many. I don't know which to use."

Roland chuckled. "There *are* a lot of them."

"Don't worry, we can show you which to use," Lillian said.

Luci brought one hand to the collar of her blouse. "I'm sorry. That I don't know."

"Don't apologize," I said gruffly. "Never apologize for ignorance unless you choose to be so." A twinge of guilt rattled me. I kept thinking what a grand life I could give her. But I hadn't thought about her feeling embarrassed or unsure, even though she'd questioned me about this very thing. Seeing her humiliated made me dislike myself immensely.

A lone tear caught in Luci's bottom lashes. "This is all wrong. I shouldn't be here."

"Nonsense," I said.

"How will I ever be your wife?" She swiped under her eyes with her gloved finger as her chest rose and fell. "I don't know about forks or whether I'm to keep the gloves on at dinner, and the champagne has made my head feel cloudy."

It pained me to see her suffer. I glanced over at Roland for help. He always knew what to say during awkward moments.

"I had to learn all this too, Luci," Roland said. "They taught us at school, and I was the only one who had no idea there was any such thing as more than one fork. Where I'm from, we were happy to have a meal and one fork each."

"They gave us an entire semester on etiquette," I said.

Roland leaned forward slightly, animated. "One of the teachers walked around during mealtimes with a ruler and smacked us on top of the head if we used the wrong fork."

"Or God forbid, put our elbows on the table," I said.

"That's awful," Luci said, seemingly forgetting her own angst for the moment. "Did you ever get hit?"

"Wes here never got in trouble, but I still have a scar on the top of my head." Roland pointed to the crown of his head.

Lillian laughed. "You don't have a scar up there."

"I do. It's given my perfectly shaped head a dent."

"I'm pretty sure it was like that before," I said.

"He's absolutely wrong." Roland grinned at Luci. "I was much better-looking before boarding school."

She smiled back at him.

"We'll teach you about the forks and whatever else," Lillian said. "It's a silly convention anyway. Who needs this many types of silver?"

Luci's gaze returned to her plate. "Are these snails? Do people eat snails?"

Roland laughed again. "In fact, they eat slugs in France. They're called escargot. But these are oysters and come from the ocean. You'll be surprised to know that people love them. A delicacy. Where I'm from, they're another thing we can steal from the sea to stay alive."

Luci looked over at Roland, then back to her plate. "Oh yes, an oyster. I've heard of them."

My sister picked up the small pitchfork-shaped fork. "Use this one. Etta has already loosened the oyster from its shell, so you just have to scoop it up with the fork and bring the whole thing to your mouth at once." Lillian demonstrated before picking up her champagne glass. "Then you follow it with a drink of champagne."

"Or water." Roland's eyes twinkled as he looked adoringly at my sister. "And leave the champagne for Lillian."

"Since it makes your insides tickle, I'll be happy to have yours," Lillian said.

"But no more than a second glass, right, Lillian?" Luci asked earnestly.

"You're a quick learner," Lillian said.

"I don't want to feel as if I want to die in the morning. All I've done all my life is try to stay alive." Luci smiled, then chuckled.

"This is a wise woman." Roland picked up his oyster fork and deftly scooped an oyster from its shell and into his mouth.

Luci imitated Roland's move, scooping the oyster out of the shell. Somehow she didn't quite get hold of it and the entire thing plopped onto her lap. "Oh no."

"Well, that's not *exactly* the way." Lillian abruptly stood, then darted around to the other side of the table. She tugged one glove off and plucked the oyster from Luci's lap and plopped it back into its shell. "They're slippery, I'm afraid. And look at you. The devil fell in your napkin, which you so cleverly had spread over your lap. No harm done."

Roland and I had both stood when my sister left her place at the table. Now, Roland assisted her by scooting her chair back in. Once she was settled, we both sat back down.

Luci lifted her chin from where it had been tucked into her

neck. "They smell like three-day-old fish heads. And the shell looks like a scary sea creature. I think I shall hate them."

I barked out a laugh. "Truth be told, I don't care for them. Let's give them all to Lillian and Roland and move on to the soup."

Luci's wide smile made me dizzy. "You won't make me eat them?"

"As I said earlier today. I'll not make you do anything you don't want to." I spoke softly as if she were an abused dog, wary and suspicious. Thinking of Sam Quick made my blood boil. I'd have loved to give him a little of what he'd been giving out all these years.

"No, I can't leave food on the table," Luci said. "That's wrong. I'll try again to get the devil in my mouth." She stabbed the tiny fork into the oyster and leaned over her plate as she lifted it to her mouth. Her eyes widened as she swallowed. "It's slippery in my mouth too, but it doesn't taste too bad."

"They taste like the sea," Lillian said. "Which is why I love them."

"I've never been to the sea," Luci said.

"We're going soon," I said.

"Do you love it there as much as Wesley?" Luci asked Roland.

"Yes, and I think you will as well," Roland said.

June returned with the second course, a cold vichyssoise. Etta was a little too French for my liking, but I put that aside for the moment. After gathering the oyster plates, June set a bowl in front of each of us. I waited for her to leave before turning back to Luci. "Is it obvious which one is used for soup?" I asked.

Luci raised the only spoon and blessed me with another smile. "This one?"

"See, there's nothing to this," I said.

"The only thing here is that you have to scoop away rather

than toward you," Lillian said as she dipped her spoon into the soup. "No one knows why, but that's just the way it is."

"Again, I had no idea about this detail until school." Roland gave Luci an encouraging smile. "I was used to scooping it into my mouth as fast as possible or risk having it stolen by a sister."

Again, Luci imitated my sister, scooping carefully away from her as instructed. The moment the soup was in her mouth, her eyebrows shot up in surprise. "It's cold."

Lillian nodded. "They love their cold soup in France."

I dipped into my bowl and took a hearty bite. The flavors of leeks and garlic were delicious. "This is good. Luci, do you like it?"

"Very much, yes." She took another bite. Such a pretty mouth, I thought, momentarily distracted. I couldn't wait to kiss her.

"Do you think Sadie's all right?" Lillian asked. "This must be disorienting for her."

Luci looked up from her intense concentration on the soup. "She's quite well, thank you." Her tone sounded both protective and leery. "Has she done something?"

"Not at all," Lillian said. "She's sweet as can be and has impeccable manners. You've done wonderfully with her, considering everything."

Luci's eyes flashed with a hint of anger at the word *everything*. My sister had meant no harm, but I could see how that could be taken as an insult. "Thank you."

"Darling, I'm sorry," Lillian said. "I'm a dolt. I meant only that she's a remarkable child, and that can only be because of you."

"Thank you." Luci lifted her gaze toward Lillian. "It's true that our circumstances haven't been ideal. However, just because we're poor doesn't mean we shouldn't have good manners or learn how to speak properly. Before my sister came, I went to school, for which I'm grateful."

"Same with me," Roland said. "I had an unknown benefactor who sent me to boarding school, where I met Wes."

"Really?" Luci asked. "You never learned who it was?"

"I've absolutely no idea," Roland said.

"It's dreadful," Lillian said. "I can't let any mystery go. Anything unsolved spins around in my head forever."

"Some things I wish I didn't know," Luci said.

"Like what?" Lillian asked.

"Nothing. Never mind." Luci held up her spoon. "What do you do with this when you're done with your soup?"

"Just leave it in the bowl," Lillian said, sounding disappointed.

During the rest of the meal, we continued to cover forks. Lillian explained that everything went from the outside inward. "Every time they bring a new course, use the next fork."

Our next fork was not used for fish as it often was, but a melon paired with thinly sliced ham.

Luci took a bite of cantaloupe and closed her eyes as she chewed. "I've never tasted anything so good."

"Dax's garden," Lillian said.

Next, June brought the main course, chunks of beef covered with a garlic butter sauce.

Luci groaned softly as she chewed the first bite. That particular sound caused all kinds of feelings to stir in me, none of them gentlemanly.

"Mother would frown on appreciative noises at the dinner table," Lillian said. "Isn't that right, Wesley?"

"Yes," I said. "I was scolded for that a few times growing up."

Luci flushed. "I'm sorry. It's just that I've never tasted anything like this."

Lillian laughed merrily. "Oh, Luci, you certainly liven things up."

"But I don't want to be lively," Luci said. "I want to be presentable."

"Proper young ladies are so boring." Lillian drew out the first syllable of *boring* for dramatic effect. "We only have to pretend to be in front of anyone who cares about such things."

"Your mother will care," Luci said. "What if she finds me lacking?"

"Who cares?" Lillian asked. "She has no say over anything Wesley does. He inherited her father's fortune, leaving him independent of any ties."

Luci looked over at me, clearly surprised. "Did it go to you because you're a man?"

"Partly," Lillian said. "But mostly as a way to punish our mother for marrying our father."

"He didn't approve," Wesley said. "Which proved to be right."

"But without him, there would be no you," Luci said. "Or you, Lillian. Which would make the world less bright."

Roland lifted his champagne glass. "I couldn't agree with you more, Luci."

21

Luci

"I'M TO SLEEP IN HERE? WITHOUT YOU?" SADIE'S EYES WERE BIG and her voice small. "But there are two beds."

"In our new life, I'll have my own room. When I marry Wesley, then I'll share a bedroom with him."

Sadie frowned as she clutched the quilt up to her chin with both hands. "I'll be scared without you."

From the doorway came Wesley's voice. "I have an idea."

We both turned to look at him. Gus was beside him in the doorway. "May I come in?"

"Yes, all right," I said.

Gus followed Wesley over to the other twin bed, where he sat. His long legs and bulk looked almost comical on the small bed. "When I was a boy, my dog, Atlas, slept with me. Right on my bed. I was never scared. Perhaps Gus could sleep here with you?"

As if all for the idea, Gus put his chin on the mattress near Sadie's shoulder. She reached a hand out and scratched behind his ears. "Would you like to stay with me, Gus?" Sadie asked.

Gus whined and wagged his tail. "I think that's a yes," Wesley said. "You'll want him to sleep by your feet. Otherwise, there won't be room."

"How do I teach him that?" Sadie asked.

Wesley unfolded himself and ambled over to her bed. He patted the spot near her feet. "You sleep here, all right, old boy?"

Gus jumped on the bed, did three circles, and lay down with his head facing Sadie.

"Good boy," Wesley said.

Gus wagged his tail twice and then closed his eyes. "I think you wore him out today, Sadie."

She smiled up at him. "Good night, Wesley."

"Good night, Sadie Bug." He glanced over at me. "Will you come say good night when you're done?"

I nodded. After he was out of the room, I tucked the quilt around Sadie's shoulders. "I have a treat for you." I reached under the bed where I'd temporarily hidden a book of fairy tales I'd found in the shelves. There were at least a hundred tales. The volume weighed as much as five pounds of flour. "Would you like me to read you a story?"

"Yes, please."

I had already decided I would read the story of Cinderella to her. It was one Mama had occasionally told me when she tucked me in for the night. "I'm going to read to you about Cinderella, but you're going to be surprised by the ending. It's not like the one Mama told me."

The story Mama had passed along from her own childhood ended with the prince marrying the princess of his father's choice. Cinderella had remained at home, mistreated by her stepmother and stepsisters for the rest of her life. The first time she'd told me that sad tale, I'd cried. "But why didn't he choose her?" I'd asked.

"Because a prince never chooses a girl like Cinderella. Girls like us are not meant for fine lives. We're meant to grasp and claw to stay alive."

I shook aside that memory to focus on Sadie.

"Please read, Sister." She turned on her side as I sat in the rocking chair next to the bed.

"Once upon a time there was a girl named . . ." I continued, reading about how she meets the prince in the woods, and later they dance at the ball, and finally he chooses Cinderella to be his bride.

"They lived happily ever after," I said, closing the book.

"It's not at all what we thought. Why did Mama lie to you?"

I took a moment before answering. "I think she didn't want me to be disappointed. Her life was hard. She knew it would be for us too. Or, at least me. She didn't know about you yet."

Sadie's eyes filled with tears. "I don't want to have a sad ending."

"You, my sweet, are not going to have a sad ending. I shall not allow it."

"Do you want to dance with Wesley? Like Cinderella danced with the prince?"

"I don't know how to dance." I scooted out of the chair to perch on the side of her bed.

"Cinderella loved the prince, didn't she? Do you love Wesley?"

I smoothed the blanket over her shoulder. How could I explain to my little sister the deep feelings I had for Wesley? "I'm as tied to him as I am to you."

"Like Cinderella and the prince?"

"I suppose so."

She turned over onto her back and looked up at me, a crease in her fair brow. "Why did Cinderella's father not take care of her? Why did he let the evil stepmother and stepsisters be so mean to her?"

"I'm not sure. I think some people don't understand how to love."

"Will you still love me even if you love Wesley?"

"I'll never ever stop loving you." I tapped my chest with one finger. "You're in here, no matter how many years go by. It's been you and me for a long time now. That will never change, even if we grow to love others too."

"Even if you have a baby of your own? Not a sister but a daughter?"

I gazed down at her, amazed by these questions. "Have you been worried about these things?"

"I guess so. I don't want you to leave me behind."

"I'll never leave you or send you away. You're my sister, yes, but you've been mine since the day you were born. I'm the one God entrusted to take care of you. You're my child. You always will be. Do you understand?"

"Yes." She yawned and snuggled deeper under the covers.

I leaned over to kiss her forehead. "Good night, precious girl."

"Night, Sister."

I stood up from the bed and walked quietly to the door, then turned back to get another look. She'd closed her eyes. The quilt moved up and down from her even breathing. A feeling of deep gratitude filled me. We'd made it. I'd managed to keep us both alive. Now Wesley was here, offering us a new life. My sweet Sadie would never have to be hungry again.

AFTER I CAME DOWNSTAIRS FROM TUCKING SADIE IN, WESLEY asked if I'd like to take a stroll in the garden. Although I was slightly nervous to be alone with him, I accepted. Dusk was the shade of dusty roses as we ambled across the lawn toward the vegetable gardens. The night was warm and still and smelled of ripening tomatoes. Tucked behind the fenced garden, the lights of Dax and Mollie's cottage peeked through. The notes of Lillian's piano playing from the main house drifted through the open windows.

"What's the ocean like?" I asked.

"Like nowhere else. The air smells of fish and seaweed and salt. When the sun shines, the water is as blue as anything you've ever seen. All day the waves crash onto the shore. At night too. I can hear them as I fall asleep. You can drift to sleep knowing that in the morning they will still be there. On summer days, you can sit on the back porch of the cottage and look and look but never find the end of the ocean. Everything's green, with wildflowers that dot the hillside."

We walked in silence for a moment. The sound of a cricket started up, background to the croak of a bullfrog and interfering with the piano notes.

"Will there be a school for Sadie?"

"Yes, it's small, but there's a schoolhouse in Castaway."

"Do you regret bringing me here?" I asked. After dinner, I'd had a hollow feeling in my stomach. Maybe he'd seen for himself how uncultured I was and had decided I wasn't for him after all.

He stopped walking and turned me to look at him. "No, why would you ask?"

"I don't know. It was an impulse, wasn't it? Not a decision you thought through? After tonight at dinner I thought you may have changed your mind."

"Knowing which fork to use is of no consequence to me. It's you I want. One of the reasons I moved to the sea was to live how I want to live. Free from expectations from my parents or anyone else. We'll make our own way. Together."

"And what would I do? As your wife, I mean."

"What do you like to do?"

I thought for a moment. Had I ever done anything other than chores? "I've no idea. There's never been a choice. I did what had to be done."

"What about before Sadie?"

My memories were dim of the time before my sister. I'd gone to school long enough to know how to read and write. "I liked school. Reading books. But there have been so few of those."

"I'll buy you books, and you can sit outside on the porch and read as the waves crash to shore."

"But who will make dinner and clean the house?"

He laughed. "You have a lot of questions tonight."

"Is it too many?"

"Never. If we decide we need help, we can hire someone."

I thought about that for a moment. What would it be like to have a maid or a cook? Or to have time during the day to read a book?

"Thank you for letting me borrow the book to read to Sadie. She enjoyed it more than I can say. As did I."

"You're welcome to any of the books. Mother won't miss them, if you'd like to take anything with us when we go." He steered us toward the fence. "Would you like a book for tonight? I like to read before I go to sleep at night."

"Yes, please." I couldn't keep the excitement out of my voice. "Could you help me pick something out?"

"What kind of stories do you like?"

I thought for a moment. Not really knowing, having read so few, I took a guess. "I might like to read a book about a girl like me."

"There aren't any books about a girl like you," he said. "You're one of a kind."

"Surely there are books about a girl rescued by a kind boy. Isn't that what fairy tales are about?"

"But that's not the kind of story we are. You didn't need rescuing. Not really. Look at what you've done, all on your own, despite every obstacle in your way. Perhaps it's the other way around. You rescued me."

"But how? I have nothing to offer."

"Your heart. Your courage. Your honor. I'm better just being near you."

I giggled. "You're silly to say such things, but I like to hear them."

"I'm not silly," he said. "I'm truthful. I'll spend my life hoping to be good enough for you."

We were quiet. Lillian's piano playing stopped, then started again. "Wesley, is it hard being here? Remembering?"

Several seconds skipped by before he answered. "I've had a few moments. Standing in my father's study and seeing that painting of him . . . was hard. Gave me pause, I guess you'd say."

"I'm sorry."

"It's all right. Don't be sad. Those days are behind me now."

"Do you still remember, though, or does it fade with time?" I asked, wondering if I'd ever be able to forget Pa.

"I could put it all aside when I was at school and over the last few years while Roland and I were building the cottages. Now that I'm here, the memories are around every corner. I don't think a person ever forgets the cruelty. But we move on with things. Dwelling in the past takes away the present. I like the present, here with you."

"I like the present too," I said. After another few seconds I asked another question. "Why did you come home for the burial?"

"I came to collect what I left behind all those years ago. You, for one. I'm not sure I knew it until I saw you again. All these years, I thought of you and remembered my promise. Somewhere inside me I guess I couldn't find peace until I came back for you."

I shivered, remembering the dark, isolated, and desperately lonely days after Sadie's birth.

"There was a restlessness inside me, a longing for something I couldn't quite fix upon. Perhaps that was the impetus for my cottage. My obsession with finishing it. Every nail I pounded—every finishing detail was for you."

I hooked my hand into the crook of his arm as we came upon the fence on the west end of the property. The sun had dipped below the horizon. Pink streaks painted the sky.

From here, the house seemed far away, and it seemed only the two of us. I'd grown increasingly comfortable with Wesley, as if we had never parted and had spent the last five years together. What would that have been like? Growing up together?

But with that ease between us, a different feeling was developing, coming alive in me. I wanted him to touch me, kiss me.

"I have one more thing I need to ask you," I said.

He leaned his backside against the fence. "Anything."

The sweet scent of roses perfumed the air and made me almost dizzy. Or was it my prince who made me swoon? "How come you haven't tried to kiss me?"

He turned to look at me, taking one of my hands in his. "I didn't want to be presumptuous. I'm trying not to scare you away." He ran the back of one finger along my jawbone. I longed to rub my entire face against his hand. "Would you like a kiss?"

"How else will we know if we're suitable that way?"

"I don't suppose we will," he said. "Shall we try now?"

"But I don't know how to kiss." Did I lift my face upward? Should my mouth be closed or slightly open?

"I don't think there's much to it," Wesley said. "Impossible to do wrong, really."

"Do you close your eyes?"

191

"Some do. I think most, actually. But honestly, I've not had much experience kissing either."

That startled me. Had he kissed others before? I hadn't thought of it until just now. "How many kisses have you had?"

He chuckled. "Only one."

"Who was she?" I didn't like this at all. "Where is she now?"

"At school we occasionally had dances with the girls' boarding school. I danced with her one night, and she invited me outside for fresh air. Somehow we escaped the scrutiny of the chaperones. Before I knew it, she'd planted a kiss on me. Quite brazen."

I sucked in a breath. If I'd been a girl who went to a fancy school, would I have been like that? Loose? Was it something I'd inherited from my mother? Because right now I would have given almost anything to have Wesley kiss me. Were girls not supposed to have these feelings? "Did you not like her after that? After her brazen move?"

"I liked her about the same before and after. Not much. She wasn't you, Luci."

I sighed with relief and giddy joy. *She wasn't you.* "Is it wrong for a woman to want a kiss?"

"I don't think so. Why do you ask?"

"My mother. Do you know about her? What she did?" My voice had grown small and afraid. I held my breath, waiting for his answer.

"Yes, I know. But that's an entirely different thing than what's between us. Your mother did what she had to do."

"Do you think? Because I think there were other ways to keep us fed. I'm ashamed for her."

"I understand, but you're not your mother any more than I'm my father."

"I guess so." I brushed the lapel of his dinner jacket with the tips of my fingers. "I didn't know what it felt like to fall in love. How wonderful it would feel."

"Are you in love with me?"

"If all these fireflies in my stomach mean that I'm in love, then I suppose I am."

He smiled down at me as he brushed my bottom lip with his thumb. "You're beautiful."

"It's dark. You can't see me."

"I see you. May I kiss you now, or would you like to hear more about my past?"

"Stop teasing me," I said. "I don't like the idea of you kissing other girls."

"If I have my way, you'll be the only one I ever kiss."

If it was possible to smile with one's entire body, as if it started in my stomach and spread throughout my body, I was doing so now. "Do I lift my face up, like this?" I raised my chin.

"That'll do," he said huskily. "Close your eyes or I'll lose my nerve."

I did so and waited. He was so close I could smell his shaving soap. I held my breath then, waiting, unsure what to do. In the next second, his lips were on mine. They were softer than I'd imagined. The kiss kept going. Soon, my lips parted all on their own. He pulled me closer to him. A small moan escaped before I could stifle myself.

Finally, he lifted his mouth from mine and loosened his arm from around my waist. "I suppose that answers our question."

"I forgot what the question was," I said.

"About whether we're compatible in that way."

"Yes, I suppose so." Just then I would have said the world was all mine. Every bit mine for the taking.

"Your laughter is my favorite sound."

"I like laughing," I said. "Especially here with you."

"Do you want to get married soon, or do you want to wait and plan a formal wedding?"

With the light fading, it was hard to see the nuances of his expression. "I'd like to do it quickly and leave for Castaway. The longer we stay, the more worried I am about Pa figuring out where we are and causing trouble."

"Roland's going to ask Lillian to marry him," he said. "But you have to keep it a secret. He wants to surprise her."

"Lillian was worried that he might not want to . . . because of money."

"I've got that worked out with him," Wesley said.

"And you approve?" I asked.

"I've known for a while now that Roland would marry her. I knew it before they even met."

"Really?"

"Like you and me," he said. "Some love stories are written in the stars."

He kissed me again, this time without preamble. When we parted, breathless, I knew it was definitely the man who made me dizzy. No scent, regardless of how sweet, could make me feel this way.

"I've something for you," he said. "A ring."

"What?"

He dropped to one knee. Once more, I held my breath and waited for what was next.

22

 esley

ON ONE KNEE, I TOOK THE RING FROM MY POCKET AND REACHED for her hand. "Luci, would you wear this ring for the rest of your life? Will you be my wife?"

"Yes to both."

I put the ring on her finger and then stood to kiss her. Soon I drew away, knowing that if I continued it would compromise us both. I was beginning to act too boldly. Being around her was intoxicating. I lost all sense of gentlemanly behavior. If I had my way, we'd be upstairs in my bed. After being married, of course. I wasn't a barbarian.

Fireflies had appeared during our kiss. They twinkled as they darted about over the lawn. "You're my firefly. My light in the dark."

She answered quietly, just above a whisper. "You're mine too."

On the horizon, a sliver of moon had risen over the valley. I took her hand in mine. With my index finger, I traced the calluses on the pads of her palm. They told the story of day after day of hard physical work. Chores that must have seemed unending. Had they been a crushing burden to her? Dax had said she'd never once complained to him.

"Are my calluses horrid to you?" she asked.

I brought the palm of her hand to my mouth. "Nothing could be farther from the truth. In fact, I was thinking how hard you've worked and that I want to give you everything you've ever wanted."

"All I've ever wanted was to keep Sadie fed and safe."

"We shall. From now on, you'll have me to help."

Hand in hand, we started out across the lawn toward the house. "Did you ever think of me?" I asked. "Over the years?"

"Yes, but I didn't think I'd ever see you again, so I didn't spend too much time wishing for what couldn't be. That's the road to unhappiness for a girl in my position. No time for daydreams. I just went day by day. One hour to the next. Still, those few minutes with you were the first time anyone had ever really looked at me, not through me or around me. That's not something I could forget."

"I'm sorry I couldn't keep my promise. I would have if I could. With the inheritance from my grandfather, I'm free to do as I wish now."

"Did you know about your inheritance?"

"No. I had no idea that he would leave everything to me. I'd never met him. Can you imagine giving money to a stranger just because you didn't want to give it to your daughter?"

"People do strange things. My father gave me away in a poker game." To my surprise, she laughed.

"It's not funny," I said. "I want to kill him with my bare hands."

"A good life is the greatest revenge."

"We still have another few days before Mother arrives. I'd like to stay so that we can tell her in person about Lillian and Roland and you and me."

"I'm anxious to go, but I understand. Even so, I'll be frightened to meet her."

"She doesn't have a say in my life." I touched her cheek with the back of my finger, fighting the urge to take her in my arms and kiss her.

WHEN WE ARRIVED BACK INSIDE, LILLIAN ROSE FROM THE PIANO. She must have spotted Luci's new ring right away because she rushed over to us. "It's pretty, Wesley." Lillian embraced Luci. "I'm so happy we're to be family."

"Me too," Luci said.

"Shall we have a drink?" I asked. "To toast?"

"Water for me," Luci said. "I do not like that floating feeling."

"Sherry for me," Lillian said.

I poured Roland and myself a whiskey as the ladies settled onto the couch. Roland wandered around the room, from the window to the piano. He'd shared with me in confidence that he would ask Lillian when he felt the time was right. He wanted a romantic, perfect setting and didn't yet know where that was. Until then, he'd said, the ring in his pocket felt as heavy as a boulder. His heart would either be broken or not, depending on Lillian's answer. No amount of talking would convince him that she was sure to accept, so I'd given up and kept silent. Nothing like love to make one's self-assurance waver.

After everyone had their drink, Roland and I sat in the chairs opposite the couch. We toasted first to my official engagement to Luci.

"We have other news as well." I raised my glass. "To our

new venture, Harris and Ford Dry Goods. Roland and I are now partners. We signed paperwork today." I shared with them the idea for multiple locations and that we would begin the moment we returned to Castaway.

"You've agreed, Roland?" Lillian asked.

Roland grinned. "Yes, but only because he agreed that I was to repay him for my half of the starting costs once we were profitable."

"He's been stubborn," I said. "But I've worn him down."

"Do you wear everyone down in this way?" Luci's mouth twitched into a smile.

"Some take longer than others." I winked at her.

"I can't wait to get started," Roland said. "Once we get the building done, we're going to have a grand opening. Every child who comes into the store will get a piece of candy."

Lillian had gone strangely quiet. She seemed to be studying her sherry with more intensity than it deserved.

"I'd have liked a store with free candy," Luci said wistfully.

"You may have a piece of candy whenever you come in," Roland said. "To make up for all the pieces you haven't had."

"Really? And Sadie too?" Luci smiled, momentarily looking as young as the day I'd first met her.

"Of course, Sadie too," Roland said.

Lillian downed the entirety of her sherry and slammed the glass down on the coffee table. "I'll be heading to bed now."

"What's the matter, Lillian?" I asked. "Do you not like our idea?"

"It sounds fine." Staring at the floor, she spoke woodenly. "Just wonderful."

Roland leaned forward. "Do you think I'm unfit for the partnership? That I'll fail? Or do you think I've exploited your brother?"

Lillian lifted her chin to look at him. "None of those things."

"Then what?" Roland asked.

"I thought you might ask me . . . to marry you, and now you're leaving to open up your precious business. How long will I have to wait?" Her voice cracked as a sob rose from her chest. "Until the first store is profitable? The second? Or third? How many will it be, Roland, before you see yourself worthy of me? Meanwhile, I'll be here, waiting. And you'll all leave me."

"Who said anything about that?" Roland asked.

"It's obvious, isn't it?" Lillian stood. Tears gone, she now seemed merely furious. "You won't want to propose if you don't have a ring, and how long will that take? Years? Do you expect me to follow my brother and his new wife and live with them like an old maid until you're good and ready?"

She was on such a rant, and neither of us could interrupt.

"I'm so very tired of everyone having a say about my life but me. I want to get married now, Roland, and I don't care one hoot about a ring. It's you who's insistent that all be done as rich people do, and I just want to be your wife."

Roland shot me a panicked look. Lillian in all her life had hardly raised her voice.

"Lillian, calm down for a moment," I said.

She turned on me, eyes blazing. "Calm down? I will not calm down. Don't you dare tell me to calm down."

"I think you'd better forgo the perfect location and ask her now," I said to Roland. "Before she hauls off and breaks something."

"Yes, I believe you're correct." Roland dropped to the floor in front of Lillian as he pulled the ring box from inside his jacket.

Lillian crossed her arms over her chest and glared at him, perhaps not yet ready to let go of her anger, even though it was obvious what he was doing.

"Forgive me, Lillian. I thought you'd prefer a more romantic setting with champagne, but I'll do it now. Will you marry me?"

He lifted the top off the box and presented it to her. "This isn't much—someday I'll get you the prettiest I can find."

Lillian brought her hands to her mouth and shook her head. "No, no, I love this one."

He stood and lifted the ring from the box. "May I have your hand?"

She held it out, and he pushed the engagement ring onto her ring finger.

"Are you saying yes?" Roland asked.

"Yes, I'll marry you."

"May I kiss you now?" Roland asked.

"Yes. I'm saying yes to that too."

Roland leaned closer and gave her a chaste kiss on the lips. I knew that was for my benefit. As if they hadn't kissed before.

"I can't believe it," Lillian said as she stared at her hand. "I've dreamed of this day for what feels like forever. I'm sorry I acted so awful. I couldn't bear the thought of Luci and Wesley and you leaving me while I was stuck here missing you."

"I'm sorry I waited. I wanted it to be special." Roland smiled gently as he put one arm around her waist. "We've had enough missing each other and endless letter writing. I want you by my side where you belong. In fact, I'd like to get married before we leave. I want you to come home with me as my wife."

"What about Mother?" Lillian asked. "Wesley, should we wait for her?"

"It's whatever you want," I said. "But it might be better to already have married so she knows there's nothing she can do to stop you."

"He's right," Lillian said.

"But do you want a formal wedding?" Luci asked. "Won't you want a dress and a party?"

Lillian laughed. "I don't care about any of that. Let's go to the courthouse on Monday."

"Us too?" Luci asked me.

"I suppose so," I said. "Monday's as good a day as any."

Today was Saturday, which meant we had a day to get everything in order.

"Let's dance," Lillian said. "I'll put on the phonograph. And you must ask me to dance, Roland." She scurried over to the phonograph and put on a waltz.

Roland bowed at the waist and then led her to a spot near the piano.

I turned to Luci, who had remained on the couch during all the excitement. "Would you care to dance?"

She ducked her head. "I don't know how."

"There's nothing to it," I said. "I'll show you."

She nodded and allowed me to escort her to a spot by the window. "Put one hand here, like this." I guided her hand to rest gently on my shoulder. "Then give me your other hand." As she did so, I encircled her waist with my other arm. "Now, simply sway to the music. We don't have to make any fancy moves." I moved my feet to the beat of the music.

For a moment, she was stiff in my arms, but then she relaxed and we danced as if we'd been made for each other.

23

L uci

WE BUMPED DOWN A DIRT ROAD IN WESLEY'S MOTORCAR. HE drove slowly, but still we bounced in potholes that lifted me off the seat as if momentarily flying. Dust billowed around us, but I wore my new duster in a soft tan color over my new white summer dress. The dressmaker had brought it that morning. How I loved the soft white material and the way it swirled around my legs. Lillian had given me a purple silk scarf to cover my straw hat, which I'd tied under my chin. Despite my attempt to remain humble, the new clothes made me feel posh and proper, as did the ring on my finger.

Gus sat on his haunches in the back seat.

"He likes the motorcar," Wesley said.

Gus barked.

"What about you, lovely Luci? Do you like riding in my car?"

"I like riding in the car with you." I smiled over at him.

"I'm glad to know. Lillian told me you were frightened."

"I was, but I'm not now." I gazed out to the countryside as the car conquered the hill, chugging along. The road had been carved out of the heavily wooded hillside. On each side trees grew wide and tall. Wesley had said it was a logging road where men came to cut down trees and haul them to the mill, where they would be made into boards for stores and houses.

My ears felt plugged suddenly, making everything quieter. "What is it, Wesley, that makes my ears feel clogged?"

"That's the altitude—a difference in air pressure causes your ears to feel plugged. Try swallowing as if you're drinking water."

I did so and immediately felt relief. "That's better. How odd."

"Yes, one of the many wonders of Mother Nature."

I settled back into the seat and looked at the trees, mesmerized by the contrast from dark to light between them. Soon thereafter, Wesley turned right down a skinnier dirt road. I sat up straighter to get a better look. Through a patch of pines and maples, a green lake sparkled under the sunlight. "Is this it?"

"Yes. Do you approve?"

"Oh yes. It's beautiful."

A picnic basket had been packed by Etta and June. Wesley had surprised me that morning at breakfast by asking if I'd like to accompany him on a picnic outing. *A picnic,* I'd thought. *What does one do on a picnic?*

So here we were. Wesley got out and sprinted around the side of the car to help me down. Gus jumped out from the back and barked.

I stepped onto the soft grass and took a good look around as he reached in the back for the picnic basket. The air was cooler here than at the house and smelled of pine needles.

Gus took off down the path, his nose to the ground. What did he smell?

Wesley reached into the back for the picnic basket. And the blanket. "The last time I was here, the meadows and shores were covered with snow and the lake was iced over."

Now, natural grasses grew tall, stretching toward the sun. Purple and red wildflowers bloomed. I breathed in the fresh air and resisted the urge to run after Gus as if I were no older than Sadie.

Wesley carried the picnic basket as we headed down a trodden path toward the water. When we reached the lake, the beauty of the crystal-clear water entranced me. I stood with my hands clasped together, taking in the scene until Wesley placed his hand at the small of my back. "Would you like to sit over there in the shade?" He gestured toward a sandy cove under a maple tree.

I agreed and made my way down the rocky path, careful not to twist my ankle, not yet fully adjusted to the heel of my new shoes.

While Wesley spread a blanket over the sand, I wandered down to the shore and peered into the water. Shiny pebbles covered the bottom of the lake. I knelt, careful not to get my duster wet as I dipped my hand into water as cold as newly melted snow.

I came back to our picnic spot. The basket was woven from twigs and had a lid that opened on a hinge. Red-and-white checkered fabric lined the inside. Wesley had taken a bucket of cold fried chicken, two oranges, and a baguette of Etta's wonderful bread from the basket. Would I ever look at a feast like this and not remember the time of gnawing hunger?

I sat on the edge of the blanket, stealing glances at Wesley. He wore a cream-colored suit with a light-blue tie. He'd tossed his hat onto the blanket. His dark hair was without the pomade he used for evenings, which made it loose and wavy. Was it as silky as it looked?

He loosened his tie and shrugged out of his jacket. As he rolled up the sleeves of his white shirt, he caught me looking at him. I flushed with heat.

"Are you all right?" His forehead wrinkled. "Too warm?"

"A little." In fact, I'd never felt warmer in my life.

"Take off your shoes and stockings. I can't have you fainting from heatstroke on our first picnic together."

"What?" How could I possibly do that in front of him? My stockings were held in place with garters attached to my bloomers. Reaching up to unhook them would be impossible without showing him my legs. "I can't. Not in front of you."

"I'll turn away and promise not to look."

The tips of my ears and cheeks seemed to have caught fire. I placed my hand over the wildly beating pulse at my neck. "It might take a moment. I'll tell you when you can turn back around."

"Your wish is my command." He bowed his head.

I giggled, nervous.

Wesley turned all the way around so that he faced the tree.

I held my breath as I unbuckled my new shoes and slipped them from my hot feet. Next, I reached up to unhook my garters and slide the cotton stockings from my legs. Immediate relief. Before my new wardrobe, I didn't wear stockings or a corset and petticoat. All these layers made me hot. Lillian had said she didn't even notice her corset. How was that possible?

I smoothed my skirt back into place, making sure to cover my feet, and folded my stockings small enough to fit into one of my shoes. Bare toes were surely inappropriate in front of a man. Even if one planned to marry him as soon as was earthly possible. "I'm done."

He turned back around. His eyes darted to my abandoned shoes and then back to me. "Better?"

"Immensely."

"I shall do the same then." With quick movements, he took off his shoes and, to my horror, his socks. He rolled up his pants legs to mid-calf. I had to look, noting it all within seconds. Not too much hair. Taut calf muscles. Nice feet too. Tidy toenails. "After lunch, we can wade in the water to cool down further."

We'll see about that, I thought. I wasn't about to lift my skirt. What if he found my feet ugly? I'd never thought about them before now. They'd simply been the tools that I used to accomplish my chores. Now I saw them in a new way. A tool of seduction? Another area of my body that I hoped Wesley admired? Alarmed at my thoughts, I flushed even further. What had become of me in such a short time? I was now a wanton woman.

During my lascivious thoughts, Wesley had pulled a bottle of wine from the basket. "Would you like to try a glass of Chablis?"

"Will it tickle my mouth?"

He laughed. "No, there are no bubbles in this one. It's dry and light. I'll give you just a swallow or two to see if you like it."

He used a contraption with a spiral metal rod to pull the cork from the bottle. I jumped when it popped out of the bottle, startled by the noise. "Have you never seen anyone open wine before?" Wesley asked.

"No, never. What is that?" I pointed at the contraption.

"This is a corkscrew. Made specifically for getting a cork out of a bottle. Thus, the name." He smiled as he poured a small amount into one glass and handed it to me.

I smiled back at him, my nervousness dissipating. This was Wesley. He was familiar to me. His smile as known to me as the back of my own hand.

He poured wine for himself and then set a flat board in the middle of the blanket, where he placed the bottle and his glass. "This is a table of sorts," he said.

I took a sip from my glass. The wine was cold and tasted of green apples.

"Ah, you like it, don't you? No tickling bubbles?"

"It's delicious. I'd like a little more, please."

He poured more for me, filling my glass halfway. "Sip slowly or it'll go to your head. Lillian will not approve if I bring you home drunk."

I laughed, imagining the scene, then just as quickly sobered. Would a small amount of wine make me like my father?

"What is it?" Wesley asked.

"Nothing, really. I was thinking of Pa. How drink ruined him."

"I don't think a small glass of wine will ruin you." He lifted a small plate from the basket and handed it to me. "Would you like to eat now?"

"Yes, please."

Wesley filled a plate for me and then one for himself. "Sit with your back against the tree. You'll be more comfortable."

I set aside my glass of wine and scooted over to the spot next to the tree, tucking my legs under my skirt. First he placed a square cloth napkin over my lap, then set the plate by my side. I ate some of the chicken first; it was moist on the inside, with crunchy batter on the outside. How could anything taste this good? I closed my eyes as I chewed, and I must have made one of my embarrassing noises because Wesley laughed. My eyes flew open to find him gazing at me.

"I'm sorry," I said. "It's just everything that Etta makes is so good." I clamped my hand over my mouth as a thought occurred to me. "I don't know how to cook any of these things. You'll hate my cooking."

"No, I'm not that particular. Roland and I have been bachelors the last few years. While we were building the cottages, we lived on flapjacks and beans."

"I know how to make flapjacks and beans," I said, cheered somewhat. "What's your kitchen like?"

"Not like the one at my parents' home. We built it on the main floor. The window over the sink looks out to the sea. While I'm washing my dishes, I can enjoy the view." He tore off a few chunks from the baguette and set one on my plate.

"That sounds nice." I took another bite of chicken and managed to stay silent this time.

Wesley grabbed an orange and began to peel away its rind. When he was done, he took a section and handed it to me. "Have you had an orange before?"

"No."

"They're juicy, so lean over your napkin."

I bit into the slice. The sweet juice awakened every part of my mouth. "It might be even better than strawberries."

"It's a worthy race between the two."

We ate in silence for a few minutes. Stuffed after half an orange, a piece of chicken, and a piece of bread, I reclined even farther against the back of the tree. Wesley busied himself by putting away the plates and other remnants of our meal. I had another sip of wine. Eating had changed the flavor and it had warmed slightly, but I still found it delicious.

"What else do we do on picnics?" I asked.

He lifted a book out of the basket. "I could read to you. I picked a novel I thought you might like called *A Little Princess*. Have you read this one?" He held it up for me to see. The cover was of a sad little girl. "I read it while I was in school, and although it's supposed to be for children, I think any age can read it."

My stomach tightened. "Did you pick it because you think I'm too unsophisticated to read an adult book?"

"Not at all. I know how clever you are. I simply wanted to find a book you would enjoy. Let me read the first chapter, and I think you'll see why I chose this one for you."

My prickly insecurities did not outweigh my desire to hear the story. "You may start," I said primly.

He came to sit beside me with his back against the tree and his legs spread out long. I rested my head against his shoulder as he began to read.

❀

TWO CHAPTERS IN, I WAS CRYING LIKE A CHILD FOR THE POOR lonely girl in the story. Her situation was worse than mine had been. I'd had Sadie. She had no one after losing her father.

Gus, who clearly sensed my distress, had come to lie by my other side. As Wesley read, I absentmindedly petted his head.

At the end of the chapter, he set the book down on the blanket. "I'm sorry it made you cry."

"The story's very sad. But so good."

He caressed my damp cheek, then leaned close to brush his lips against mine. "Do you want me to read more or should I stop?"

"No, you can't stop. We have to find out what happens next." I sighed with joy, forgetting the unfortunate girl in the novel as I stared into the eyes of my love. "Oh, Wesley, this is just the best day. Thank you for bringing me here."

"We'll have more like today, I promise."

"Sometimes, when I was feeling sorry for myself, I would think that if I only had a book to read, a story to fall into and escape my problems and worries, then I could bear all this."

"You shall have as many books as you desire now. I'll fill our house with them."

I laughed as I wiped under my eyes. "You said your cottage wasn't large. Where would you put all those books?"

"All right, then. How about if we start a library in Castaway?"

"Wesley, that's not something to tease about." I tapped his chest with my fingertips.

"Who says I'm teasing?" He kissed me again. "I would never joke about books. We could take my father's books and donate them all to the library. Some good would come of his obsession."

"Would *anyone* be able to borrow them?"

"Yes. You said yourself that a story was what you longed for. Wouldn't it be nice if everyone has access to books if they want them?"

"It would be. Truly."

"Then it shall be done." He moved to lie on his back with his head in my lap.

I put my fingers into his thick, silky hair. "I know every part of your face."

He closed his eyes. "I can see you even like this."

I brushed my fingers along his cheekbones. "Soon, my fingers will know you as my eyes do."

His mouth curved upward in a lazy smile as he opened his eyes to look into mine. "One short day away and you'll be my wife."

"I can hardly believe it to be true."

"It was Atlas who led me to your house," Wesley said. "As if he knew I was meant to meet you."

"Or wanted you to," I said.

"That may be true."

Gus lifted his head briefly before placing his chin back onto his paws.

"I think Gus believes the latter," I said. "Or should we call you Atlas?"

Gus wagged his tail.

"Do you believe in that which we can't see with our eyes?" Wesley asked. "Do you believe in miracles?"

"Yes, with all my heart. I can remember the moments before

you appeared. I'd prayed as hard as I ever have for help. I knew we were in deep trouble. And then, there you were." I played with a lock of his hair that had fallen over his forehead. "My Christmas miracle."

"My purpose for everything. That's you, my love."

We were quiet for a moment. He closed his eyes as I played with his hair. Gus snored softly. Overhead, a flock of birds flew in a mass so thick they seemed to be one creature. A breeze rustled the leaves of the maple.

"I've had this dream since I was young," Wesley said. "I'm very small, sitting on a woman's lap. She's singing to me and calls me Jonathan. It's like from another lifetime. Do you ever have dreams like that?"

I thought for a moment. "No, not like that one. I dream often of a man at the door. A bad man. Sadie's behind me, and I'm trying to lock the door before he can get inside."

"Do you lock it in time?"

"I always wake up just before I know."

"I won't let him in, Luci. Never again."

Before now, I'd not thought the hard, lean times served a purpose. Sitting here now with Wesley, I realized they had led to a deeper understanding of gratitude. Without the sour, I could not savor the sweet. Pain and struggle had made the good as vivid as the blue sky above me.

"You're a good man, Wesley Ford," I whispered.

"For you. All for you."

24

esley

WE WERE MARRIED AT THE COURTHOUSE IN ROCHESTER MONDAY afternoon. Our witnesses were Roland and Lillian, as we were for them. All was done by three that afternoon. The four of us went back to the house together and were surprised with a party of sorts, organized by Mollie and Sadie.

They'd decorated the table on the back porch with flowers and the good silver and china. Etta and June had baked a beautiful white cake, and we brought up bottles of champagne from Father's cellar.

June, who had surprised us by bursting into tears when we told her that Lillian would be moving to Castaway with Roland, had been quickly persuaded to come with us. I'd dangled the idea of eligible bachelors and few women in Castaway. She'd dismissed that with a grumpy huff, saying she had no need for a man, thank you very much, but that she would very much like to come and work for both our families.

We all sat around the table enjoying Etta's roasted chicken, baby red potatoes, and carrots. Dax's garden continued to provide a glorious bounty. June had poured us all champagne, and even Mollie was having a glass.

"What would it take to convince you to come with us?" I asked Mollie.

"We have work here. What would we do? Live on a wing and a prayer?" Mollie asked.

"You'd work for me," I said.

"Managing a cottage?" Mollie sniffed. "That's hardly enough work to keep me busy. Do you even have a wine cellar?"

I laughed. "No, but we could make one with your help."

"Wouldn't you like to have your own cottage?" Lillian asked.

"We have our own cottage," Mollie said.

"But not really," Lillian said. "Everything here belongs to Mother. In Castaway, it would be yours and yours only. And don't you want to be with us? We're your family."

Mollie and Dax looked at each other from across the table. "I suppose it's something to consider," Mollie said.

Dax grinned but didn't say anything further. We knew what "something to consider" meant. We'd finally convinced her.

I glanced at Luci. She'd barely touched her dinner, which was not like her.

"Are you all right?" I asked, leaning close to her ear.

"Everything tastes like sand," she whispered back.

Sand? For a moment, I was stumped. Then it occurred to me. She was nervous for our wedding night. Did she even know what would happen? Was she not ready? I would not push her. If she needed more time, I would give it to her, even though it would be difficult to do so. I'd thought of nothing else all day but to have her in my arms, touching her bare skin.

Was my sister nervous? No, I wouldn't think of my sister with Roland. These things needed to be separate in my mind.

I squeezed Luci's hand under the table. "It doesn't have to be tonight," I whispered in her ear.

She met my gaze with her innocent eyes and gave me a slight nod. I wasn't sure what the nod meant, but for now I would be content to have her by my side.

June came scurrying out to the porch. "There's a telegram." She handed it to me.

Will arrive tomorrow. Love, Mother.

"It's from Mother," I said. "She'll be here tomorrow."

"Thank goodness we married today. Not a moment too soon," Lillian said.

"Oh dear, and me in the drink the night before her return," Mollie said.

I waited for Luci to come out of the bathroom. While we were at the courthouse, June had moved what Luci needed for the next few days to my room. Other than that, everything was packed into a trunk, ready for our journey home. Our plan was to leave the day after tomorrow. Lillian had decided to take one of the motorcars that had belonged to Father for the trip. She said that if Mother minded, she could come get the blasted thing herself.

To keep myself distracted from my ungentlemanly wedding night thoughts, I finished packing the rest of my clothes back into the suitcase I'd brought from home.

Finally, Luci came out of the bathroom. I had to hold back from exclaiming over her beauty. I'd never seen her this way. Her hair was loose and reached the middle of her back. She wore a white cotton nightgown that hinted at what lay beneath.

She stood near the bed with her arms by her side. "What do I do now?"

I crossed over to her and put my hands in her hair. "Not a thing. Leave it all to me."

"Do you know what to do?"

I smiled before leaning closer to kiss her neck. She shivered. I wasn't sure but I thought that was a positive outcome. "I have a good enough idea."

"I know it will hurt the first time."

"I'll be as gentle as I can." Roland and I had discussed this at length back in our school days. Neither of us had firsthand experience, but one of the boys on our floor was from the country and had participated in the act with a neighboring farmer's daughter up in the hayloft. He'd assured us that after the first time, the girl could enjoy herself too. But maybe that wasn't true for every girl?

I kissed her gently on the mouth. "We're in this together. That's all that matters." With more urgency, I kissed her again before moving to her ear and down her neck to her collarbone.

"Wesley." She whispered my name as she wrapped her arms around my neck and pressed her hips against mine.

Dizzy with desire, I broke free and moved to the bed and lifted the covers. "Climb in. I'll get the light."

She did so as I crossed over to the windows to pull the curtains closed. I took the lantern with me to my side of the bed. Luci was under the quilt with just her head sticking out, watching me with eyes that were apprehensive but also excited.

"Are you ready for me to join you?" I asked.

"Yes."

I blew out the lantern and cautiously got into bed. The room was pitch-black for a moment. I turned on my side, waiting for my eyes to adjust. "Are you there? I can't see a thing."

She giggled. "Yes."

"Is it better in the dark?"

"I think so."

I scooted closer. Her silky hair was splayed out on the pillow. I felt rather than saw her move onto her side to face me. "Here we go," she said.

"For better or worse."

W E'D BOTH FALLEN ASLEEP AFTERWARD, DAMP BODIES ENTANGLED. All in all, it had been better than expected. As always, my Luci was stoic. An hour or two later, we'd both awakened and tried again. The second time was glorious. Just as my friend from school had promised. Women liked to be touched a certain way in various places, and if done correctly it created a life-changing response. I'd never felt like more of a king than in Luci's arms.

We lay together with her head on my chest. I kissed the top of her head.

"Do you want children?" Luci asked.

"I'd like to fill up the cottage with our children, yes, but if God chooses not to bless us in that way, I'll be fine having you all to myself."

"Sadie's so smart that she's like at least three children."

I smiled. "She is indeed.

"When I was a little boy, my mother had this collection of snow globes. She'd bring them out every Christmas, and I'd spend hours looking into the imaginary worlds. One of them had a cottage with a dog that looked just like Atlas, and I loved to pretend I was inside, living that life. I vowed to myself that someday I would have a cottage like that one and a yellow Labrador and a wife who loved me just inside the glowing windows."

"What was your wife doing in there?"

"Depended on the daydream. Sometimes she was making dinner. Other times she was curled in a reading nook as the snow fell outside her window."

"I'd like either of those. What were you doing outside?"

"Manly things, of course. Chopping wood or dragging home a Christmas tree."

She sighed. "That sounds lovely. Maybe your wife was making ornaments while you were bringing home the tree. Or stringing popcorn."

"We shall do all those things."

She propped herself on my chest with an elbow to peer down at me. "That thing that happened to me just now. How did you know what to do?"

"You mean . . . ?" I didn't know what the word was for the way she'd tensed and arched her back and let out a primal moan, but I figured it was akin to what had happened to me right afterward.

I chuckled. "There was this boy at school who had experience. He tutored us, so to speak."

"God bless him, wherever he is." She planted a kiss on my mouth before plopping back onto my chest.

I played with her hair, content and warm and feeling quite pleased with myself.

"Lillian has a married friend who told her she quite liked it, so we had hope."

"I'm glad we now know for sure."

"I'm so happy, Wesley." Her voice sounded sleepier than a moment before. "More so than I ever thought I'd be."

"As am I. Now, go to sleep, my love. We have a big day tomorrow."

25

L^{uci}

I WOKE THE DAY AFTER OUR WEDDING NIGHT SORE BUT BLISSFUL. Why had I worried so about the physical act of marriage? Other than the initial pain, the entire experience had been better even than eating Etta's cooking. That I would never have believed until I'd experienced it myself.

I rolled over, expecting Wesley to be there, but he must have risen earlier. What time was it? He'd closed the curtains, perhaps wanting me to have the extra sleep. Last night, I'd taken in every inch of his masculine body. His muscles were hard and taut from his labor, and I loved every bit of him.

Lillian and I had been so naive about the entire process. No one had mentioned that pinnacle where everything seemed to stop except for the incredible urge to keep going until the explosion. I stretched and let out a moan as I remembered the third encounter of our wedding night. Had anyone heard the noises that had come out of me? I desperately hoped not.

I sat up and pulled my wayward nightgown over my head, then trotted off to use the bathroom. Once there, I decided to run a bath to soothe the soreness between my legs. Was that normal? I hoped so. Why was all this such a secret? Or were women with mothers privy to all the information before their wedding night? I would tell Sadie when it came her time what to expect. I'd also tell her not to be afraid. Nothing but goodness waited.

I scrubbed in the tub, almost sorry to wash Wesley's scent from my skin. *Tonight, you will have him again,* I told myself. Every night until the day death parted us.

Thank you, God, for sending him to me, I prayed silently. *I'll do my best to be a good person and pay back all you've blessed me with.*

I dressed in the robe that June had hung by the door for me. I stood before the mirror to brush out my wet hair. What a luxury it was to sleep in a soft bed and then wake to a bath. This life I'd fallen into was so luxurious. However, none of it would have been the same without Wesley. No comfort in the world was as good as being in love.

I'll come tomorrow, he'd said that first day. Despite all the obstacles in his way, he'd made good on his promise. *Tomorrow had come.*

Still in my robe, I went back into the sunlit bedroom. Wesley had set a stack of books on the desk for me to choose from. While my hair dried, I looked through them and decided on a mystery set in England. I sat in the chair near the window. With the sun warm on my head, I was completely lost in the first chapter when Wesley came through the door carrying a tray.

He halted for a second, staring at me, then shoved the door closed with his foot.

"Good morning," I said.

"Morning. I've brought breakfast for my bride." He set the tray on the bureau.

"Thank you. I took a bath and was waiting for my hair to dry before putting it up, and then I started this book. I've completely lost track of time."

"It is the day after our wedding. I think sleeping in is allowed. Would you care for coffee?"

I nodded. Coffee was now a part of my morning routine. How quickly I'd become spoiled.

He set two cups and saucers on the square table between the two armchairs, then poured coffee from a silver pot into them.

"Are you hungry? There are berries, some eggs, and toast."

"Coffee first," I said. "Come sit with me."

He brought a bowl of berries and a plate of toast with him. When he finally sat, he gazed over at me, his right cheek resting in the palm of his hand. "I don't think I've ever seen anything as beautiful as you are right now. Your hair in the sunshine, all down about your shoulders. You're like the painting of Aphrodite."

I flushed, both embarrassed and pleased, even though I had no idea to which painting he referred. "Thank you."

"My wife. I still can't quite believe my good fortune."

"Or I mine. Now tell me what was going on downstairs. Was Sadie awake?"

"Yes, she and Gus were already with Dax in the garden. Mollie fed them both breakfast and then sent them outside."

"And the other newlyweds?"

"No sign of either of them. I don't want to think why."

I smiled, thinking of Lillian. As good as it was to bask in the glow of Wesley's loving smile, I looked forward to chatting with my new friend about the delights of the wedding bed.

"Do you have any idea when your mother will arrive?"

"I assume sometime this afternoon. We'll spend the evening with her and then plan to head out tomorrow morning."

"Will she be mad we're not staying?"

"I'm not sure how she's going to react to any of it. Whatever it is, it won't bother me."

We talked briefly through our plans for the morning. "If we leave early, we can arrive in time for supper. Roland and I have our work cut out for us to get a cottage built before Dax and Mollie come in September."

"September? They've decided?"

"Yes, Mollie told me this morning that she and Dax talked it all through and decided it was time to make a change. They've saved through the years and have a tidy sum to live on."

A fat robin redbreast landed on the window's outside ledge.

"There's something I wanted to tell you about your father. June said the word around town is that he thinks you two ran away and abandoned him. He's told the sad story to anyone who'll listen. Not that anyone feels a bit sorry for him. Anyway, that he thinks you're already gone works to our advantage. I'm hopeful no one saw us."

My stomach churned. I set my cup back onto the saucer. There was a part of me that wanted to walk away and never think of him again, which of course was impossible. As much as he'd hurt me, he was still my father. A loyalty to him remained. There were memories, too, not so easily forgotten. Ones that would haunt me for years to come.

"Where would we have gone? What a fool."

"Yes, but his delusion is for the best." Wesley set aside his piece of toast to pick up a berry. "I have a theory. I suspect he doesn't remember the poker game or what he did. Do you think that's possible?"

"Yes, very possible. If he knows our new situation, he will want to exploit it somehow." I looked out at the robin, squatting happily on the ledge. Did she have baby birds somewhere waiting for their breakfast? "We must walk away and hope he never finds out what happened to us."

"All right, as long as you're sure."

I looked into the eyes of my husband. There in his eyes was the future. One in which Sadie and I would be safe and far away from Pa. "I'm sure."

THAT AFTERNOON, LILLIAN AND I HAD LEMONADE ON THE PORCH while Wesley and Roland went into town to get a few items for our trip home. My new home. Although I'd never seen it, I knew it would be the place I would always want to stay. Everyone I loved would be there, and that made it a home, no matter the location.

I hadn't yet had a moment alone with my new sister-in-law. But now Sadie and Gus were down by the pond, too far to overhear.

Lillian lounged on one of the chaises with her skirt spread out over her legs. She didn't look different than she had the day before. I felt different, but perhaps it was not obvious.

"Are you going to ask or shall I?" Lillian's eyes twinkled at me from under her hat.

I giggled from my own chaise and turned on my side to get a better look at her. "Well?"

"My married friend did not lie."

"Oh, thank goodness. I was afraid it was only me," I said.

"Now what will we wonder about?"

I laughed again. "I suppose there's nothing left. We know it all now."

"Darling Luci, can you believe all that's happened since you came here?"

"I cannot."

Her expression sobered as she rolled onto her back. "I can't help but think about Mother. Will she be sorry when she comes home to us married without even telling her?"

"I don't know."

"I wish I didn't care," Lillian said.

"She's your mother. Of course you do."

"Were you ever angry at yours for leaving you with a baby? And then to find out what she did to make money?"

"That was when I was the angriest," I said. "Now, however, I can understand how desperate she must have been to keep us alive. I don't suppose it's my place to judge her. We all do what we have to in order to survive."

"I suppose we do."

I shuddered. "Can you imagine doing what we did last night with our husbands with strangers?"

Lillian hugged herself. "There but for the grace of God go I."

Yes, I thought. But for the grace of God.

"Do you ever wonder who Sadie's father is?" Lillian asked. "He might be living right here in this town and doesn't even know she exists."

"I never think about him." This wasn't entirely true. Sometimes I was thankful for him. Without him, there would be no Sadie. Other times I hated him with a hot, hard rage.

"None of it matters now, anyway," Lillian said. "You have Wesley. A new life."

Was that true? Or did the demons from our past continue to haunt us all our lives?

26

Wesley

I'd just come downstairs to the sitting room after changing for dinner when I heard a motorcar in the driveway. Assuming it was Mother, I walked out to the porch. Indeed, it was. Her Cadillac was packed full of suitcases. A driver and her maid had come along as well. Mother didn't travel lightly.

I went down the porch stairs to greet them as the driver killed the engine. Seconds later, Mother emerged from the car. She wore a light-yellow dress instead of black. There was no one to pretend to, I supposed. We all knew their marriage was on paper only. She was not the grieving widow.

"Darling, it's good to see you." She placed her hands on the sides of my face, peering up at me from under her enormous hat. "You're looking well."

"Thank you, Mother. You too." Indeed, she was as pretty

and slender as ever but without the wary eyes she'd had when I was small. "How was the trip?" Actually, she seemed happy.

"Exhausting. I'm sorry I wasn't here sooner. The drive from Florida seemed to go on forever."

"It's all right. We took care of the burial. Or, rather, Mollie did."

"What would we do without her?"

I said hello to Ruth, who was as prim and straight-backed as ever. "Mister Ford, it's nice to see you," she said. "All grown up, I see."

"It's nice to see you too," I said.

The driver was young, with dark hair under a chauffeur's hat. Mother introduced him as Walter just as Mollie scurried down the stairs toward us. "Mrs. Ford, I'm sorry. I didn't hear you arrive."

Mother smiled and held out her hands. "Dear Mollie. Thank you for taking care of everything."

"We're glad to see you here safe and sound," Mollie said. "Ruth, we have your room ready for you downstairs. I'll have June come out to help you with the luggage."

I took Mother's arm and left Mollie to supervise the unpacking. "Come inside, Mother. We have a lot to catch up on."

As we crossed over the porch toward the front door, Mother said quietly, "Walter's the son of a friend's housekeeper. Very good behind the wheel, despite that he's just over sixteen. I only thought we were going to perish two or three times."

I chuckled and held the door open for her. "Come inside. How does a drink before dinner sound?"

"Heavenly." We walked down the hallway toward the sitting room. "Has it always smelled this way?"

"What way?" I asked.

"Like dried flowers and despair?"

"Don't let Mollie hear you say that. She wouldn't sleep for a week."

Mother smiled as she unpinned her hat. "True. Where's your sister?"

"She's upstairs getting ready for dinner." My stomach churned with nerves. How would Mother react to the news of our marriages? "What would you like to drink? Chablis?" Mollie had chilled a bottle earlier, anticipating Mother's arrival.

"Vodka. Neat."

Vodka? When had she started drinking vodka? Mother wandered over to the piano and picked up a framed photograph of Father. "He was handsome, wasn't he?"

"I suppose." I poured vodka from one of the crystal decanters into a glass.

"You can't imagine how in love with him I was."

I couldn't imagine, but I kept that to myself.

"Would you like to sit?" I asked.

She nodded absently, as if she was deep in thought, but then she sat in one of the armchairs. I handed her the drink, then went back to pour myself a whiskey.

When I returned to her, she was running her finger over the rim of her glass.

"Mother, are you all right? Is it hard being here?"

She patted my arm and gave me a faint smile. "There's something about Florida that makes the memories fade. Maybe it's all that sunshine, like bleach to the mind." She downed half her drink before putting the glass on the table. "But the one thing I haven't been able to forget was how he treated you. I'm sorry for that."

"You were as trapped as I was."

"It's a poor excuse, but true. Anyway, I won't dance on his grave, but I'm not mourning him. I can't say I'm sorry he's gone. His death solves a lot of my problems."

I wanted to ask for details but remained silent. If she wanted to share with me, she would.

"In the end, my father was right. A philanderer is always a philanderer."

Did she mean adultery?

As if I'd asked the question, she nodded. "Your father was never faithful. Not even in the beginning when I thought we were actually in love. Later, I realized I was simply a conquest. One that he was particularly keen on because my father was so against us."

Shocked, I glanced over at his photograph, as if he were there to answer.

"There was a maid here or there. One time it was the wife of his friend, staying here as our guests. I'm not sure who else. I didn't know about all of them, I'm sure." She rubbed her temples, then picked up her glass to finish her drink.

"Is that why you fought?" I could hear the raised voices then, as if it were yesterday.

"Yes, as if my anger could change him. That's what one learns over time. No amount of love changes a person. But when I was young, he was like a sickness to me. I couldn't let go of the idea that if I loved him enough, he would be faithful. Finally, though, I'd had enough. After we sent you and Lillian away for school, I left. Broke free from the cycle and traveled to all the places I'd dreamt of going with him. To Europe. Down to Florida."

"Mother, I'm sorry."

"It's all right now. I'm still young. I can marry again if I want. At least he had the decency to leave me the money. I half expected it would go to the latest mistress."

"Was there one?"

"I've no idea. I don't care. Not anymore."

"Will you return to Florida?" I asked. "What about the house?"

"I'm planning on selling it. I feel badly about the staff, but every inch of this place reminds me of your father. Since she's done with school, I'll invite Lillian to join me. If she doesn't want to, maybe she can go with you to Maine."

"Yes, about that. Lillian's fallen in love with Roland."

"Your friend? The poor one?"

"They've married, Mother."

She raised both eyebrows. "I see. How will they live? Does he know what Lillian is accustomed to?"

"He and I are going into business together. They'll be fine."

She pulled a handkerchief from her wrist and dabbed at the corners of her eyes. "I don't suppose I deserved to be invited to the wedding."

"It was at the courthouse. Functional only."

"I would have thought Lillian would want a dress."

"She only cared about the man, not the ceremony."

Lillian appeared in the doorway. "Hello, Mother." She crossed the room as Mother rose up to greet her.

"Darling, are you sure you know what you're doing?"

Lillian kissed Mother's cheek. "I do. I promise. He's the best man in the world, besides Wesley," Lillian said. "I'm very happy."

They both sat on the couch. Mother kept hold of Lillian's hand. "I should have liked to throw you a lavish wedding."

"We didn't think you'd approve."

"And that I'd interfere?" Mother asked.

Lillian nodded. "I'm sorry."

"It doesn't matter, I suppose. As long as you won't have regrets, as I did, from marrying for love."

"Roland isn't like Father," I said. "He's as steady as they come."

"We thought you'd be angry," Lillian said. "Because he's poor."

"I would be a hypocrite if that were true. I'm in love with a poor man too. I've been living with him for the last three years in Florida."

She'd been living with another man? For three years?

"He's poor as a pauper. A painter—brilliant but without a dime to his name. I've been supporting him on my allowance your father gave me. We have a small house near the beach. There's a studio on the second floor where he paints beautiful landscapes of the sea. At night we eat alfresco under the stars. For the first time in my life, I've been happy."

Lillian and I both stared at her.

"I plan to marry him," Mother said. "The moment I return. I've already told your brother, but I'm selling this estate."

"I can't believe it," Lillian said, finally. "I'm happy for you, I suppose, but this will take a moment to grow accustomed to."

"Touché, dear," Mother said. "Where is Roland? I'd like to congratulate him. Perhaps you'll allow me to throw you a party."

"Mother, there's something else," I said. "I'm married too. I wed Luci Quick yesterday."

Mother's face turned ashen. "Luci Quick? No, Wesley. It can't be. Not her."

Just then, Sadie and Gus came running into the room slightly out of breath. "Wesley, we found a bird's nest on the ground, and you have to rescue the eggs." Sadie came to an abrupt halt when she saw Mother. Gus, too, stopped in his tracks.

From the hallway came the sound of Roland's deep voice and Luci's laugh. I looked over at my sister, who returned my gaze with a panicked widening of her eyes.

"Who is this?" Mother asked, her voice high-pitched as she rose to her feet.

"This is Sadie, Luci's sister," Lillian said. "And Gus, our new dog."

Sadie placed her hand on Gus's head. He pressed close to her side.

"Wesley?" Sadie whispered.

I went to Sadie and placed my hand on her shoulder. "This is my mother, Sadie. She's just come from a long car ride."

"How could you do this?" Mother's eyes were wild with rage and hurt. "Why, Wesley? To punish me?"

Out of the corner of my eye, I saw Luci and Roland in the entryway. My instinct was to run to Luci, but I didn't want to leave Sadie.

Mother's gaze fixated on Sadie. "My God, she looks just like him."

"Like who?" Lillian asked as Roland came to stand at her side. "Mother, what's gotten into you? Sadie's just a little girl. She's Luci's baby sister. Now she'll belong to our family, just as Luci will."

"Don't you see it?" Mother asked. "Can't you see she has his eyes?"

And then it all came tumbling down upon me. The truth. The reason for Mother's intense response to my desire to help a little girl and her baby sister. It should have been obvious. I looked over at my bride. She had her hands covering her mouth as if to hold in a scream and was shaking her head in tiny back-and-forth motions. The truth had occurred to her as well.

Sadie was my father's child.

"ROLAND, WILL YOU TAKE SADIE DOWNSTAIRS TO MOLLIE?" I asked. "The adults have something to discuss."

He nodded, looking perplexed but knowing now was not the time to ask questions. I spoke softly to Sadie. "Take Gus downstairs with Uncle Roland, all right?"

Fat tears slipped from her eyes. "I don't want to leave Sister with the mad lady."

Luci rushed to her and fell to her knees. She wiped Sadie's tears with her handkerchief. "Don't worry, I'll be down shortly. Go with Roland, please?"

"Yes, Sister." She took Roland's outstretched hand, and they walked toward the doorway with Gus right behind.

Mother had sunk back into her chair by then. Her hands shook as she reached for her drink. Finding it empty, she slammed it back onto the table. Lillian, who had clearly not come to the same conclusion as Luci and I, jumped at the noise.

"Lillian and Luci, please sit," I said.

Like they were in a trance, both of them obeyed, sitting close together on the couch.

"What is it, Mother? What's wrong with you?" Lillian's voice shook. "How could you be so cruel to an innocent child?"

Mother raised her head to look at Luci. "Did you know?"

Luci's gaze slid to me first and then back to Mother. "No. I was twelve years old. I had no idea about my mother's . . . occupation. I knew Sadie wasn't Pa's."

"Know what?" Lillian asked.

"For God's sake, Lillian, are you really so dense?" Mother asked.

"Apparently I am," Lillian said under her breath.

"Your father is that bastard child's father." Each word from my mother's mouth sounded like the firing of a bullet.

Lillian reeled backward as if someone had hit her. "No, it's impossible."

"How do you know?" Luci asked. "She was with other men. I think, anyway."

"She wasn't," Mother said. "For a whole year he was her only client."

"Mother, how would you know that?" Lillian asked.

"He told me." Mother sighed. Her shoulders slumped. All

the anger suddenly seemed to drain from her. "Wesley, can you refill my glass?"

I plucked it from the table and went to the liquor cabinet. No one spoke as the vodka splashed into the glass. When I handed it to Mother, she took the glass without looking up at me. "He told me in a moment of anger as a way to punish me. As if it wasn't already bad enough, he actually enjoyed telling me that he'd gotten his whore pregnant. For a year he'd paid for her exclusive company. He didn't like to share, he said. I asked him if he planned on running off with her or bringing her into this house, and he laughed in my face. His exact words were, 'Why would I do that? She's nothing to me. Merely someone to play with since you're a cold shrew.' Once he learned that she was to have his child, he no longer requested her company."

"Sadie's our sister?" Lillian asked, mumbling to herself.

"Something to *play* with?" Luci's eyes snapped as her voice rose.

"How have you wormed your way into this family?" Mother turned toward me. "Have you really married this . . . this girl?" The word *girl* sounded like an expletive.

"She was a person," Luci said. "A woman who had to make choices to keep her daughter alive."

"What do you expect? That I'd pity her?" Mother's shoulders straightened as she stared right back at Luci. "A better person might have been able to, but all I could see was that she took the final piece of dignity I had left. She was having a baby with the man I loved. After all the prayers and hopes for a baby and nothing, and then he makes one with her. Do you know, even that didn't soften him. Even after he knew how badly I'd wanted a baby of my own."

What did she mean? She had Lillian and me.

"I always wondered who he was." Luci twisted her handkerchief into the shape of a snake. "I wondered if he knew about the baby, and if he did, had he made a deliberate decision not to provide for her?"

"He said he'd had enough of providing for bastards." Mother folded her hands in her lap and seemed to study them as one would a map.

"Mother, what are you saying?" Lillian asked, her tone sharp.

Mother raised her gaze to my sister and then to me. "You're both adopted. We got you from the nuns who ran an orphanage. Wesley, you were already two by the time you came home to us. Lillian, you'd only just been born."

Lillian stared at Mother as she reached for Luci's hand. "No, that's not true. How could that be true?"

Mother's face twisted in pain. "It's true. I never wanted you to know."

"But why?" Lillian asked.

"You were mine," Mother said. "What good would it have done you to know that a woman had given you up?"

"What happened to our mothers?" My mouth had gone so dry I could barely speak. The dream of the woman holding me, the warmth of that embrace. Had it been real? Was she my mother?

Mother rested her forehead in her fingertips. "You have the same mother. They took you from her because she was living on the streets. The nuns let her live with them while she was carrying the child. When Lillian was born, they gave you both to us."

My legs had weakened to the point I might collapse. I sank into a chair.

"Did she want to give us away?" Lillian asked.

Mother flinched, and one eyebrow twitched upward. "I've no idea. The details were never disclosed to us. I didn't want to know, anyway. The Catholic Church has strict rules about these things. Two children born out of wedlock to a teenage girl? You were better off with us."

The memory of the sound of the whip across my back echoed through my head. "I disagree." I wanted to hurt her. "Is this why Father hated me?"

"Your father never really took to either of you. I'd hoped for years to have a child of my own, but apparently your father was right. My womb was too cold to host a baby. I thought children would bring us together, make your father a family man. That idea didn't work. Obviously."

"So many things make sense now," Lillian said.

She didn't say out loud what I knew we were both thinking. This was why he hadn't loved us. Especially me. Was it because I'd already bonded with my own mother? Had he sensed that and rejected me because of it? Or were they monsters who should never have been entrusted with children? Was our real mother still alive? Had we been ripped from her by the nuns?

Luci was sitting very still. Too still. I could feel the silent fury in her. Before last night, I'd only known her soul. Now I knew her body. She lifted her eyes and leveled them on Mother. "Dax did what your monster of a husband should have done. Because of Wesley and Dax, Sadie lived. Do you understand that without him, both of us would have died?"

"I was heartbroken," Mother said. "I'd already suffered enough humiliation from the man I loved with all my heart. And then, while the wound was still fresh, Wesley comes traipsing in from one of his nature walks and tells me he's found a girl and a baby in the woods and can we take care of them. Can you imagine the rage and grief I felt? Can't any of you understand any of this from my perspective?"

"I can, actually," Luci said. "I know what it feels like to be betrayed by a person who should love you."

Mother laid her hand flat against the front of her dress. "Yet still, even with my complicated feelings, I gave permission to Dax and Mollie to take care of you."

"You did?" Luci asked.

"You knew about Dax helping them?" I asked Mother.

"Yes. When he returned from the train station that day, he came to me. He said he would do it with or without my permission because he'd promised you, Wesley, but that he'd like my blessing. I told him if he wanted to help, I wouldn't stand in his way. I advised him to keep it from my husband and to be careful. Then I left. I never thought I'd have to confront it all over again."

"Did Dax and Mollie know the truth?" Luci asked. "About Sadie's father?"

"I never told them," Mother said. "But that doesn't mean they didn't know."

Lillian hadn't taken her attention from Mother. "Did you meet her? Our mother?"

Mother shook her head. "They gave you to us. That was all."

"Where's the nunnery?" Lillian asked.

"If it's still there, outside of Boston," Mother said.

"Would they have records?" I asked.

"I doubt it. They were secretive."

"Isn't that what this whole family's been built on?" Lillian asked. "Secrets and lies?"

Mother looked at my sister for a long moment, then walked over to the secretary desk. She scribbled something on a piece of stationery and handed it to me. "This is the name and directions to the nunnery. If it's still there, you can ask them what they know. I truly doubt she's still alive."

"We have to try," Lillian said. "If they know anything, we have to get them to tell us."

"I can understand why you need to chase after all this." Mother dabbed at her eyes. "But remember, I'm still your mother. I haven't been the best, but I tried. I hope you can forgive me for my failings."

"We do, Mother," I said. "We've all come through to the other side."

"Be happy, Mother," Lillian said. "There's nothing to be done about the past, only the future."

27

L uci

After I'd put Sadie to bed that night, I went downstairs but found no one. A quick glance outside told me that Wesley and Roland were packing the cars. Lillian, too, had gone to her room to pack the rest of her wardrobe. The dressmaker had agreed to send my final items to the house in Castaway. For now, I had a few dresses that would suffice until the rest arrived.

During dinner, Wesley and Lillian had filled Roland in on what he'd missed. Wesley's mother had asked for her dinner upstairs and gone to her room. Who could blame her? The more I thought about her position, the more I realized she'd been as much a victim as Sadie and I were. Just the idea of Wesley doing what his father had done made me sick to my stomach. I could easily understand her anger. That she'd relented to Dax's request to help us had softened me to her as well.

Still, there was the big secret. Had she worried over the years that if Wesley and Lillian discovered the truth, she would lose them too? How ironic that Sadie was Matthew Ford's only real child. The only one he hadn't provided for.

I went out to the screened back porch. The sun had set, but twilight lingered. I ventured out to the lawn and walked to the pond and sat on the bench. The ducks were tucked under shrubbery, apparently retired for the evening, taking a break from their endless search for food. The pair of swans floated out from behind a bush to glide across the water.

Thoughts of Pa came then. Leaving tomorrow meant that I would never see him again. As bad as he'd been, he'd made it so I could keep Sadie. For that, at least, I would be eternally grateful. Dax had said to leave it be, but it was hard to do so knowing that he would surely perish without me.

Still, I would leave and not look back.

I heard footsteps behind me and turned to see Mrs. Ford headed my way. Turning back to the pond, I waited. Seconds later, she appeared at the side of the bench. She had one hand wrapped around an object. "Luci, I saw you out here from my room. May I sit?"

"Yes, please." As much as I wanted to run away, I stayed put. This was Wesley's mother. I would respect her.

"I have something for Wesley and wondered if you could give it to him for me." She handed me a snow globe. "This was his favorite when he was a little boy."

I held it up. Even in the dim light I could see the cottage and yellow dog. "He told me about this one."

"He used to stare into it for long chunks of time. I always wondered why. I suspect he was dreaming of his future. It sounds like he's found what he wanted in you and his cottage. I'm grateful he's happy."

"I'm sorry about . . . what my mother did."

The swans made ripples on the water as they swam closer.

"None of it was your fault. What you've done is remarkable. I'm sorry they left you with a mess."

"I got Sadie out of it."

"Is she a blessing to you instead of a burden?"

"Yes, Mrs. Ford. I never once thought of her in any other way than a Christmas miracle. Wesley too. And Dax."

"I've found in my life that there are two kinds of people. Some are like my father, who couldn't think of anyone other than himself and how he wanted things. Anyone who went against him was either punished or disposed of. My husband was this way too. And then there are those like you and Wesley. You've both faced many difficulties through no fault of your own, and yet you see the blessings."

"I despaired many times," I said. "But I knew I was all Sadie had, so I kept going. Life's easier when you know what you're fighting for."

"Yes, well, I should go. I'll say goodbye in the morning." She rose to her feet. "What a long, strange day it's been."

"Will you ever be able to visit us?"

"You mean because of Sadie?" she asked.

"Yes."

"I'm not sure. That's the best answer I have for now."

"Fair enough."

"Good night, Luci."

"Good night." Her skirts swished as she walked away, startling the swans. They turned and swam the other direction.

A LITTLE AFTER NINE THE NEXT MORNING, WE SAID OUR GOODBYES and headed down the driveway.

"Do you really think it's a good idea to stop and ask questions?" Wesley asked me from the driver's seat. "Maybe it's better for Lillian and me to forget all about finding her. As Mother said, there probably aren't any records."

"If the nunnery's still there, it's on the way. Why not stop and ask questions? They might have records. Or maybe one of the nuns will remember her. It's only been eighteen years."

Wesley grimaced. "Eighteen years is a long time."

"What's on the way?" Sadie asked from the back seat, where she and Gus were snuggled together. He had his head on her lap, asleep. He'd been anxious as we packed the last of our things into the back of the car until Wesley told him to get in next to Sadie. In hindsight, I realized he'd been afraid we were leaving him.

I hesitated before answering Sadie. Since the shocking revelation of her true heritage, I'd been bouncing from one thought to another. Should I tell her? If so, when? She was too young to understand now. Someday, though, I'd want her to know the truth. What an odd family we were. Wesley had been right all along. We were inextricably connected. He and I. Lillian and Wesley and Sadie. We were meant to be together, even if the ways in which we found one another were astounding and convoluted.

"Do you know what *adopted* means?" I asked her. "When a mother and father take a baby who isn't theirs and raise him or her as their own."

"Like what Wesley's doing with me?"

"Yes, exactly. How did you know that?"

"Wesley's taking me and you together. You're like my mother, so he'll be like my father." She said it with such assurance I was speechless.

Wesley coughed into his fist. Was it to hide a laugh or a sob?

"Yes, well, we've just learned that Wesley and Lillian had a mother that they were taken from so that Mr. and Mrs. Ford could adopt them."

Sadie nodded, her eyes as round as quarters.

"So we're going to the place where his real mother gave birth to Lillian to see if they know anything about where she might be now."

"I hope they do," Sadie said.

"Me as well," Wesley said.

We'd all agreed on the plan before we left. Roland had strongly agreed with me that Wesley and Lillian should at least try to find answers by visiting the nunnery. "You've been in the dark long enough," he'd said. "Whatever it is we find, we'll go through it together."

Now we grew silent, lulled by the engine and the bumps in the road. I fell asleep. When I woke, I had a cramp in my neck. We turned down a long driveway. A minute later, a two-story brick building appeared.

"It's still standing," Wesley said. "We'll see if anyone's there."

Wesley parked and killed the engine. Small windows were shuttered against the afternoon sun. But in the back, on the lawn, several young women were sitting on benches or walking along the flower beds. Several were noticeably pregnant, their protruding stomachs obvious despite smocks over their dresses.

"It's still here," I said. "And in use."

"Yes, yes, it is." Wesley gripped the steering wheel and bowed his head. "I'm afraid to go in and be disappointed."

"We won't know unless we try."

"I'll hold your hand," Sadie said. Gus barked. "Gus says he'll be there too."

"Well, that's a nice offer, but how about you two stay out here and play in the grass. Gus needs a break from the car." He turned to grin at her, then patted Gus's head.

By then, Lillian and Roland had arrived. We all got out of the car and gathered near the steps that led up to the front entrance. "No time like the present," Roland said.

"We can't expect much," Lillian said to Wesley as we walked up the stairs.

"Quite right," Wesley said. "Very unlikely we'll know anything before we go."

I turned back to make sure Sadie and Gus were all right. She'd already found a stick to toss. "Stay close here and don't talk to strangers," I called down to her.

Sadie waved and then returned to Gus.

Roland used the iron knocker on the front door, tapping it two times. Seconds later, a young nun appeared. She had a round, sweet face. "Welcome. I'm Sister Mary. May I help you?"

No one said anything for a moment. Roland took the lead. "We've come to inquire about one of the women who gave birth here. These are her children." He gestured toward Wesley and Lillian. "They've only just learned of their adoption and are interested to find out if their real mother is still alive. From what we know, they have the same mother."

Sister Mary's mouth puckered in surprise. "Dear me, yes." She peered at Lillian for a moment. "I see. Yes, you'd better come in. I'll have to ask Mother Superior if she can help you."

We were led down a long, dark hallway to a closed door. Sister Mary tapped softly. A low-pitched voice said to enter.

"Wait here," Sister Mary said. "I'll have to ask her first."

Ask her what?

We stood awkwardly in the hallway. Minutes passed. I could hear the murmur of the voices but couldn't make out what they were saying. Finally, the door opened and Sister Mary slipped back into the hallway. I caught a glimpse of a woman in a habit looking down at a paper on her desk.

"Mother says we're not allowed to share any details about our adoptions." She said this in a clear, almost loud voice. Then she gestured toward the front door and motioned that we should follow her.

Once outside, she led us over to a seating area on the long

porch. Chairs were arranged in a circle around a low table. "Please sit. I have a few questions," Sister Mary said.

I took a quick look at Sadie and Gus, still happily playing fetch on the lawn.

We all took seats. Lillian's hands were visibly shaking. She placed them together on her lap. Roland covered both of them with his large hand.

"Do you know anything about your mother?" Sister Mary asked.

"Only that we share her," Lillian said. "Wesley was two and I was newly born when our adoptive parents took us."

Sister Mary looked out to the lawn, her expression contemplative. "Was your childhood a good one?"

Lillian barked out a laugh. "We wouldn't describe it as such, no."

"Our parents were not quite suited for the job," Wesley said. "And fond of the strap."

The petite nun rocked back and forth, her lips pursed. "Oh dear me." Her gaze darted to the door and then to the other side of the porch, as if she was worried about being seen or overheard. In a quiet voice, she continued. "There's a woman here who works in the laundry. She's been here for decades, as far as I know. She recently confided in me that she came here in desperation when she was pregnant with her second child. She was only eighteen, having had her first child at sixteen. Her family had kicked her out when she had the first child. I'm not sure what happened in the years between your births. Perhaps she can tell you that story. All I know is she had nowhere to go but here. She'd not understood that they would take the children from her. For whatever reason, whether they were lied to or not, the girls believed they were only here for shelter." She paused and turned to my sister. "Lillian, you look so much like her that it's startling."

"What's her name?" Lillian asked.

"Rose Miller," Sister Mary said.

"Rose," I said. A pretty name.

"Why is she still here?" Lillian asked.

"She's long held the belief that if her children ever learned of her presence and wanted to meet her, they would come here first, which is why she's continued to work here all these years. Because of the privacy of the adoptions done here, she understood you would never be able to find a lead, other than that she'd given birth to Lillian here. Every evening after her shift, she comes out here to sit, watching the driveway. 'They might come tomorrow,' she says to me when I tell her to come in for the night. And now it seems you have."

Lillian and Wesley were both in tears. I had shivers and goose bumps. Like Atlas, she'd waited for Wesley to come home. Like me, who had waited for the boy with the kind eyes, who'd sent Dax in his absence. All this waiting and hoping for a tomorrow that never came. But now we were here. All the tomorrows we'd wished for had arrived.

"May we see her?" Wesley asked.

"Not here," Sister Mary said. "The eyes are many and see everything. I'm taking a great risk to tell you all this. In town, there's a park. Can you wait for her under the gazebo? She'll be able to walk there after her shift."

For the first time, Wesley spoke. "Tell her to bring whatever she wants to take with her. She'll not be coming back here."

28

esley

As instructed, we waited in the park. The town of Maud was having some kind of summer festival with live music and dancing. The gazebo, built for just such an occasion, was packed with people, all out for the festival.

We lingered around the edges of the crowd. If we hadn't been waiting for such a somber meeting, I would have taken Luci out to the dancing area to enjoy the music in the evening light.

Instead, we'd spread a blanket out on the grass and had eaten cold sandwiches we'd bought from a shop in town. I had my arm around Luci. Lillian had her legs curled under her dress and leaned against Roland's chest. Gus lay with his chin resting on my foot.

Sadie danced not far from our blanket, oblivious to the

strain of the adults. *As it should be,* I thought. She'd seen enough hardship.

The locals had strung festive lanterns around the dancing area, which I assumed would be lit after the sun went down. Now, it hung just above the horizon, casting a magical glow over the park so that everything was tinged with orange.

"How will she know us?" Lillian asked. "With all these people here?"

"Yes, what if she can't find us?" Luci asked.

"She'll find us," Roland said. "She's been waiting eighteen years. I imagine she'd crawl here on her hands and knees to see you."

From the crowd of people surrounding the beer and lemonade stand, a lone woman emerged. She wore a simple black skirt, a white blouse, and a modest hat. My heart thudded in my chest as I took in her high cheekbones, green eyes, and hair the color of a copper cup. Lillian looked just like her. Finally, we knew the source of that hair.

Carrying a small satchel, she drew nearer, looking this way and that, scanning the crowd.

"There she is," I said, my words strangled by the lump in my throat.

Roland and I scrambled to our feet and then helped the ladies to stand. I tried to steady my breath, but I felt as if I'd just run up a hill.

"Her hair," Lillian said.

"You look like her," Luci said. "Now I see how Sister Mary knew right away."

Sadie stopped dancing and came to stand next to Luci. Gus woke from his nap and stood, wagging his tail. A rowdy song from the musicians ended, and a mournful Irish ballad began.

About six feet from us, Rose stopped and stared at me. She pressed one hand against her mouth.

I waved, as if she and I were an ordinary mother and son meeting for a picnic.

And then she was before me, her eyes so like those of my sister, searching for the toddler in the face of a man. "Jonathan?"

The dream. *Jonathan.* My name. My original name. "They called me Wesley."

"Wesley." She placed a hand against my cheek. "Your eyes. I know your eyes."

"Mama?" I whispered as hot tears traveled down my cheeks. "Do you remember me?"

"I've had dreams about you. Dreams I didn't understand. They didn't tell us we were adopted. We came to find you as soon as we learned the truth."

"I hoped you'd come." She pulled me into her embrace. She was petite like Lillian, but her arms were strong and tight around my chest. *Mama.* This was the scent in my dreams. The smell of my mother.

Lillian stepped forward, visibly shaking. "I'm Lillian." My sister's voice shook as much as the rest of her.

"Sister Mary said she knew who you were the moment she saw you." Rose began to cry as she gazed into my sister's eyes. "I never even saw you. They gave me something during labor. When I woke, you were gone. All I knew was they kept you together."

Lillian put her arms around Rose, and they held each other tightly. "We had no idea about any of this."

Rose stepped back and placed her hands on Lillian's shoulders. "I never gave up hope that you would someday find me."

I gestured for Luci and Roland to join us. "This is Luci. My wife." I loved how the word *wife* sounded coming from my mouth. "And Roland, my best friend and Lillian's husband."

"Nice to meet you," Luci said. "We're happy to have found you. I think it's a miracle."

"I'd have to agree," Rose said.

Roland took Rose's hand and lightly kissed her knuckles. "It's a pleasure."

I introduced Sadie and Gus next.

Sadie smiled shyly. "Hi."

"Hello, Sadie," Rose said.

"Do you like children, or are they a nuisance?" Sadie asked.

"I like them very much," Rose said.

"Wesley's my dad now. And Sister's always been my mother because ours died. Would you like to shake Gus's hand? No one taught him. He just knew how to shake."

Never one to disappoint, Gus sat on his haunches and raised his front paw.

Rose leaned over to shake Gus's paw. "It's nice to meet you, Gus."

Gus barked and wagged his tail, then licked her hand for good measure.

"Did you bring your suitcase because you're coming with us?" Sadie asked.

"Wesley left a message for me to bring my belongings." Rose straightened and smoothed the front of her skirt. "I wasn't sure if he meant forever or only for overnight, so I brought what would fit in this bag."

"He meant for you to come with us forever," Sadie said. "We're all going to live in a cottage by the seashore. When Christmas comes, we'll have a big tree that Wesley cuts down himself. Sister, Lillian, and I are going to make decorations. Probably birds made out of paper. Lillian and Roland have a cottage very close by, and we're going to have family dinners every Sunday. Wesley says the sound of the ocean makes you fall asleep at night and wakes you up in the morning."

"That sounds nice," Rose said, smiling.

"Will you come with us?" Lillian asked, sounding younger than Sadie in that particular moment.

"Would you want me to? Truly?" Rose asked.

"We want to make up for all the lost years," Lillian said. "More than anything."

I nodded. "We have plenty of room for you."

"You can stay with us," Lillian said. "Roland and Wesley built cottages with three bedrooms, with an additional room for a maid."

"I can work," Rose said. "I won't be a burden."

"In this family, we all work together," Luci said.

"And play together," Sadie said. "Don't forget playing."

AFTER STAYING OVERNIGHT AT AN INN IN MAUD, WE LEFT THE next morning for the drive home. We arrived at the cottages in the late afternoon. Rose had ridden with Roland and Lillian. We'd separated along the way, but I figured they weren't far behind.

"This is it," I said as I shut off the engine.

From the back seat, Sadie squealed. "Sister, look at the ocean."

Gus barked and put his nose in the air.

We all got out to walk around the cottage to the back garden, which overlooked the water. A gentle breeze caressed my face as we stood looking over the cliff. God had blessed us with a cloudless day on which to introduce Luci and Sadie to its charms. The Atlantic was a deep blue with whitecaps that crashed to shore. Seagulls screamed as they circled above the sea.

Gus lifted his nose as if to familiarize himself with the scent of his new home.

"The air smells fresh," Luci said. "Better than my imagination."

"It's the smell of salt, seaweed, and sea-foam," I said, proud, as if I'd made the scent myself.

"Can we see inside?" Sadie asked. "I want to see my room." She'd been talking about her room for most of the morning, asking me all kinds of questions.

"Yes, let's do just that." I tapped the top of her hat with the pads of my fingers.

As we walked back around to the front door of my cottage, I tried to see it as they might. Would they like the white paint and black shutters that framed the windows and dormers? Two skinny columns held up a covered porch. Pink rosebushes wove their way through lattice on the sides. Would it seem a disappointment after my parents' estate?

"It's so perfectly charming." Luci placed her hand in the crook of my arm. "Do we really get to live here?"

"Yes, we really do."

"Show us inside," Sadie said. "Please, Wesley?"

"Wait one moment." I stepped away to unlock and open the front door and then came back to Luci. "I'm supposed to carry my bride over the threshold."

She squealed as I lifted her into my arms. "Sadie, lead the way."

Sadie and Gus bounded indoors as I crossed over the porch with Luci. I set her down in the sun-drenched living room. They all drifted immediately toward the window seat that looked out to sea. Sadie knelt on the cushions, pressing her nose against the glass. Gus followed her.

"Oh, Wesley," Luci said as she turned back to me. "You said it was small."

"Smaller than the Ford estate."

"Just the right size for the three of us," she said.

"If there's anything you don't like, you may change it." I gestured around the room. "This is your home now."

I'd decorated the living room sparsely, with comfortable furniture in light colors. I'd wanted my home to be the opposite of my parents' formal one. Two cozy chairs faced the brick fireplace. I'd already imagined Luci and me sitting in the two armchairs talking or reading after Sadie had gone to bed.

Luci walked to the shelf to the left of the fireplace where my modest book collection was on display.

"We'll fill them up," I said.

"Stop apologizing. I love every inch."

"The dining room's through there." I gestured toward a set of French doors. A long rustic table filled the space, as well as a buffet between the pantry and dining room. "Through here is the kitchen. Would you like to see?"

Luci nodded. "Yes, please."

The kitchen was about half the size of the living room, with a door that led out to a screened porch. Luci ran her hands over the modern icebox and sink.

"Will it do?" I asked.

"Yes, and then some." She kissed my cheek. "But I could live anywhere with you and be happy."

I wrapped both arms around her waist and kissed her properly.

Sadie came running in, breaking us apart. "Can we go upstairs, Wesley? I want to see where Gus and I are going to sleep."

"Gus will be sleeping with you?" I asked, teasing. "What about me, old boy? Are you abandoning me for this pretty girl?"

Gus wagged his tail in answer. He apologized by trotting over to lick my hand.

"All right, the lot of you—upstairs," I said.

We took the stairs off the kitchen up to the second floor and into a hallway. To the left, the maid's quarters, where June would stay when she arrived, were directly over the kitchen with access to the screened porch. Parallel to the stairs was a bedroom, which now stood empty. "For a nursery someday?" I said lightly as we passed by.

"If we are blessed that way, then yes," Luci said.

I showed them the bathroom, which was across from the first bedroom. Luci exclaimed over the claw-foot tub. "I've grown spoiled already, but I'm quite happy to see a tub."

"Running water. I spared no expense to make everything modern."

Our bedroom was above the dining room with a window directly above the front porch. Next to it, a slightly smaller bedroom had the same view. "This is for you, Sadie." I opened the door. A twin bed and dresser were the only pieces of furniture. Roland had stayed there when we were building his identical cottage.

Sadie ran into the middle of the room and twirled around. "Mine, all mine!"

"We'll decorate it as you wish," I said. "Perhaps some pink and lace?"

"Or yellow and white, like a daisy," Sadie said.

Having already discussed the details, Roland and Lillian had agreed that Rose should live with them, since we had Sadie. June would live with us but would help Lillian as needed.

I showed Luci our bedroom next. She didn't say much, other than to comment on the luxury of two closets, but I could tell she was pleased. "We'll be close to Sadie, in case she needs me. I like that."

"Sister, did you see the flower boxes?" Sadie asked, referring to the ones that hung off the bedroom windows.

"Perhaps you and Luci can plant them for me," I said. "Thus far they've remained empty under the supervision of a bachelor."

"A former bachelor." Luci tucked her hand into the bend of my elbow. "I'll be delighted to fill them with flowers."

"Wait until you see the best part." I took her hand as we headed out to the hallway and through a door to the upstairs balcony, situated between the two bedrooms. "We can sit out here and have our morning coffee if we like and watch the sun rise."

Sadie put her face between two of the steel bars that ran the length of the balcony. "It's like a jail."

"That's so you don't fall off, Sadie Bug," I said.

Luci took off her hat and curled the fingers of one hand around the railing. She leaned forward, jutting out her chin. "Not a jail, Sadie. This is freedom. Can't you smell it?" Fine locks of her hair had broken loose from her bun and swirled about her face.

Sadie and Gus both put their noses in the air and sniffed. "Yes, Sister. I do." She patted Gus's head. "Can you smell it, boy?"

Gus tilted his head as if unsure of the question, but he wagged his tail anyway.

The sound of a motorcar drew my attention. It was Lillian, Roland, and Rose. They drove past our house to park outside their own cottage. We all waved as they got out of the car. Lillian blew us kisses.

My dream had come true. I felt in the pocket of my jacket for the snow globe. Still there. I took it out and shook it before holding it up to the light. The snowflakes swirled about the cottage and the yellow dog. Inside, I imagined us all gathered around the fire.

All my life, my father and mother had emphasized wealth as the most important aspect of a man's life. Who you were and who you knew were king. Your character didn't particularly matter. If you were wealthy, then you could play by a different set of rules. But I knew that those were lies, as so much of my childhood had been. The simple things in life and those you loved were what sustained you, gave you a life to fight for.

"What's that, Wesley?" Sadie asked.

"This is a snow globe. When I was a kid, I used to spend hours peering into the glass and wishing for the life inside it. Now I have it."

"But it's not snowing and it's not Christmas," Sadie said.

I handed Sadie the globe. "Not yet. Wait a few months and we'll have exactly this."

Sadie squinted into the glass ball. "Gus, you're in there too." She held it out for him to see.

He barked, obviously pleased.

"You found us again, old boy." I scratched behind his ears. "Just like I hoped you would."

I put an arm around my wife and took Sadie's hand. Gus leaned against my leg. "Thanks for having enough faith in me to take this leap. We're going to have a lot of good times here together."

"Shall we unpack and then head into town for supplies before supper?" Luci asked.

I gave my practical wife's shoulder another squeeze. "As you wish, my queen."

THAT NIGHT WE DINED ON SOUP LUCI HAD PUT TOGETHER WITH potatoes, carrots, and chicken we'd gotten from the butcher shop in Castaway. Sadie had called it stone soup without the stone.

After Sadie had been tucked into her new bed, Luci, Lillian, Roland, and I sat with Rose in my living room. She'd said we could ask her anything. Yet I was fearful to ask too many questions. Were there things I didn't want to know?

Rose's hands trembled as she lifted a cup of tea to her mouth. "What would you like to know?"

"Our father," Lillian said. "Who was he? Was he the same for both of us?"

She set her cup back onto the saucer and gazed into the fire as she spoke. "Yes, his name was Michael O'Keefe. He was from the neighborhood in Boston where I grew up. We'd known each other as kids from Catholic school. Not well, but he was always one of a gang of boys who ran around together. When I was fifteen, he started asking to walk me home from school. I was charmed by him, even though my mother didn't approve because his family was poor. We started spending time together in secret. I fell in love with him, and we eloped when I was only sixteen after I discovered I was going to have a baby. My parents said they wanted nothing more to do with me. Michael had already dropped out of school by then, and his friends were rumored to have ties to the gangs. Irish criminals."

Lillian reached for Roland's hand. "Criminals?"

"Yes. They ran certain neighborhoods back then. Still do, I'm sure. A little over a year went by. He never told me about his work, and I pushed it out of my thoughts. We lived in this tiny apartment, but Michael always kept us fed and clothed. I was very young but also in love and only too happy to be with him and my precious baby. I became pregnant again. One night when I was about six months along, Michael didn't come home. Often he would come home late, but he always returned before sunrise. By morning, I was frantic. I bundled you up, Jonathan . . . Wesley . . . and went looking for him. I walked all over south Boston and asked shop owners and anyone else if they knew anything. No one did."

"Are you saying he was killed by the bad people he worked with?" Lillian asked, eyes wide.

"Or their enemies. Two days later one of the men from the neighborhood came by to tell me they'd found his body floating in the river." Rose's eyes glassed over for a moment. "He'd been shot."

"That's awful," Lillian said.

"You must have been very frightened," Luci said.

"I was. I had no money of my own. No place to go. I was evicted when I couldn't pay the rent. I tried to see my parents, but the maid told me they didn't want me. For a few days, we lived on the streets." Her voice shook as she continued to tell her story. "I had to beg for food. Someone told me of a nunnery where they took care of single mothers. I managed to hitch a ride on a delivery wagon out there. I asked if they'd take me in just until I had the baby and could get on my feet somehow." Tears gathered at the corners of her eyes. "I didn't know they took girls like me in only to steal our children and give them to rich people. They sedated me, and when I woke you were both gone. I didn't even get to see you, Lillian."

Roland handed Rose a handkerchief, which she used to dab her eyes. "As I said before, I asked if I could stay on and work for them. They agreed, perhaps out of pity or maybe because I was a hard worker. All these years I've been in the basement of that building doing laundry." She held up her rough, chapped hands. "The work has made me old."

Only your hands, I thought. The rest of her was beautiful.

"I believed my only hope to see you again was to stay. Knowing how unlikely it would be that the family who took you would ever tell you the truth, I held on to a small glimmer of hope. Until, finally, you arrived."

"We would've come sooner had we known," Lillian said.

"What prompted that woman to tell you the truth?" Rose asked.

Keeping it brief, I told her how everything had unfolded. "With my father dead, perhaps she felt it was safe to tell us. There were a lot of secrets in our house, including our connection to Sadie and Luci." I conveyed the rest of the story.

"Sadie's your sister, then?" Rose asked. "Or, not really, depending on how you look at it."

"Doesn't matter either way," Lillian said. "We're all together now, where we belong. That includes you, Rose."

Rose dabbed at her eyes. "When I was working, I'd daydream about a reunion to pass the time. One like this."

"What about your parents?" Lillian asked. "Have you ever heard from them?"

"No. I've no idea if they're still alive," Rose said. "It took a lot for me not to succumb to bitterness. I didn't want to become a hard person."

Dax had asked that very thing of me all those years ago. Not to become hard, despite my circumstances.

"But for them—there is only hardness and no forgiveness," Rose said. "If they'd taken us in, we would have been together."

"We are now," I said. "No one can change that."

PART III

———————

December 1910

29

L uci

CHRISTMAS EVE MORNING, WE WOKE TO A FRESH LAYER OF SNOW. I was putting the finishing touches on a pumpkin pie when I looked out to see Wesley dragging a fir tree across the yard. Sadie and Gus bounded excitedly behind him. "They're back," I said to June.

She was at the cookstove, basting the turkey Wesley had brought from the butcher shop in Castaway. "It's a pretty tree. Just the right shape."

She and I had spent the better part of two days cooking for the feast tomorrow. Lillian and Rose had done the same in their kitchen, as Mollie had in hers. There were cakes, pies, cookies, potato casseroles, and vegetable dishes. Enough to feed the whole town, which was our plan for tomorrow. We'd partnered with the pastor at the church to arrange a dinner for anyone who wanted to come. The pastor's wife had agreed to cook a

261

TESS THOMPSON

turkey in her kitchen too. Mollie and Lillian were doing the same. There would be no hungry children in Castaway this Christmas. Or any night, if my plan worked.

We would eat our holiday meal tonight here as a family. Wesley had built two long benches for our dining table so that we would all be able to gather together.

"I'll make sure they know it needs to dry first," I said to June as I put the pie in the oven and hurried to the front door.

By the time I arrived, Wesley had managed to get the tree to the porch steps. He lifted it upright and grabbed the trunk in the middle, then shook it to get the snow off the branches. I shivered in the cold air, having come out without my shawl or coat.

"Do you like the one we chose?" Wesley asked.

"It's large," I said. "Will it fit?" The tree was as tall as Wesley.

"Yes, yes, Sister. It's just the right size."

I backed up as Wesley brought the tree up the stairs and leaned it against the wall. The scent of fir needles and pitch filled my nose.

"I'll nail some boards to the bottom for a stand." Wesley took off his cap. "I worked up a sweat getting it here."

Gus and Sadie trudged up the stairs to stand beside me. She wore a knit cap, mittens, and a red coat. Her cheeks and nose were pink from the cold. Since we'd come here, she'd filled out and no longer looked as if a good wind would blow her away from me. "We didn't have to go far to find it," Sadie said.

"Just to the edge of the woods," Wesley said.

"When can we decorate?" Sadie asked at the same moment Gus decided to shake all the snow from his body.

"Gus, you're making a mess," I said, laughing. "As soon as the tree dries a bit, we can bring it in."

For most of December, we'd been working on ornaments for our first family Christmas. Wesley had coerced delicate twigs into crosses and stars. Sadie and I had cut tissue paper into snowflakes. Lillian, in front of her own fire, had knitted red yarn into miniature stockings and wreathes. Mollie had strung red berries I'd collected in the fall.

Luckily, the men had been able to finish Dax and Mollie's cottage by the first snow. They'd wanted a small one-bedroom without a second story, and the work was quick with three men working together. When spring came, they would help Dax build planting beds and fences to keep out the deer.

"Come inside for now. June's made hot chili for lunch. Everyone's coming over at four to decorate the tree before our Christmas Eve feast."

"And presents?" Sadie asked.

All over the house, I'd hidden surprises for Christmas morning. A set of paints for Sadie and a book of birds of the Northeast, her latest fascination. For Wesley, I'd ordered a new pair of leather driving gloves. We'd had a new coat made for Rose cut from soft pink wool. I'd found a beautiful scarf for Lillian. Wesley had ordered a spyglass for Roland to match the one we had.

DAX AND MOLLIE ARRIVED FIRST, CARRYING TWO WRAPPED packages.

"I thought we said no gifts," I said, dismayed.

"Don't fuss, now," Mollie said. "It's just a few trinkets for the lass."

"You'll spoil her," I said.

"All the more reason to have a baby," Mollie said.

Dax caught my eye, and we laughed. "My wife needs more to do."

"I'm growing fat as a piglet in retirement," Mollie said. "There's nothing to keep me from cooking and eating all day."

"You are not growing fat," I said. Anyway, I had an idea

about what she could do to keep busy. I was going to propose the idea at dinner.

Lillian and Rose, who had brought presents earlier, arrived with a bowl of smashed potatoes and a basket of rolls. Last year, Sadie and I had shared a few slices of bread and two potatoes. It was hard to believe that was only a year ago.

"Merry Christmas, beautiful Luci," Rose said.

"Same to you." I kissed her and helped her out of her coat. Since moving in with Lillian, she'd lost the haunted look in her eyes. Roland and Wesley had promised to build her a cottage in the spring. She'd confided in me that she liked being with Lillian, even though she worried she was in the way of the newlyweds. Lillian had said nothing of the sort to me. In fact, she loved having Rose there, not only for the company and the running of the house but because it had given them a second chance to know each other. Also, Lillian was going to have a baby. Only I knew. She'd told me just yesterday and had asked me to keep it secret so she could announce it at Christmas Eve dinner.

Sadie came running up to hug Rose and then Lillian. "The tree's here already," Sadie said.

"Isn't it exciting?" Lillian's cheeks glowed from the cold.

"Where's Roland?" Wesley asked as he hung up her coat.

"He's on his way. He only just got home and wanted to clean up a bit. He opened the shop early so he could close and get home before dark. He didn't want to miss out on any last-minute shoppers."

June came out from the kitchen with a tray of hot toddies for the adults and a cup of cider for Sadie.

"Is it time yet?" Sadie hopped from one foot to the other by the tree. We'd set it near the window seat to keep if far away from the fire.

"Yes, it's time," I said.

Sadie hung the ornaments on the bottom of the tree, while

Lillian focused on the top. Mollie supervised what went where. Rose and I sat together on the window seat and watched. The men chatted by the fire, not paying much attention to us.

"I had a letter from Mother," Lillian said.

"Really?" I asked. None of us had heard from her since the day we left. "What did she say?"

"She married the artist, and the estate has been sold. She's having the piano sent to me."

"That's nice for you," Rose said. "You've missed it so."

"And for us," Sadie said. "Now we'll have music."

"Be careful, little Sadie." Lillian pointed at her with one of the knitted ornaments. "I'll be giving you lessons."

"I'd rather listen," Sadie said, quite seriously.

They continued chatting about favorite Christmas hymns and how next year we could have Lillian play for us. We'd also have a baby added to the family. I could hardly wait for Rose to learn of the baby that was coming.

"Quite a thing, isn't it?" Rose asked me. "That we're here."

I patted her hand. "It's a miracle, if you want to know the truth."

WE WERE ALL SEATED AROUND THE TABLE, WESLEY AND I ON either end. I'd insisted that June sit with us for our meal, even though she'd protested. She seemed happy sitting between Mollie and Lillian. I hoped she wasn't too homesick for her family. She wasn't the kind to ever say a negative word, so I couldn't be sure.

"Shall we pray?" I asked.

"Yes, I'll do the honors," Wesley said.

We took one another's hands. I held Sadie's small warm hand in my own and Rose's strong one in the other. We bowed our heads.

"Thank you, Lord, for the food we are about to receive," Wesley said. "And that we're all together, warm and healthy. Our hearts are full and thankful."

A chorus of *amen*s followed, and then we began to pass the food around. When all the plates were full, Lillian raised her glass. "I have something to say."

Everyone turned to look at her. She and Roland were sitting across from each other on either side of Wesley. She fixed her gaze on her husband. "I'm happy to announce that Roland and I will be having a baby right around May, if my calculations are accurate."

Roland's expression went blank, as if someone had punched him. Thankfully, in the next moment, he broke into a grin. "I'm going to be a father?"

Lillian beamed back at him. "Isn't it wonderful?"

Roland leapt up from the end of the bench and crossed over to pull his wife up from her seat to hug her and then twirl her around.

"Be careful," Mollie said. "She has a baby in there."

Roland set Lillian back on her feet and kissed her before escorting her back to the end of the bench.

Wesley clapped his best friend on the shoulder. "Congratulations, brother."

"Does this mean I'm an aunt to the baby?" Sadie asked. "Or a cousin?"

Lillian laughed. "In this family, who knows? Let's just say cousin, since you're only five."

"Six," Sadie said. "Remember, my birthday was last week."

"Right, excuse me," Lillian said. "I forgot."

I snuck a glance at Rose. She was dabbing at her eyes with a napkin.

"What do you think, Mama?" Wesley asked her. "Is this a good Christmas gift?"

"I'm going to be a grandmother," Rose said. "A dream come true."

"You'll be a great one, Mama Rose," Roland said.

"Another chance," Rose said. "And to think I'm here with you all. It's . . . just . . . there are no words."

There were no words to describe my joy, so I understood what she felt but could not say. After Lillian's happy news, we all dug into our meal, laughing and talking. When we'd stuffed ourselves, I asked Sadie to take Gus outside for a potty break. "Afterward, we'll open presents."

She squealed and ran out of the room, with Gus at her heels.

"We have something exciting to share with you, but we wanted to tell you about it without Sadie being here," I said. "Wesley and I, along with Roland and Lillian, have come up with an idea—a way to give back for how fortunate we are. We're opening a home for unwed mothers. Only, unlike the nunnery, we're going to do it the right way. They'll be provided a place to live and give birth but with the understanding that it's their choice about whether or not they keep the baby or give it up for adoption."

"In addition, we'll provide them the opportunity to learn skills while they're there," Wesley said. "Ways for them to support themselves if they decide to keep the child. Or, if they have no family to go back to."

"How would you do this?" Rose asked softly.

"Each of the young ladies would be assigned a role when they arrive: cooking, laundry, maid, dining hall, seamstress, nurse, typing, gardening, depending on their interests and aptitude. After the baby's born, they would have a skill they could use. We've hired a doctor and a nurse, who have agreed to work for us full-time. They'll take care of the girls but also teach medical skills to any who want to be nurses or home-care providers."

"How will you fund this?" Mollie asked.

"We've lined up a few benefactors," Wesley said. "Through contacts from school."

"We pulled in some favors," Roland said. "And got in touch with some wealthy widows who are sympathetic to the cause."

"Also, because the girls will work while they're there, it requires less than it otherwise would," I said.

"I'm donating the land and building," Wesley said. "We're drawing up plans now to start in the spring."

"What about the other skills?" Mollie asked. "Who would teach them those?"

Wesley flashed her his best smile. "That's where you come in."

"Me?"

"Who better qualified than you to teach domestic skills? You could train them in proper housekeeping etiquette for working for wealthy families, as an example," Wesley said. "Or how to set a proper table."

"All the forks," Lillian said as she smiled at me.

"Or how to keep the books for a household," I said. "And manage a wine cellar. We're hoping that, over time, our school will develop a reputation and people will want to hire the girls simply because they know they're well trained."

"Also, we've hired a head cook," Wesley said. "I've been in touch with Mrs. Walker, and she's agreed to come."

"I'm going to teach sewing," June said. "But only the kind where they need to learn to sew for themselves."

"There's a seamstress in town who said she is willing to take an apprentice."

"We're hoping Dax will teach gardening," I said. "As a skill for either their own use or for a job."

"I'd be happy to," Dax said.

"We want to help young women who are in the situation I was in," I said. "Alone with a baby and no skills."

"Or like you, Mama," Wesley said. "Not given the chance to keep your children."

"We're still looking for a typing and shorthand teacher," I said. "But Lillian's agreed to help us find someone from her friends at school."

Dax looked from one of us to the other. "I couldn't be prouder than I am right now."

"We learned kindness from you," Wesley said. "It's we who should be thanking you."

CHRISTMAS MORNING, I WOKE EARLY. INSTEAD OF JUMPING UP AS I often did, I remained in bed for a few minutes, luxuriating in the warmth trapped beneath the down comforter. Wesley slept on his side facing away from me. I curled myself around him. He caught hold of my arm and pulled it close to his chest, then returned to the steady breathing of sleep. For a few minutes, I listened to the sound of his breathing and felt his heartbeat against my arm.

Then I scooted away from him, disentangling my arm and moving to my side of the bed. I shivered in the cold room as I reached for my robe. As quietly as I could, I tiptoed out of the room in my stocking feet. The Maine winters were bitter, and even newlyweds wore socks to bed. I peeked in on Sadie. She was still sound asleep, but Gus lifted his head. He must have been hungry because he decided to follow me down to the kitchen.

I'd instructed June to sleep in and that I would get the fires started. I started a fire in the hearth and in the cookstove.

"Come on, boy. Go out and then I'll give you some breakfast." I opened the kitchen door, and he ran outside, traipsing through snow that reached his belly.

I left the door open an inch. He knew how to open it fully

with his paw. I scooped coffee into the percolator and set it on the stove. My husband liked his coffee first thing.

Gus pushed open the door and sauntered in, looking up at me with pleading eyes. "I know, you're hungry."

I put food in his bowl and set it near the stove so he would be warm.

He scarfed it all down in what seemed like two bites.

"You eat too fast. Don't you want to savor it?" I asked him.

He wagged his tail as if that would get him a second breakfast.

I tossed together a pan of biscuits using fresh butter we'd gotten from a local farmer. While they baked, I fried up bacon slices. The smell, no matter how many mornings we were blessed with it, made my mouth water. Such abundance. I hoped I'd never take it for granted.

When the bacon and biscuits were done, I covered them with towels. We would eat when everyone was up. It was Christmas, after all. I poured a cup of coffee, then went out to the front room and sat on the window seat to watch the snow fall. On mornings such as this, the ocean and horizon were a study of grays and whites. The only sounds were the crashing of the waves onto the shore, until the creak of the stairs told me Wesley was awake.

I turned from the window as he crossed the room toward me. My stomach fluttered at the sight of him, as it always did.

"Merry Christmas, my love." He hadn't yet shaved and was dressed in a flannel shirt and the denim pants he wore for his morning chores. I was perfectly capable of bringing in firewood or shoveling the walkways, but he wouldn't have it.

"Merry Christmas." I smiled up at him and waited for his kiss. In our cottage by the sea, we were creatures of habit already.

He left me to grab a cup of coffee. I heard his familiar movements in the kitchen—the rattle of the coffeepot, an opening of a drawer to get a spoon, the clank of it against the cup as he stirred. He liked his coffee with a teaspoon of sugar. I smiled to myself. These small daily rituals added up to a happy life. One neither of us took for granted. I didn't think we ever would.

Wesley joined me, spreading his legs out long and entangling them with mine so that we were bookends on the window seat.

"I've dreamt of this moment since the first time I ever saw you," he said. "Just like this."

"That's the difference between you and me. I never had enough hope to dream of such a happy life. To me, hope was dangerous."

"Perhaps I hoped with enough conviction for the both of us."

"Perhaps you did."

And so we stayed thus, watching the snow fall and waiting for Sadie and Gus to scamper down the stairs. I hadn't known until Wesley had come back to me that my heart could feel actually swollen with love.

"I knew it would be this way. If I could only find my way back to you."

"Tomorrow finally came."

A pairing of souls could not be kept apart. No matter how hard the world, love would find its way. Even to a girl like me. One simply had to keep living, breathing, carrying on until tomorrow came.

CLICK HERE TO DOWNLOAD THE NEXT BOOK IN THE SERIES, PROMISE OF TOMORROW!

Join Tess's newsletter and never miss a sale or new release HERE!

ALSO BY TESS THOMPSON

The Innkeeper

ABOUT THE AUTHOR

Tess Thompson is the USA Today Bestselling and award-winning author of clean and wholesome Contemporary and Historical Romantic Women's Fiction with nearly 50 published titles. Her stories feature family sagas, romance, a little mystery, and a lot of heart.

She's married to her prince, Best Husband Ever Cliff and is the mother of their blended family of two boys and two girls. Cliff is seventeen months younger, which qualifies Tess as a Cougar, a title she wears proudly. Her bonus sons are young adults working toward making all their dreams come true out in the world. Oldest daughter is at college studying Chemistry. (Her mother has no idea where she got her math and science talent!) The baby of the family is a junior in high school and a member of a state champion cheer team as well as an academic all-star, including achieving a 5 on the AP World History exam during her sophomore year.

Tess is proud to have grown up in a small town like the ones in her novels. After graduating from the University of Southern California Drama School, she had hopes of becoming an actress but was called instead to writing fiction.

Tess loves lazy afternoons watching football, hanging out on the back patio with Best Husband Ever, reading in bed, binge-watching television series, red wine, strong coffee, Zumba, and walks on crisp autumn days. She never knows what to make for dinner and is often awake in the middle of night thinking about her characters and their stories.

She's grateful to spend most days in her office matchmaking her characters while her favorite cat Mittens (shhh...don't tell Midnight) sleeps on the desk.

She adores hearing from readers, so don't hesitate to say hello or sign up for her newsletter: https://tesswrites.com/. You'll receive a free ebook just for signing up!

Made in the USA
Middletown, DE
30 October 2023